# Felix Roth

A Novel by

Cary Fagan

Stoddart

0015

Copyright © 1999 by Cary Fagan

All rights reserved. No part of this publication may be reproduced or transmitted in any form or by any means, electronic or mechanical, including photocopying, recording, or any information storage and retrieval system, without permission in writing from the publisher.

Published in 1999 by Stoddart Publishing Co. Limited
34 Lesmill Road, Toronto, Canada M3B 2T6
180 Varick Street, 9th Floor, New York, NY 10014

Distributed in Canada by General Distribution Services Limited
325 Humber College Blvd., Toronto, Ontario M9W 7C3
Tel. (416) 213-1919 Fax (416) 213-1917
Email Customer.Service@ccmailgw.genpub.com

For information about U.S. publication and
distribution of Stoddart Books, contact
180 Varick Street, 9th Floor, New York, NY 10014

03 02 01 00 99 1 2 3 4 5

**Cataloguing in Publication Data**

Fagan, Cary 1957–
Felix Roth

ISBN 0-7737-6049-0

I. Title.

PS8561.A37F44 1999 C813'.54
C98-933087-7 PR9199.3.F33F44 1999

Portions of this novel, in an earlier form, first appeared in
*Parchment* and *Paragraph.*

Cover Design: Angel Guerra
Design and Typesetting: Kinetics Design & Illustration

Printed and bound in Canada

"I Am" by Mani Leib, translated by John Hollander, published by Holt, Rinehart and Winston in *A Treasury of Yiddish Poetry*, edited by Irving Howe and Eleizer Greenberg. Every effort has been made to secure permissions for quotations of previously published material.

*Stoddart Publishing gratefully acknowledges the Canada Council for the Arts and the Ontario Arts Council for their support of its publishing program.*

*To my brothers, Mark and Lawrence,*

*for all you taught me*

*We must believe in free will.*

*We have no choice.*

— Isaac Bashevis Singer

# 1

# The Very Air of the City

My first view of Manhattan was from above, and no matter how often I had imagined that moment, how many novels I had read that were set in the city, I was not prepared for it. For the *realness* of it, the dark glittering grittiness, the street canyons shadowed by so many miles of aggressively vertical buildings; the clumsy lyrical sweep from the southern point of Battery Park up past the fluted towers of the World Trade Center, the etched white arch of Washington Square, to the darkening rectangle of Central Park, striped with shadows cast by the descending sun against the West Side apartments. I hadn't expected the airplane to get so close. I could see the most remarkable details in the failing light — round wooden water towers with their pointed roofs, an umbrella on a penthouse garden, tiny specks moving on a grubby basketball court squatting in the middle of red-brick public housing.

Did I really see so much, did the plane actually touch the very air of the city? Or has my memory made everything more acute, more vivid than it really was? But that is how I remember that moment and every other of those five days. Well, at the age of twenty-one everything *is* more vivid. Back home in Toronto I had affected an air of world-weariness, *Weltschmertz* or existential gloom, and the stories that I was writing were more tragic than *King Lear*. But looking out the oval window of that plane I suddenly realized what a ridiculous sham I'd been putting over myself and how happy I was to be alive. I felt my youth just then as a physical sensation, almost a trembling, or as if my skin were being touched everywhere by delicate fingers. I felt close to weeping ecstatically.

And then I reached over to touch my brother's arm. He had given me the window seat and I wanted to make sure he saw the view. Immediately I regretted having spoiled the moment.

Reaching out, I felt not his arm but the hard and knobbly cover of a book. I turned to see him gently rocking in his seat, holding the small Hebrew prayer book against the armrest but not looking at it, as his eyes were half closed. His yarmulke, which he had begun to wear only three or four months ago, was askew on the back of his head, not quite covering the bald spot; like our late grandfather, he was already losing his hair in his mid-twenties. Perhaps he was praying to atone for the sin of having agreed to travel on the sabbath — it was Friday eve — for he was half-mumbling, half-singing as he rocked. Outside, Manhattan beckoned like a delicious oyster and my brother was *davening* so that we might have a safe landing! I wanted to snatch the prayer book from his hand and if I could have opened the plane window, I would have tossed the damn thing into the troposphere.

The plane rose over the bridges connecting Manhattan to Queens and I had a last dazzling view of the red sun reflecting off the Empire State Building. I knew all about the Empire State, I could have recited a host of facts (date of construction start April 7, 1930; height 1,250 feet; cost $40 million) or told how the needle that topped it had been intended as a mooring post to tie up passing zeppelins or of the day in 1945 when a B-25 bomber crashed into the seventy-ninth floor. And then we were banking away towards La Guardia and the city was replaced by feathery clouds of scarlet. Over Flushing Meadows I looked down to see Shea Stadium like a round hat box with the lid off, illuminated a brilliant green inside for the Mets game in progress.

The plane began vibrating almost violently as it started to descend. I pushed myself back into the seat. From this angle I could see part of the wing, a patchwork of screwed-together pieces with arrows painted on it, as if the crew might otherwise have attached it to the plane backwards or upside down. Maybe one of the engines was tearing itself from the wing or the wheels had stuck or the pilot couldn't ease back the speed enough. I was prone to nausea and sudden fears; even as a child I had disliked car rides, boats, merry-go-rounds. To take my mind off the landing I removed my wallet from the pocket of my corduroy blazer and took from it the photograph I had been carrying around for months. It was a small square cut from *Time* magazine the week the Nobel Prize for literature had been announced the previous fall, a black-and-white photograph of Isaac Bashevis Singer, his elfin face peering at the camera with a mixture of surprise and suspicion. He looked old and not old. I thought that he resembled a little my late uncle Mort, who had worn the same kind of hat over his own bald and mottled head. But Uncle Mort had been famous only for his habit of drinking a glass of vinegar every night, not for writing stories and novels.

My parents had subscribed to *Time* for as long as I could remember; my father considered it more authoritative on international news than any of the Toronto papers. According to the article on the Nobel Prize, when told that he had won the most prestigious literary award in the world, Singer had raised an eyebrow and said in his Yiddish accent, "Are you sure?" I loved that "Are you sure?" and repeated it to everyone I knew — my university friends, Aaron, my parents, my increasingly unhappy girlfriend, Theresa Zeitman — it so beautifully captured Singer's blunt skepticism, his directness, his rich human qualities. No one else seemed to read quite so much into those three words, nor to be quite so excited. But I had long worshipped Singer's work and considered him not just the greatest Jewish writer ever but the greatest living writer, period. His work seemed to live in the world of the living and the dead simultaneously. He was both an uneasy modernist and an entrancing old-fashioned storyteller. His writing was tragic and funny, rich with the ache of sex and mortality. He was part philosopher, part psychoanalyst, part vaudevillian. And his books were vivid with the life in Warsaw before the war and New York after.

And this writer, this man who looked as if he might have been a jeweller or a dealer in used furniture but who in fact was a literary sorcerer, actually lived in the city of New York. He was down there at this very moment, on this first Friday in July 1979, getting up from a chair in his apartment on the Upper West Side, or taking a walk down Broadway. Well, my brother had his superstitions and so did I. I rubbed the picture between my fingers like a talisman of good fortune and slipped it back in my wallet. For everything I had to accomplish here, I would need it.

The plane dropped, levelled, dropped again. My heart lodged in my throat. Through the window I could see drab row houses rushing up at us, then a highway clogged with cars, then suddenly the end of the runway. We hit it with a jerk, forcing the back of my head into the seat rest. I could see the flaps on the wing shoot upwards as the engines roared furiously into reverse.

"*Boruch Hashem,*" Aaron said.

I thought of Singer's short story "The Blasphemer," about a man driven insane by his lack of faith. But wasn't Singer saying that faith too was a kind of insanity? That was what I thought about Aaron; that he had found God and gone crazy.

We had a reservation at the Schraft Hotel. I'd seen a small advertisement for it in the *New York Review of Books*, which described it as quaint, central, and especially welcoming of "showpeople." More important, the cost was thirty dollars a night, and while I wasn't sure about Aaron, my own resources were limited, especially as our father had refused to bankroll the trip and our mother, in deference to his stubbornness, had resisted the temptation to slip us some extra cash. I had $250 to last me from Friday evening to midday Tuesday.

In the airport we passed through customs and then just stood there with our carry-on bags, both of us looking bewildered as people streamed past. I stared at them going by — luggage handlers and janitors in overalls, businessmen with newspapers under their arms, women with coiffed hair moving rapidly on their heels. They didn't look like people back home to me; they looked both more grim and more amused, sharper and wearier. None of them seemed amazed to be in New York.

"Let's take a cab," I said to Aaron. "We'll get into the city faster."

"No, we'll take the bus. There's no reason to waste money."

"Come on, Aaron. Aren't you anxious?"

And right there, standing in a corridor of La Guardia Airport, Aaron proceeded to give me the sort of lecture that had become infuriatingly common lately. I can still remember precisely the list of ethical values that he urged me to hold to during our stay in the city: cleanliness of mind, zeal, abstinence, personal humility, fear of sin, love of holiness. He spoke in a low voice that nevertheless carried above the noise, and it came to me that although his lectures had taken a religious turn only lately, he had always taken it upon himself to instruct me on how to live. He was four years old when I was born and, according to the accounts of my mother, had made himself my watchful guardian from the day my father drove us back from the hospital. I had been his dedicated and admiring pupil for the first fifteen or more years of my life but I wondered now, with a sadness not untouched by impatience, when exactly I had stopped listening.

But I listened now, looking into his face which appeared younger than my own though he was all of twenty-five, in part because he was fair and I was dark. Also, his face was rounder than mine and he was a little on the heavy side, while I was more the undernourished type. He preferred loose clothes, such as the oversized law-school sweatshirt he was wearing and which only made him look bigger and slower than he really was. Those words he used — abstinence, humility — meant nothing to me. I wasn't interested in them, certainly not at this particular moment of my life, and if I had been honest with him I would have said that were I to follow his rules there would be no point in coming to New York at all. What was New York if not temptation? Not that I had any real hedonistic desire; I already knew that my temperament leaned towards the ascetic, even if it manifested itself in a different way from my brother. Actually, thinking about it, I realized that I too yearned for a life of purity, only I believed it was literature that would provide it for me.

"Please, Aaron," I said when he was finished. "I don't want to discuss moral behaviour or defending the faith or anything else right now. All I want to do is look down Broadway."

Aaron sighed, like a teacher who knew his pupil wasn't ready to get the message. "All right. Let's find the bus."

He picked up his bag and I followed him, just as I had been following him all my life. The airport was rundown and grimy, not spanking clean like Toronto's. Even the airport workers looked somehow slovenly in their uniforms, jackets wrinkled, shirts hanging out. A black man with a shaved head was leaning against a high, brimming garbage bin and smoking. He was stern and handsome and he looked very strong even in repose. I couldn't tell whether he worked at the airport, as he wore workman's pants but a black satin bomber jacket, and when he turned around to toss the cigarette up into the bin I saw that the back was embroidered with words.

WHEN I DIE I'LL GO TO HEAVEN

CAUSE I ALREADY DONE MY TIME

IN HELL.

68–69

LONG BINH, VIETNAM

I stared at the man in awe, feeling the angry weight of his history as he leaned back again and gazed into space. In Canada we hadn't experienced such collective trauma, and I felt the charismatic pull of this country's dark past.

"Felix, please don't dawdle," Aaron said. I hurried after him, inwardly bristling at his tone. We went through the doors into the evening dusk, the sun having sunk farther since our landing. The air smelled of diesel and also cheap perfume wafting from one of the women waiting on the platform. Three men in greasy overalls were sitting on a pile of luggage and laughing as they played cards. "You see that? Get *outta* here. Man thinks he's Donald Trump." The garish musical tone of Brooklynese! In Toronto people didn't have accents, unless they came from somewhere else more interesting. My own voice sounded to me scrubbed clean of character, as if my tongue had been run through the washing machine with extra bleach.

From out of nowhere the bus roared up, halting with a shriek of brakes at the curb. The door opened and a man in a blue uniform stepped down to take our money, stooping because of his height. He had a gaunt face, acne-scarred and marked by sporadic tufts of beard. "Five dollars," he said, pronouncing the two words as one: *fiedollahs*. He spoke a continuous patter as the line moved up into the bus. "No matter who you are, fiedollahs. The towel boy at the gym, fiedollahs. The king of Persia, fiedollahs. Welcome to the greatest democracy in the world, ancient Greece included. Cost to get in, fiedollahs."

Aaron and I dragged our bags onto the ratty bus and found places near the back. The upholstery on the seats was a hideous brown check. I took the window without asking, since Aaron clearly had no interest in his surroundings. We drove through silent residential Queens and onto an ill-lit highway. A billboard of the Marlboro man flitted past. I felt myself brooding still about not taking a cab. This was my first trip to Manhattan and Aaron was unconsciously trying to ruin it for me. Where was the romance of entering the city on a damn bus? I had studied the various ways of crossing onto the island and had planned to ask the taxi driver to take the Queensboro Bridge in order to get a view of the city. But I could hardly tell the bus driver what route to take and felt a fatalistic gloom as we descended instead into the Queens-Midtown Tunnel. The tile walls vaulted narrowly over us, like some medieval catacomb, and the white lights flashed by in a disorienting strobe effect. When the line of cars ahead slowed up I imagined the watery filth of the East River bearing down on our heads. Next to me, Aaron appeared to be sleeping, his head tilted and his mouth slightly open. On car trips he used to fall asleep almost as soon as we were off. I could remember my mother leaning over from the front seat to brush the hair from his eyes.

The bus angled up and suddenly we were moving slowly along a dark Manhattan street. I pressed my face to the window to see a liquor store with glowing signs for Schlitz and Miller beer, the canopy of an apartment house. As if watching a mime play, I saw a man in a tuxedo and a woman in an evening gown having a terrible argument, their faces distorted with rage, the woman weeping. Another man walked past them, reading a book close to his face, oblivious. I thought to look at the street signs just as we turned from Thirty-seventh Street up Park Avenue. From somewhere came music, a Latin beat seeping into the bus only to be drowned out by the sudden blare of automobile horns. I wanted to bang on the window and shout: I belong here! I was born in the wrong place! Let me in!

I looked at Aaron. He was awake now and staring calmly at the seatback in front of him.

# 2

# I Am Named

My last name, of course, was inherited from my father, Saul Roth, sole owner and manager of Roth Cement and Gravel, but it was my mother, Miriam (née Kronish), who chose my first name, not before I was born as is usually common, but when I was three days old. She did the same thing for my older brother, Aaron, for she believed that she had to "feel" our personalities before bestowing on us the name that would mark us for life. Mine came from my mother's adoration of Felix Mendelssohn. Her favourite work of all time was Mendelssohn's Violin Concerto, which I no doubt heard while still idling in the womb, as my mother had the Jascha Heifetz recording and played it often on the hi-fi in the sleek walnut cabinet that my father had bought for her. Maybe I even liked it then, although in my teens I came to despise its sweet melody and sweeping crescendoes.

It's possible that my mother looked into my large,

wondering eyes and decided that I would turn out an artistic prodigy of some kind. She never said as much, she wasn't a stage mother at all, but she had a worshipful attitude towards artists that came, I think, from certain Hollywood biopics she had seen as a young girl. While she was the first woman in her family to achieve a higher education, taking classes at the University of Toronto where she read *The Wasteland* and studied Impressionism and life in Pompeii, she never got over those early romantic images of the creative artist.

My mother loved all the arts, but music was to her the most divine because of its immediate access to the emotions. Naturally she loved the romantic composers above all, and among them Mendelssohn ranked number one. It did not hurt his standing that Mendelssohn was a Jew; she would not have named me Wolfgang Amadeus or Ludwig or Frédéric, even if one of them had been her favourite instead. And so when she looked into my eyes and saw some spark of the creative spirit flicker there, she must have felt it only right to name me Felix. I have long wondered why she did not see this same spark in the eyes of her first-born, Aaron. How did she know that as Aaron grew up there would emerge in his character not a single shred of artistic sensibility? How could she see that her real kinship would be with me, her youngest? Or did all mothers feel that way towards the last child?

Of course, what my mother did not know was that Mendelssohn had been baptized a Lutheran when still young, so that his religion would not impede his musical career. When I discovered this at the age of fourteen (I had got it in my head to read up on him in the *Encyclopaedia Britannica* that a builder client of my father's had extravagantly given to me for my bar mitzvah), some devil made me run gleefully downstairs to tell my mother. She was in her blue-and-yellow kitchen, her dream kitchen, in the house my father had custom built for her, and she was standing at the stainless steel island dipping chicken parts into beaten egg and then bread crumbs while listening to Gordon Sinclair on the radio. Breathlessly I told her about Mendelssohn's conversion and she listened, wiping her hands on a towel. Then she sat down on one of the George Jensen stools and burst into tears.

Nevertheless, I thought Felix Roth was a pretty good name for an author. Often when I was supposed to be doing my homework, I would draw a rectangle in the margin of my notebook, using a plastic ruler to make it neat. And in this rectangle, which was meant to represent a book cover, I would carefully print the title of a novel I would someday write. *Sigh of Death by Felix Roth. The Boy Who Could Fly by Felix Roth.* My room in the new house was enormous, but I had made a space for myself by hauling up an old rug from the basement and putting it against the wall opposite the foot of my bed. Then I built a bookshelf from boards and leftover bricks that I found in the garage. On the shelves I put my Penguin Classics, and in this little space of my own that might have been in some high Parisian garret I would lie on the rug with a notepad writing my stories.

I know exactly at what moment the Parisian garret turned into a Greenwich Village flat. In October of my sixteenth year my parents' issue of *National Geographic* arrived in the mail with a three-foot-long map of Manhattan tucked inside its cover. I took the map for myself and thumbtacked it up over the brick-and-board bookcase where I could study its cross-hatching of streets and the way Broadway curved up the island like a supple spine and the poetic names of its neighbourhoods — Gramercy Park, Chelsea, Murray Hill and so on, all the way up to Washington Heights. I had already read *The Great Gatsby*, a book I was mad about, and so had a feeling for the ambience of the city, its tremendous power and the collective anguish of its inhabitants' heartbreak. Also, it seemed a great metropolis to write about, unlike my own city, which everyone said was such a nice place to live but which I believed lacked any sort of grand or racy or tragic character.

It was about this time that another important influence came into my life, a woman teacher (I was the sort of boy more likely to be influenced by women than men) who taught me grade twelve English, The Modern Novel, and whose stern and demanding temperament was almost a thrilling antidote to my mother's doting. She bore the unfortunate name of Mrs. Springbottom, a teacher's curse to be sure, but she assigned to us novels that I felt, even as I read them, were changing my life. *A Portrait of the Artist as a Young Man. Of Human Bondage. Sons and Lovers.* She was a big woman, stocky and wide-shouldered as a stevedore and equally deep-voiced, who favoured silk scarves and flowing dresses. A childless widow of twenty-five years, Mrs. Springbottom told us that life was cruel and that the best novels presented this reality unflinchingly while offering the compensation of art. This was a step up from my mother's simple devotion to the beautiful and rang closer to the truth to me, despite my own life so far having been without the slightest hardship.

Mrs. Springbottom's lectures were more passionate than anything I later encountered at the University of Toronto, but it was not she who introduced me to the great novels of New York. These I discovered on my own, sitting on my little rug over a copy of *Washington Square* or *A Tree Grows in Brooklyn* or *Miss Lonelyhearts*. I discovered Singer on my own too, or rather I found a copy of the novel *Enemies* on the study bookshelves, my father having abandoned it after twenty-five pages as "sordid" and "full of lies about Jews." I charted the lives of the characters from all these books on the *National Geographic* map. I also read histories of New York, literary studies, guidebooks.

As for wanting to be a writer, that desire came so early that its origins are lost to me. Perhaps it seemed easier than composing music or playing the violin or painting. I felt that the word itself — *writer* — had a luminous glow. But I do remember the Sunday night when, at the age of eleven, I announced at the dinner table my intention to be one. My father said, "Does nobody at this table want to take over the business?" Aaron rolled his eyes and kicked me under the table. My mother's reaction was the one I really waited for, but she said nothing. Only that night when I was already in bed did she come into my room and kneel down to kiss my forehead. "My writer," she whispered. "I always knew." I blushed in the darkness with pleasure, though I knew that even she didn't understand the strange, humbling power I felt inside me.

I courted my first girlfriend, Theresa Zeitman, who sat behind me in French class, with my talk of New

York and a promise, never fulfilled, to take her there. I find it difficult to explain why I did not apply to Columbia or NYU, or at least take one of those cheap bus-tour packages and spend a weekend in the city I had been imagining for so long. The only answer I can think of is fear — of leaving home, of growing up, of replacing my dream version of New York with the real thing. By the time I got on that airplane with Aaron, Theresa and I had not seen each other for five months. We had been a couple from that last high-school year until not long before university graduation, when, in the front seat of my father's Lincoln Continental, she told me that it was over. I was the one who wept, while Theresa stroked my hair to comfort me. "It's all right," she kept saying evenly, "everything will be okay." But I didn't think it would be. I drove her home, and after sitting in the car outside her house for a while I drove back to my parents' house. Aaron was already asleep; I could hear him snoring in his room. I threw myself on the rug in front of my bookcase and knew that my old teacher was wrong and that art was not compensation for life, that nothing was compensation.

An hour or so later I picked up a pen and began to write. I managed only two or three pages, but I picked it up again the next day. And after several months, after rewriting and rewriting, it became the story that I would take with me to New York. Art was not compensation but it was necessary anyway, I decided, and this sudden truth gave a severe and tragic quality to my chosen calling.

# 3

# The Cockroach

Ahead of us on Park Avenue I could see Grand Central Station, lit up like the Parthenon and with the statue of fig-leafed Mercury posed above its enormous clock. I could not help thinking of all those John Cheever characters, woollen-suited men commuting home on the trains from their advertising jobs, mildly drunk and guilt-ridden over their adulterous affairs. The bus pulled up beside a tarnished green bridge that led car traffic around the station, an oddly cloistered space I knew was called Pershing Square.

The door opened with a hydraulic whoosh and the driver said, "Welcome to the greatest show on earth. Remember folks, watch your wallets." We waited for the passengers ahead of us to shuffle off and then dragged our bags out the door and stood on the side-walk beside the dim subway entrance. An acrid smell of urine rose up the stairway. Garbage swam around our ankles — paper cups with a Greek geometric design around their rims, tattered pages from the *New York Post*, cigarette butts, gum wrappers. I didn't even bother to suggest that we take a cab from here, but for the first time Aaron hesitated, so I picked up my bag and started down the entrance. Halfway down the blackened stairs sat a man who appeared to have no legs; he sat in a cardboard box with a ragged blanket over his lap and looked up at us with plaintive eyes. Back in Toronto I rarely saw anyone begging, and certainly never one so miserable. Aaron stopped behind me and found some change in his pocket, which he placed carefully in the man's filthy hand.

"What kind of money is that?" the man said, peering at it.

"Canadian," Aaron answered. "It's all the change I've got right now."

The legless man shrugged and put the money some place among his clothes.

A woman coming up the stairs began shouting at us. "What you giving him money for?" She was a large woman, with a big face and tremendous hips, but with two long braids like a young girl. "You think that does any good? He makes a better living than I do, cleaning those damn toilets. That Jew mayor ought to do something."

Aaron and I stood there with our jaws open while the woman, fast despite her size, pushed past us, whacking my leg with her purse, and was gone. We continued more slowly down the stairs and I said, "That couldn't be, could it, Aaron? Do you think there are honest beggars and dishonest ones?"

Even as I asked I realized that I was appealing to Aaron for the truth, just as I had done when we were young. We had only set foot on Manhattan ground a few moments before but already I had my first disquieting doubt about whether I would find myself quite as at home as I had expected.

Aaron said, "Don't listen to such talk. For all we know, the guy might be a *lamed vavnik.*"

"A what?"

"One of the thirty-six righteous men. That woman is doing the work of the Evil One by trying to destroy the charitable impulse."

My brother now took the lead down into the subway. He had sounded so sure of himself. He could not see into the heart of the beggar and he didn't care to; he needed to know only his own duty. I almost wished such a response was adequate for me, but I already knew it couldn't be.

The subway felt so much like a cave I would not have been surprised to see stalactites hanging from the ceiling. At the ticket booth I slid a five-dollar bill through the slot. The Plexiglas separating the ticket-seller from the masses was scratched and cracked, as if some beast had torn at it with its claws. She pushed out a small pile of metal tokens and I gave half to Aaron. We each put one in the turnstile and followed the signs to the Forty-second Street shuttle. Above our heads a web of girders and rivets made it feel as if we were in the hold of a battleship. Trains we couldn't see vibrated the stairs as we climbed to the platform. A crowd was waiting — babies wailing, teenage boys cutting up, women reading magazines. Two short Hispanic men who looked like brothers were carrying a naked mannequin without a head. The shuttle pulled in and even before the riders had gotten out our crowd began pushing its way inside. Aaron and I were too slow and the others forced themselves around us so that we were the last to get on and Aaron's bag got caught in the closing doors. The two of us had to yank it into the shuttle, ripping open the side pocket. Yellow pamphlets scattered onto the floor. As we gathered them up I read the title:

The Mashiach Is Close
and Your Good Deeds
Bring Him Closer

"Who's the Mashiach?" I said, mangling the word.

Aaron looked down at the floor. "The Messiah."

"Where did you get the pamphlets?"

"A Lubavitch gave them to me."

"But what do you need with so many?"

"I leave them around. On car windshields or in mailboxes."

"Aaron, please, don't tell me that. That's like the Jehovah's Witnesses. It's so —"

"What? In bad taste? Embarrassing to you?"

"Frankly, yes. And do you believe it? Do you really believe that the Messiah is coming soon?"

Just then the lights flickered off. I felt a sudden irrational panic, as if I would be crushed by the other bodies in the train or would feel strange hands pulling at my clothes. The lights blinked on, off, then on again, and as the thumping of my heart subsided the door connecting our car to the next slid open and a man with sores on his face came in. He was dirty and emaciated, his cheeks hollow, his eyes dull and glassy. Despite the crowding, people moved aside to allow him to limp past with a paper cup in his hand, and I saw a cardboard sign hung around his neck with a string.

PLEES HELP

VICTIM OF A NEW DISEEZ

A few people gave him change — someone even pushed in a bill — but he didn't acknowledge them and when he passed us and reached the other end of the car he opened that door and passed through to the next.

"Now that I'm here," Aaron said, "I believe it even more."

Aaron assumed that the only reason for my coming to New York was to watch over him during his visit to meet the Kovner Rebbe in Brooklyn. But I had my own reasons as well, and if one of them was forced on me against my will it nevertheless excited me, and I was anxious to deliver my brother to the Schraft Hotel and then leave him as soon as possible. We hauled our bags up out of the subway and along Thirty-ninth Street to the hotel. It had an enormous and dismal front, old but uncharming, with half the letters on its neon sign frizzed out. It was not, as I had faintly hoped, a once grand hotel now fallen on hard times; it had never been grand, just big. We pushed our way through the revolving door, the glass of one panel having been shattered and replaced by chipboard, and entered the cavernous lobby. I imagined that at one time, in the forties and fifties, the lobby had been crowded with all kinds of people — sheet-music salesmen, hopeful chorus girls, unknown playwrights — but it was all but deserted now. It seemed as large as a football field, and the groupings of dusty armchairs with their worn velvet upholstery hardly seemed to fill it. The place smelled of mildew and rancid milk. It was dim inside, as if the management had put bulbs of insufficient wattage into the ghoulish chandeliers to save on electricity. I knew that New York had come close to bankruptcy four years earlier and it seemed to me that the entire city had merely descended to the condition of the Schraft Hotel.

The only other person in the lobby, besides the desk clerk, was a small wrinkled woman with jet-black bangs and black circles painted around her eyes like an aging Sally Bowles. Beside her on the sofa sat three tiny dogs, hairless chihuahuas by the looks of them, and every few moments one of them would do a somersault into the air, landing again on its spot on the sofa. I remembered that the advertisement had declared the hotel friendly to showpeople, but wondered what sort of work a dog act could possibly find so many decades after the end of vaudeville. As the fill-in between strippers in some lousy grind joint? The woman stared at us as she cracked sunflower seeds and put the shells into a little purse in her lap.

We went up to the front desk where the clerk was reading a copy of *Variety*. He stroked his goatee as he looked up and gave us a cheerless smile.

"We have a reservation," Aaron said. "Roth."

"Roth the somnambulist?" His voice was lugubrious.

"No, we're not performers."

"I see." He looked disdainful but reached back to

pick a key from the rack. "Twelfth floor. I'm sorry, but the bellboy is indisposed at the moment."

We carried our bags to the elevators and watched as the big hand rotated on the overhead dial. "What the hell does that mean — indisposed?" I whispered. But Aaron didn't respond. If this had happened a year ago we would have been suppressing giggles, would have turned the undertaker clerk into a story, a piece of our shared mythology of brothers. The elevator arrived but the door stuck halfway and we had to push it open. On the way up Aaron seemed to be saying something under his breath and I hoped that at least he was praying for us to survive the trip to the twelfth floor.

To find our room we had to go down a long corridor, turn right, and down another. Aaron unlocked the door and turned on the light, which cast a jaundiced haze over the two single beds, a dresser with its thin veneer chipping, an armoire, and a television set with rabbit ears. The carpet appeared green, although under that light it was hard to tell. A small window looked directly onto the window of the building across the alley, through which I could see three bored-looking women with telephone sets on their heads.

"What a dive," I said.

"It doesn't matter." Aaron put his bag on the bed next to the window. "The holy light shines from within."

"Are you going to talk like this the whole trip? Because if you are I'll buy a notebook to write it all down. I think the Old Testament could use another chapter."

"What do you want to talk about, Felix? How we used to build balsa-wood airplanes?"

"We used to talk about philosophy when you were an undergrad. Sartre and Hegel."

"Those two were both egomaniacs. The only thing they believed in was themselves."

"And science. You were always trying to get the basic principles into my dim head. The theory of relativity. Black holes. Genetic evolution."

"The Almighty said, 'Let there be light.'"

I shook my head and sat down on the edge of the bed that was mine by default. The mattress groaned under me, a fair imitation of the way I felt at that moment. "It really drives me nuts when you talk like that. It isn't natural. It isn't human, Aaron. I know we aren't the kind to talk about our brotherly relationship, but I always used to look up to you. I mean, you acted like it was your *duty* to educate me."

"Well, I didn't deserve it. The things I knew, Felix, they were just facts. What did they add up to? What good were they? They didn't tell me how to live or what to believe in. And all that philosophy just left me dissatisfied and angry. What did I learn except that every value was relative and there was no real truth but just aimless speculation? That's not enough for me. And what kind of values did Mom and Dad give us? I don't blame them — they grew up after the war, when everybody just wanted the security of a home and a decent job. It made sense for them to equate material success with happiness. But it isn't enough. Maybe going to law school and being surrounded by all those students strutting around like they were already senior partners was the last straw for me. I want faith. I've always wanted it. I need to be able to pray and believe that God hears me. Not to ask for anything, but to give thanks. I want to live a righteous life."

He tried to suppress a yawn and then bent over to untie his Wallabies, those shapeless suede shoes that he had been wearing since junior high, replacing each worn-out pair with an identical new one.

I said, "You want easy and secure answers when there aren't any."

"You think what I'm trying to do is easy? Every step is excruciating to me."

"That's not what I mean. You want to shut off your own natural intelligence and believe in something blindly, a truth that gets handed to you on a platter."

"It isn't like that, Felix. I want to open my eyes, not close them. It's really a matter of what you choose to believe and what you choose to be skeptical about. Think of it this way. You believe that you're the one with the open, questioning mind, right? But do you really question everything you see or think you know? What about that ashtray on the dresser?"

"I see they neglected to clean the butts out."

"That's not what I mean. What colour is it?"

"This is a trick question."

"In a way it is. But what colour is it?"

"Blue."

"And do you question its blueness?"

I hesitated. "Well, no."

"But what is blue? It's the wave of light that's not absorbed by the ashtray. It's what the ashtray turns away, but you think that the ashtray is blue. And yet you refuse to believe in God. Why, because you can't see Him? But what we can see is highly suspect."

"I never said that God doesn't exist. I said that it's

a matter of indifference to me because it has no effect on my life. Also, God is simply not interesting."

"I see, He doesn't matter. He's irrelevant." Aaron leaned back on the pillow and covered his eyes with the back of his hand to shield them from the yellow light. "And His commandments don't matter either."

I felt my heart seize. Was Aaron trying to tell me that he knew what I had worked so hard to keep from him? But he went on, "All those novels you read are so important, so wonderful, but the word of God — that you can't be bothered with. I think we should go to sleep. Better to be fresh for tomorrow."

No, he didn't know. He couldn't. This was my chance. "There's just one little thing I have to do," I said, dragging my bag to the armoire. It was painted a diarrheal brownish green, perhaps to match the carpet. I opened one of the twin doors, only to see some *thing* skitter across the bottom.

"Shit!"

"What is it?" Aaron sat up.

"I'm not sure." Peering into the gloom of the armoire, I saw it: a cockroach the size of a man's thumb. It was crouching — that was the only possible description — at the back, its triangular head cocked to one side as if waiting for my next move. We did not have cockroaches in the suburbs of Toronto, and even if we did they could not have survived the warfare waged by our cleaning lady, Marie, and her arsenal of deadly cleansers and sprays. This was the first one I had ever seen and, despite my revulsion, I could not resist studying it with interest. The damn thing seemed eerily thoughtful, as if my sudden presence raised a philosophical dilemma of its own. When I moved slightly forward it scuttled into the corner. For the first time I understood why Kafka had Gregor Samsa turn into a giant insect in "The Metamorphosis." Thinking of it reminded me of a terrific story by Isaac Bashevis Singer, "A Friend of Kafka," about an old Yiddish actor who had met Kafka when his troupe performed in Prague. If the actor was based on a real person whom Singer had met, and I managed to meet Singer in New York as I hoped, then a human chain would link all of us, from Franz Kafka to Felix Roth.

"Well?" Aaron asked. "What is it?"

"A cockroach."

"Also one of God's creatures."

"Yes, but I would rather it seek other accommodations. Listen, Aaron, you go to bed. I have to go out for a little while."

"Where to?" He looked at me suspiciously. "New York is dangerous at night. Every other person on the street looked like a mugger to me."

"Even muggers are God's creatures," I said.

Aaron smiled, the smile that I had always sought to win when I was a kid, that meant he thought I had said something clever or funny. "Don't be so smart," he said. "I still don't like you going out. Mom wouldn't either."

"Mom sent me to look after *you*. She didn't say anything about the other way around. I'm too excited to sleep. If I don't take a walk and get some air I'll lie awake all night. I promise to be back soon."

In the bathroom I put my hand on the tiled wall in search of the light switch. The wall had a filmy sheen. When the light went on I saw that the toilet had a crack in the seat and the mirror was slowly desilvering itself. I ran my hand through my hair and straightened the tie that I had bought at Goodwill. The corduroy blazer I had purchased new at Eaton's just after graduation in the spring; with the paisley tie, blue shirt, jeans, and running shoes, it made a uniform of sorts, a compromise between the way I imagined a writer might look and the way I had dressed since high school.

Back in the room, Aaron was unpacking his own bag. He took out an extra shirt, a pair of pleated trousers, a small velvet bag that held the tefillin he used for morning prayers and another for his tallis, and his pocket chess game. Even though he had given up playing against real opponents, Aaron still liked to work through famous matches and chess problems. That he brought it seemed to me a good sign; he still had one foot in this world.

I unzipped my own bag and pulled out the manuscript that I had brought, careful to hold it rolled behind my back so that Aaron wouldn't see it. Perhaps it was guilt about going out that caused me to make the parting speech that I did, a sense of obligation to my mother that I had to do something more to keep him with us.

"Aaron," I said. "Do you want to know what I really think? Don't even answer, because I'll tell you anyway. I think this new religion of yours is embarrassing. Yes, I really do. It's one thing to want to go to synagogue, even to wear a yarmulke. But to come all this way to see some wonder-working rabbi? It's as if you want to dismiss hundreds of years of progress and civilization and return to the Dark Ages. Those religious Jews dress like it's still medieval times. They do everything possible to keep themselves apart from the rest of the world when they no longer have to. What do they want? Ghettos? Pogroms? A reason to huddle all by themselves? And they think the rest of us aren't even real Jews. It's pathetic and shameful, that's what I think. And if you become one of them, well, I'll feel sorry for you and I'll feel contempt."

My face was burning. Aaron sat with his head lowered for a long moment and then slowly unlatched the little portable chess set and poured the miniature pawns and kings and knights onto the bed. "Be careful, Felix," he said. I watched him begin setting up the pieces and when it was clear he didn't plan to say anything else I went out.

# 4

# Fun City

Times Square at night was a circus of grotesque desire, its audience a swarm of hungry and raucous faces lit by the throbbing marquees. The old Broadway houses on Forty-second Street had once been home to what my mother still called the legitimate theatre, but now they were pornographic cinemas and strip shows with names like Peepworld and Club Sexotica. This was not the sort of temptation that much interested me, though I stopped by one of the doors to look at some photographs of women caught in mid-wink as they presented their totemic breasts. They seemed too aggressively voluptuous, a certain kind of male fantasy or nightmare. This club was called Fun City, and the name brought back the time that Theresa Zeitman told me that I suffered from an inability to enjoy myself, to have fun. For me, everything had to be meaningful, profound, she said; it put too much pressure on things. I deeply resented this accusation and later that day I looked up that suspicious word, *fun*, in both my Oxford and Webster dictionaries. I was not surprised to discover that its original meaning was a cheat or hoax, but when I telephoned Theresa to tell her she hung up on me.

A gaggle of middle-aged male tourists went through the doors and I moved on. At the corner of Seventh Avenue a young man with hyped-up movements was working a game of three-card monte, using a cardboard box as a table. He was handsome but for the scar that began under one eye and travelled across his cheek, under his lower lip, and right up to the opposite ear. A jittery crowd blocked the sidewalk, and I remembered reading somewhere that while the cardsharp let some dope win a few dollars his partner would be lifting wallets from the onlookers. I checked my own wallet in my blazer pocket, but just as I tapped my breast the young man kicked over the box, scattering the bent cards, and slipped away from the crowd. Then I saw why: a police car was just rolling up the curb lane. Back in Toronto police cars were always spotless, as if to represent the honest hearts of the officers within, but this one was unwashed and had a substantial dent in the hood, as though a body had fallen on it.

By the time I reached Sixth Avenue the porn cinemas were gone and a low granite wall topped by an iron fence appeared, behind which rose the dusty foliage of a row of plane trees. This was Bryant Park, I realized with pleasure, which meant that the building behind the trees was the back of the New York Public Library. A figure in the darkness sitting on the wall spoke: "Hey, you looking for some weed?" When I declined to answer he said, "Don't be a snob, even college graduates get high these days." But I wasn't interested in his version of Fun City either, and I hurried the last few steps to Fifth Avenue and turned the corner to face the library with its massive columns crowned by corinthian heads, its triangular pediments over the three doors, and the glass and iron orb hanging over the centre entrance. I thought of the countless writers who had dreamed their books at the long tables of its vast reading room. And I couldn't help myself, but had to dance up the steps to reach up and touch one of the lions — Patience or Fortitude, I didn't know which — on its stony paw.

And then I upbraided myself, for these meanderings were making me late and each extra minute was painful to the woman who waited for me. I simply — yes, some emotions were simple — I simply couldn't believe that I was here in New York and the night was beautiful and I had a manuscript rolled up and wedged in my blazer pocket. Suddenly I didn't want to delay anymore. I had a great happy need to see Alice, and I started up Fifth Avenue.

Fifth Avenue in the forties was darker than I expected, with fewer street lights and half the shops shuttered with metal grates and iron doors. Across the avenue I saw the Scribner bookshop, with a slanting canopy above the glass and delicate wrought-iron front. Through the bright windows I could see the arched ceiling and hanging lights and stairway to the second floor and the rows and tables of books. But I resisted the temptation of crossing over and dreaming that one of the books in the window had my name on it, instead continuing up the avenue as the shopfronts became swankier and also brighter, beating the night away. There was Saks Fifth Avenue, stately and festooned with American flags, and then, on my side, Rockefeller Center, a coolness blowing off the fountain with its golden Prometheus at the end of the promenade of benches and palms. I passed St. Patrick's Cathedral, like some fragment of medieval France dropped onto the main street of the new world. And then I crossed Fifty-first Street and Fifth Avenue awoke like a ballroom when the chandeliers are lit, for here was Cartier and Fortunoff and Elizabeth Arden and Gucci and Rizzoli and Ginori and Steuben and Bonwit Teller and Tiffany. I felt as if I were about to run into Holly Golightly and dance with her up the sidewalk. Perhaps it was true that back home I would have denounced this materialist heaven, but on the other hand, who would have thought to write a book called *Breakfast at Holt Renfrew*? What was crass in Toronto sparkled in New York with bright, embraceable meaning.

And then there it was, the Plaza Hotel, not visible until I rounded the corner of Bergdorf's and saw it set back in its own protective circle, with the shadowy trees of Central Park just behind it on the other side of Fifty-ninth Street. It was as elegant as I had imagined, Parisian almost, from the illuminated entrance to its coppery mansard roof, and gazing up at it I wondered in which room Fitzgerald had imagined Daisy and Tom and Jordan Baker and Gatsby and Nick Carraway spending a stultifying summer afternoon drinking mint juleps and arguing over who Daisy really loved, Tom or Gatsby. And here I was, fifty years later, and now the Plaza had air conditioning and every other modern amenity, but I was still going up to see Alice, only I didn't have to argue with her husband, who happened to be my boss, because he was staying back in Toronto.

I tried to affect an air of nonchalance, though I half expected the doorman — dressed in white and black like an Allsorts licorice candy — to laugh in my face and bar the way. But he merely smiled and opened the door. The first thing I noticed was the lobby's mosaic floor, then the scent from the colossal vase of flowers on the table in the otherwise empty space, and finally the marble columns leading to the Palm Court from which the sound of a tinkling piano came. A party of young people jostled by, the girls tittering in their satin gowns and the boys, hair shaved above their ears, fiddling at the bow ties of their tuxedos. I guessed they were debutantes and stared as if at some rare species of marmoset until they were out the doors and gone into the night. Then I took quick strides past the concierge desk to the gold and mirrored elevators.

I knew Alice's room number, for just yesterday she had passed my desk and casually dropped a folded note even as she spoke to Arthur Lowenstein, her husband. She had dropped it and then, turning from him in midsentence, had let her emerald eyes light on me for just a moment. From where she stood I could not see that her right eye had a flaw, a pale streak across the iris. But I knew it was there, for I had looked at it often enough lying in bed beside her. Her daring shocked me. I was terrified that Arthur had noticed the note, but Arthur never seemed to notice anything, and a moment later I slipped it into my pocket. At lunch I had unfolded it. "Room 718. Meet me there at ten." I hadn't even known it was possible to arrange the exact room in a hotel before arriving.

Now in the elevator, panelled like some miniature library, I was suddenly bursting with impatience. How I wanted to see Alice, to tell her of everything I had seen in New York so far, to imitate the bus driver from the airport, to describe the crafty look of the cockroach in the hotel armoire, just as I had been telling her everything for the past two months, speaking to her more freely than I had ever spoken before. Of course, there was also the slight problem of telling her I thought the relationship had to end, but I would figure out how to do that at the right moment. My plan had been to be firm and tell her as soon as I arrived, but now, as the elevator doors opened, I thought it might be best to wait a little while. After all, we were in New York. Why spoil things right away?

I found room 718 and knocked on the door. Almost immediately Alice opened it, as though she had been hovering just behind it.

"Felix," she said, so softly that I saw my name on her lips more than heard it. She looked at me strangely, as if I were a mirage or had risen from the dead, or perhaps she had just not expected me to show up. Her face was pale and narrow, and her straight and slightly pinched nose always seemed so poignant to me. She wore a silk dress of a beautiful dusty grey, cut very slim, her legs and feet bare. Every time I saw her I thought of a line of Masha's in Chekhov's *Seagull*: "I am in mourning for my life." Alice was thirty-five, which made her fourteen years older than me, was married to a manic depressive who happened to be my employer, and she had a seven-year-old son who stole from her purse and said terrible things. She was an expert in porcelain restoration for the Royal Ontario Museum and could make broken objects appear whole again, although this wholeness, she had told me, was illusion.

"I'm sorry to be late," I said, stepping inside. She had a suite and we were in the living area. I could see her gin and tonic on the coffee table by the sofa.

"You're always late. You ought to have cards printed up with an apology. Then you could just hand me one."

"I'm not that bad, Alice. At least, I don't mean to be."

"I know you don't. You never mean to hurt anybody. You'd like to make everybody happy if you could so that everyone would love you. Do you want a drink? The bar is under the television. But of course you don't. You wouldn't want to lose any of that self-control of yours."

"Alice." I stepped towards her but she turned away to pick up her glass. I could see that she had worked herself up while waiting for me as she sometimes did and that I would have to manoeuvre carefully. I had never met anyone so difficult, but this difficulty also meant an exhilarating intensity that I had never experienced before. She deliberately looked away from me towards the window, but the curtains were closed to the view. I noticed a vase of unopened roses on the coffee table, and just to fill the silence I said, "Nice flowers. In our hotel they wouldn't even give us dandelions."

"Arthur sent them."

"Ah. And I've never bought you flowers. The truth is it never even occurred to me."

"Good. Don't ever start."

More silence. We were already at such a level of

discomfort it might have been a good time to go all the way and break off the relationship, but I could not find the courage to do it.

Alice said, "Do you know the book *Eloise*, about the little girl who lives at the Plaza? She gets into mischief and drives everyone crazy and is absolutely spoiled. When I read it as a kid I thought it was the saddest book in the world. Because Eloise's parents were never there. I also wished I could be as bold as she was. When I was young my parents used to bring me here every fall; my father had some annual conference of heart surgeons. Can you imagine so many arrogant men in one room? My mother loved coming because she could at least be sure that his mistress-of-the-week was staying behind. Did I ever tell you I used to hear her crying at night and begging him to stop seeing other women? But never once did she leave him or even threaten to. The awful thing is I'd rather be like my father than my mother. I *am* more like him."

"I don't think you're like him, Alice. Not from what I know."

"When we were here they would go every night to the theatre or the opera and leave me with a different sitter hired from some agency. Some of them were nice enough, but I still resented them. God knows why I still come back here. I suppose it's my desire to retreat somewhere safe, or that I pretend is safe. Maybe I'll just stay in this room for the next few days and not come out." She let herself half fall onto the sofa and crossed her legs.

"You can't stay in," I said as I sat down on the other end, careful to keep some space between us. "You've got a reason for being here."

"Which you don't believe. You think I just made it up to follow you."

"I don't, Alice. It was just an amazingly lucky coincidence, that auction coming up."

"You're too damn in love with yourself."

"I don't think I am in love with myself."

"You are. And I've only made it worse by paying so much attention to you."

For the first time she smiled. In truth, I was doubtful about her reason for the trip and the way it suddenly came up. Perhaps she *had* followed me and now felt foolish or vulnerable and that was the real reason for this tension. Would I have followed her anywhere? Would I have risked appearing the overeager one? I felt remorse for not having rushed breathlessly to see her. My own shallowness was disgusting to me; it made me doubt that I would ever write anything of importance.

I moved over a little.

"Alice, you look very beautiful tonight."

"Oh, shut up. My drink's all gone but I'm too lazy to get another. Anyway, I've had two. Before you arrived I was thinking about the first time I saw you. In that horrid office that Arthur keeps, I don't know how he can stand it. You were sitting at the typewriter with your back to me and didn't turn around."

"Because I didn't hear you, I was concentrating so hard. For some reason I'm always terrified of disappointing Arthur with what I write."

"You're terrified of disappointing everybody. You work too hard for that silly rag he publishes. Sometimes I think you do it to secretly compensate him for screwing his wife."

"I can't stand when you talk like that. It's demeaning to all of us."

"Yes, it is. I wouldn't want to demean anyone. Anyway, the first thing I noticed was that your hair needed brushing. It made me feel very tender towards you. You have that effect, did you know? I think women will always want to take care of you."

I moved closer so that my leg was brushing her thigh. "I'm glad Arthur had to do his dog-and-pony show for that advertising client. I'm glad he couldn't take you for lunch and I got to instead."

"You never stopped talking, Felix, not for the whole two hours. Going on about your stories and your terrible breakup with your first girlfriend and about your family. It was so sweet. I didn't even realize you were beginning to seduce me."

"I wasn't!"

"I'm sure you didn't let yourself know that you were. That's part of what makes you so naive. You think you know everything about yourself, that you're so self-analytical, but you miss all of the important things. You wouldn't believe yourself capable of even being attracted to a woman who was married, and certainly not to your boss. And in spite of what a son of a bitch Arthur is to you, you quite worship him. Sometimes I think you're more in love with him than with me. Of course when you came to the house and discovered me there because Arthur's trip had somehow slipped your mind —"

"Now it's you who doesn't believe me. He told me he wanted that article as soon as possible. I thought it would be better if I didn't wait until Monday. I just forgot that he had gone."

"I believe you, Felix. I'm glad you showed up at the door. And I'm glad Everett was sleeping. And I'm glad you kissed me."

"I want to kiss you now."

"Are you waiting for my permission? Felix, you don't need to pretend to be the good boy anymore when you're not."

I did kiss her, leaning over to slip my hand around her slim waist. I was shocked by what she had said, that *I* had been the seducer, even as I wondered whether it was true. We kissed a long moment and her lips parted; how sweet her tongue was. I pressed myself almost on top of her so she could feel my arousal and she pulled at my shirt and tie, hungry to get them off. We hardly had the patience to get to the bedroom. Our clothes fell to the carpet along with my manuscript and then Alice was pulling herself over me on the bed. She deftly slipped me inside her as I reached up to caress her small breasts and then somehow I managed to draw myself up so that we were face to face, knees up, holding on to one another as if for dear life.

We made love with a hungry, angry, desperate energy, in ways we had never dared try back in Toronto, as if New York had suddenly liberated us, as if after living under some dictatorship we had taken our little homemade raft and sailed it to this island of freedom. I held back and held back so that when I finally came it was excruciating, as if my soul were being torn from my loins. Afterwards I slipped down the bed and gave my absolute attention to Alice, who was always slow, until she climaxed with her own mad wailing, grasping my hair and pounding on my shoulders. I feared a house detective might come bursting through the door.

We lay a long time, unable to speak, panting in the dark. The curtains were open and I turned my head to look out at the radiant Manhattan night. I could not say anything of what I felt, so I made a joke instead.

"God, there's nothing like a first-class hotel."

Alice didn't laugh. She rarely did, and never because something was funny. She just turned and ran her hand through my hair. "You're a smart and talented boy, Felix," she said. "I love listening to you talk. And the endearing way you've taken *us* so seriously, right from the beginning. If one of my friends found out about you she would just make some comment about being satisfied by a younger man. But this isn't about your being young and beautiful, which you are —"

"I'm completely ordinary looking."

"Don't interrupt. They wouldn't understand that what's so beautiful about your being young is that you still believe that everything is possible. You haven't experienced all the shit. You don't have scars. I remember when you came in the doorway and kissed me that first time. You looked at me as if something extraordinary had just happened. And I know you suffered over it afterwards. You were shocked to discover what you're capable of feeling. And now that we've gone this far you can't reconcile yourself to the wrong of it. You still believe there ought to be a way to reconcile everything, to make it add up correctly so nobody is hurt. It doesn't help to have read *Madame Bovary* and *Anna Karenina.*"

I kissed her. "Let's make a promise that nobody takes poison or throws himself under a train, all right? You think too much of me, Alice — I'm not as good as you say. I feel ashamed to be who I am."

"Shhh — " She put her finger to my lips. "Here, I want to show you something." She sat up, letting the covers fall away from her, and turned on the reading lamp on the night table. She picked up a magazine from the table and put it on the bed before us. "This is the catalogue, I wanted to show it to you." The cover read "Hines and McCutcheon, Auctioneers" along with an address on Spring Street, the date of the auction, two days away, and "Objets d'art from the Estate of Herbert and Ethel Prangle." I hardly felt ready to return to the world beyond bed, but she turned the pages and I saw grainy photographs of small bronze statues, silver-headed walking sticks, mechanical penny banks, inkwells, art nouveau chandeliers, clocks, glass dogs.

"Who were the Prangles?" I asked.

"I wondered that myself. Mr. Prangle was a trucker from Atlanta who figured out a way to compress garbage more efficiently into landfills. He made a fortune late in life and he and his wife began to buy indiscriminately, without any knowledge of what they were getting. The museum gets all the auction catalogues and we take turns going through them. And this is what I saw."

She put her finger to a photograph of a porcelain figurine, a miniature woman in an ornate gown with tight bodice, smiling as she held a rose against her luminous white bust. Because porcelain meant so much to Alice I tried to appreciate such pieces, but for the life of me I could not see anything of interest in them.

"At the office you said it belonged to Napoleon. Were you serious? And nobody but you has realized it?"

"Not Napoleon, his mistress. It's mentioned in the diary of one of his officers. Napoleon gave it to a certain married court woman named Madame de Desmarets in 1803. There are hundreds of others like it, of course — the 'Lady with the Rose' was made by the Limoges workshop for years. But in every other example I've seen the rose is always red. Napoleon had his officer order one with a yellow rose as a sly reminder to his mistress of what a jealous lover he was. After her death it disappeared. I just happened to remember the story when I saw the catalogue and read the description of the yellow rose. You see what the catalogue says — that the rose has 'apparently' been repainted and glazed. They couldn't think of any other explanation. Tomorrow I'll go and take a close look. Then I'll be more sure."

I looked again at the photograph, in which the rose looked grey, holding the edge of the page so that my hand touched hers. Alice had never mentioned any such figurine before coming into the office yesterday to tell Arthur that she had to leave for New York as soon as possible. Arthur had given me the time off to accompany my brother only reluctantly and I had a sudden fear that he would look up from his desk, suddenly realize what was going on between Alice and me, and then plunge his letter opener into my throat. Instead, he merely said that since I was going to be there at the same time, perhaps I could take Alice out for dinner.

"Isn't she lovely?" Alice said. "If I can determine she's really the one Napoleon ordered, the museum can make a whole period display around her."

"*You're* lovely," I said, gently trying to pull Alice down to me.

She put the catalogue back and slipped beside me. "Poor Felix," she said. "Do you know how old-fashioned you are at heart? In spite of what you pretend you believe that somewhere out there the perfect soulmate is waiting for you. And I can't be that woman, how can I? So you are fundamentally unable to explain us."

"But I can explain us. Come here and I'll kiss you and that will explain everything."

"All right, but it won't explain anything."

As we kissed my hand moved slowly down from the angle of her shoulder blade to her back and on to the rise of what Napoleon would have called her *belle derrière*. I realized that I was afraid to give Alice up, for if I did I might never feel this electric clarity of experience and desire. I could not imagine someone else thinking about me, caring about me, as much as Alice did. Maybe she was right and my moral compass had gone haywire, but I felt more alive than I ever had in my life. I had an extreme awareness of my body at this moment, the heel of my foot, the downy hairs on my belly. Did that mean this was narcissism, a form of self-love? If so, it was also Alice, the sad reality of her, the intensity of her need, the feel of her skin, the beating of her heart beneath her breast.

And even as I entered her again I thought: I have to give her up, I have to.

I wish I could record here that in the heat of love-making I forgot all about the manuscript of my story that had landed among our underthings by the bed, but that is not the case. Alice wanted me to stay the night, a luxury we had never enjoyed, but I could not leave Aaron on his own and, besides, did not want to explain to him where I'd been. So I dressed again and kissed Alice and sheepishly asked her if she would read the story. She had already read my other stories but nothing as new as this and nothing, I hoped, as good. If she had wanted to read it right then I would have stayed despite how late it was, but instead she told me to meet her in the Palm Court at four the next day — or rather, that day, for it was well after midnight.

When I got back to the Schraft Hotel the lobby had the atmosphere of a morgue. The effect was enhanced by the presence of what appeared to be a corpse propped on one of the armchairs, an old man with rouged cheeks and a very bad toupée. His eyes were open but glassy, and they followed me as I crossed towards the elevators. As I passed by he made a flourish with his hand and a bouquet of flowers appeared, which he pretended to offer me. In fact, they were made of silk, looked soiled from decades of service, and I had seen him pull them from inside his sleeve.

In the room, Aaron was asleep. As a child he had been a sleepwalker, speaking urgently but incomprehensibly as my parents trailed after him around the house, afraid to wake him up. I could still remember standing inside my door and crying as I watched. Although he had grown out of it years ago, I double-locked the door and moved a chair in front. I didn't want him roaming the corridors of the Schraft along with the regular ghouls. It did not occur to me that when I awoke again his bed would be empty, and not because he was sleepwalking.

# 5

# Lowenstein's Sheet

In moments of stress Arthur Lowenstein would shout, "Who do those bastards think they are? Treating me like that! Why, I turned down a membership in MENSA! Do they know what that means? MENSA!" He had a monstrous arrogance and a secret fear that the world was mocking him. I tried to understand why Alice had married him but the best I could come up with was that she wanted to punish her parents. She had never gotten over what they had done to her, or hadn't done, and had made a faith of her grievances. Perhaps she punished them also by punishing herself and marrying a man she did not love. I wanted to believe that love and misery could not commingle so, although I was no longer sure.

My own upbringing being so different, I wondered whether I was drawn to Alice because of her early and sustained unhappiness. Did I feel a kind of sick envy? If writers turned their lousy childhoods into great novels, then what could I possibly make of my own? If my parents had a fault, it was the all-too-forgivable one of sheltering Aaron and me too much, so that we were unprepared for adult struggle. It seemed to me that a writer ought to feel reality *more* vividly than other people, not less. For example, no matter how hard I tried, I could not quite grasp how money entered into things. Of course I knew I had to make a living, but I never really believed it. Perhaps I thought my father would always be there, looking at me adoringly and offering me a twenty-dollar bill from his rough hand. I suspected that this loving protectiveness had some unconscious connection to both my desire to be a writer and my brother's hunger for spiritual faith.

The practical result of this advantaged upbringing was that well into my final undergraduate year, and despite the urgings of Theresa Zeitman that I take our future "seriously," I had no idea of what I was going to do. It was more to prove myself to her than for any other reason (at least in my imagination, for by then we had already broken up) that I cobbled together a résumé and sent it out to a dozen publishers and magazines, including *Lowenstein's Sheet*. I only knew about "The Most Exclusive Business Newsletter in the Country" because my father had received in the mail an invitation to subscribe (at a cost of two hundred bucks a year) and, snorting with disgust, had dropped it into the kitchen trash. The sample copy was printed on cream laid paper and had no photographs but a few small illustrations that looked like engravings, and I imagined the editors in some oak-panelled office, wearing fedoras and using shields on their cuffs to protect them from the ink of their Waterman fountain pens.

"I might be willing to give you a chance," Arthur Lowenstein said gravely into the phone, as if my future depended solely on his generosity. "Come down and we'll have lunch." I could not know that Arthur had just fired his third assistant (and only staff member) in six months and was struggling to get his newsletter out by himself. We met not in the Victoria Room of the King Edward Hotel or some other power-broking lunch spot but at the basement soup counter of the St. Lawrence Market near the office. Arthur was waiting for me and as he vigorously pumped my hand in his own big paw I saw that he had one of those youthful faces that didn't age well. He wore a blue blazer with an Upper Canada College crest, a striped shirt, chinos, and beat-up boating shoes, just the way (or so I imagined) that someone with old money would dress. Over our bowls he told me that *Lowenstein's Sheet* was not the usual sort of business rag offering stock tips and economic forecasts and flattering profiles of the head of General Motors. Instead of giving advice on how to get rich, the *Sheet* instructed readers on the proper way to behave once they got there. Its silent motto, Arthur said, was Live Without Guilt. "The businessman still has the little boy inside him," he confided in a voice so low I had to lean forward, a trick for forcing intimacy that I would later see him use on others. "He still wants three things. To be king of the castle. To eat all the candy in the window. And to suck on his mother's tit. We assure him that he's earned everything he wants. Everything. You see what I'm saying? Most businessmen don't know how to enjoy their own power. We give them the courage to be true merchant princes. Do you sympathize, Felix? Can you write to deadline?"

I could only nod yes, for Arthur hardly gave me room to speak. That was something else I learned about him; when anyone else talked for more than a couple of minutes he would grow agitated and begin rapping a pen on his desk or glancing about the room as if looking for something. Nor did I know that he was a Harvard Business School dropout, that he could not tolerate working for anyone else, that *Lowenstein's Sheet* was his fifth business venture or that his mother (the widow of a paper-mill magnate) was constantly bailing him out.

I did find out, on starting work the next day, that Arthur had a nervous stomach and would spend the first half-hour of every morning locked in the tiny washroom. The office was on the Esplanade, in a Victorian building that had been converted into a warren for small-time importers and dubious mail-order businesses. Our space was a single room divided by movable fabric walls into a reception area for the assistant, an art department with a layout table where Arthur had taught himself to lay down columns of type, and Arthur's office. The furniture was metal castoff, the fluorescent lighting too bright, and the washroom had no window or fan so that every morning as Arthur emerged again he would apologize for the stink that invaded the office. On my first day, he let me read the back issues. On the second day, he told me that he needed nine hundred words for the next edition and that I had until five o'clock.

That was one of the worst eight hours of my life, but by the end of it I handed him five typewritten pages with the simple title "The Chair." Taking his words about merchant princes at face value, I had begun my article with a quotation from Bellow's *Herzog*: "A man is born to be orphaned, and to leave orphans after him, but a chair like that chair, if he can afford it, is a great comfort." What followed was a primer on how to buy the perfect, the most luxurious, the most expensive executive chair imaginable. I considered all kinds of styles — Louis XIV, Bauhaus, Windsor, Queen Anne, Biedermeier — and also fabrics, although about this I concluded that only leather, smelling richly of the hunt, would do. Arthur put his feet up on his desk and chuckled to himself as he read. When he finished he swung down his big feet, put his arm around me, and offered his first and last compliment. "Felix, my boy," he said. "You're a natural."

Which was just what began to worry me. Before long I had written "Seven Rules of Etiquette You Should Break" and "The Homburg: Dare Them Not to Laugh." Soon after came "How to Make Everyone Think You've Just Made a Mint in Futures (or Gold or Short-Term Bonds) When You've Really Lost Your Shirt." Arthur ran me hard; he would come up with a subject while in the bathroom and then demand that I have a piece done by a certain arbitrary deadline, noon or five days from then. He sent me to the library to find some obscure statistic or research some arcane corner of business history or a strategy of General Patton's that might be applied against aggressive junior partners. He usually demanded two or three rewrites and accused me of being too soft, of lacking balls. But he always printed my pieces and I would stare at the new issue of *Lowenstein's Sheet* and get a nauseating thrill as I saw my words, thankful that Arthur did not believe in bylines. I did not understand how I could write in a style so smirking and authoritative, so foreign to my nature. I began to feel I had turned into a kind of ventriloquist's dummy, with Arthur's voice emerging from my mouth. Worse, it felt as if I had actually *become* this voice, for while I was writing I almost believed what was appearing on the page before me. It was my first experience of this transformation, for I noted ruefully that a similar feeling had never come over me when I was writing a story. (Not, that is, until the story I ended up taking to New York.) It shook my sense of who I was. And it made me wonder uneasily just how much this advice I was offering to the readers of *Lowenstein's Sheet* was contributing, if even in a small way, to the world's meanness. I thought of Aaron, who lately had begun to speak of the need to perform mitzvoth, good deeds, and felt shame.

I began work at the end of April. And it was in the last week of May when into this fetid little office that we shared like a demented master and his hunchbacked servant Alice entered one day. Before long we were meeting at her studio in an industrial building on Lansdowne Avenue. It had a slanted, north-facing window that gave her the indirect light she needed for her work and that cast a soft glow on our bodies when we made love on the futon sofa. During afternoons when I was supposed to be researching at the library or doing interviews, we would be entangled on that warm bed, panting with disbelief at how far we could go. In retrospect, it seems that I spent my mornings and evenings (when I would make up for lost time) trying to please Arthur and my afternoons trying to please Alice.

But I did love trying to please her. I became sore from the abrasion of our skin and exhausted to the point of near fainting, but my desire always renewed itself. It was another country we entered in that studio, and it was Alice who took me there.

When we weren't making love I sometimes coaxed her into letting me watch her work. She had a long work table with a Formica top and shelves loaded with solvents, glazes, adhesives, tweezers and calipers, palette knives, wire brushes, sandpapers. The objects to be mended waited in wooden boxes filled with straw: English teapots and dishes, miniature Meissen Harlequins and animal orchestras, blue-and-white Chinese vases, Austrian centrepieces in the form of little pleasure gardens with chipped flowers and trellises. Some came from private collectors, some from dealers, some from the museum where she worked part-time. I watched as she bonded broken pieces, modelled a missing handle or petal, painted and gilded. She explained the difference between earthenware, stoneware, bone china, soft-paste, and hard-paste. Her thin fingers worked with amazing precision, as if she had inherited her father-surgeon's touch. Her real forte was painting; she used hair-thin brushes to recreate missing bits of landscape on a restored plate or a classical pattern around the rim of a cup. I asked why she did not paint for herself, but she said that she felt no need for self-expression.

It was never long before we were back on the futon. Not that we made love only. We talked before, after, and sometimes during sex. Alice told me about her father's mistresses, often nurses at the hospital, and her mother's one retaliatory affair, resulting in a nervous breakdown. Also about meeting Arthur at a sorority party just before leaving for Columbia University, where he had roses delivered every day to her dormitory room. And her two brief affairs before me, both with older married men, which she regretted as she said she would never regret us. I asked if Arthur had ever had an affair and she said no, that he had never thought about it and was doggedly loyal to her. She wished that he would, if only to make her feel less guilty.

No doubt I would have benefited from listening to her even more, but in truth *I* was the one with the great compulsion to tell, despite having lived so much less. What she heard from me was the Life Story of Felix Roth, from Birth to Early Manhood, Including His Loving Awe of His Gruff Father and Natural Closeness with His Mother, His Worship of the Older Brother, His First Poem Read Aloud by Grade Three Teacher Mrs. Lobash, the Humiliation of a Summer Camp Bedwetting Incident, and Not Leaving Out His Prepared Speech to Theresa Zeitman on Sex as the Ultimate Expression of Love, Which Faded on His Lips as She Locked Her Bedroom Door and Began Unbuttoning Her Blouse.

It does not embarrass me to recall how ardently I spoke to Alice of these matters, and how I tested the boundaries of my self-consciousness. Alice never seemed to tire of listening, as if the enthusiasm I felt for my own young life was vicariously exciting to her. She gazed rapturously at me as I talked on and on, although I think now her silent reading of all I said must have differed from what I intended. But then a talker — like a writer — can never be certain of what the hearer makes of it all.

# 6

# Each According to His Talents

When I woke in the morning, the first time I opened my eyes to the city, a haze filled the room like the light in a saloon after dawn. A restless tingling, like little sparks, started in my toes and slowly moved up my body, just the way it had as a kid when I woke up on my birthday. Here it was just morning and all of Manhattan waited for me.

I saw that the blind had been pulled up. Aaron wasn't in his rumpled bed, so I called out to him in the bathroom. Sitting up, I could see through the window to the next building, where a different set of women from the night before sat at their desks talking into their headsets. Selling South American real estate, maybe, or talking suicides off their window ledges. One with her dark hair pulled back looked up and seemed to see me. I waved but she just stared blandly, probably bored of watching men pad around naked or couples in their cheap honeymoon frenzies.

I realized that Aaron hadn't answered me, so I called again as I got up. There was no sound of running water either and I saw that his shoes were gone from the end of the bed where he had neatly placed them. My excitement drained away, to be replaced by a sinking feeling in my stomach. "Aaron? You in there?" I called but knew even before I looked that the bathroom would be empty. Next I thought to check the armoire; sure enough, his bag was gone. "Damn," I said to nobody except the cockroach who was still there, waving his antennae and looking as sympathetic as something with an exoskeleton could. I closed the armoire door and started pacing up and down the small room, two and a half paces in each direction, wondering what to do. I remembered the chair that I had placed against the door and saw that it was back in the corner. Maybe my speech the night before had backfired and calling his new faith pathetic and shameful had only made him more stubborn. Instead of keeping him with me, I had chased him away. What an unfeeling idiot I was! And then I noticed a scrap of paper on Aaron's pillow and lunged for it so wildly that I banged my knee on the iron bedframe.

I knew Aaron's handwriting almost as well as I knew my own, a peculiar alternation of printing and script that slanted in the wrong direction.

> *No two persons have the same ability. Each man should work in the service of God according to his talents. If one man tries to imitate another, he merely loses the opportunity to do good through his own merit.*
>
> — Baal Shem Tov

"That's just great, Aaron," I said aloud, tossing the note into the wastepaper basket. We had been in New York for some twelve hours and already I had lost him. Instead of leaving me a useful note to let me know where he was going, he couldn't resist offering this cute piece of wisdom, this message from a Jewish fortune cookie. I went into the bathroom and pissed furiously, then ran the tap and splashed my hot face with icy water. I squeezed out too much toothpaste so that when I peered in the narrow mirror at this *Portrait of the Artist Brushing His Teeth* I looked as if I was rabidly foaming from the mouth. Just what was Aaron trying to tell me in that note, anyway? That I was a bigot against my own kind? That he accepted the different roles we had to play even if I didn't? Incautiously I stepped into the bathtub before pulling up the shower knob, and the spray hit me like a boxer's jab. The crazy idea came to me that Aaron's note contained another, secret message — that he had read the manuscript of my story and had decided that I was a mere imitator, a copyist of more gifted writers and would contribute to the world only if I took up some other profession.

I was fixing my tie when somebody started rapping on the door. Could it be Aaron? But when I opened it I saw a bellboy in a remarkably worn and patched uniform — a *real* bellboy, for he could not have been more than twelve years old. His ears stuck out beneath his cap and he suffered from an epidemic of freckles.

"There's a telephone call for you, Mr. Roth."

"It didn't ring."

"The room phone ain't working. None of 'em do. You got to come to the lobby."

"All right. Hold on a minute."

I took a last glance about the room to make sure I wasn't forgetting anything, even though I knew that I'd left my manuscript with Alice. That did not strike me as terribly wise, considering that I needed it this morning. The bellboy and I walked down the hall and he held the elevator door for me. After it closed he said, "You ever had a slingshot?"

"Pardon?"

"You ever had a slingshot?"

"I don't think so."

"I read about 'em in a book. You can kill squirrels with a slingshot, rats and birds too."

"What about cockroaches?" I said.

"Maybe if you're a crack shot. So I guess if you never had a slingshot you wouldn't know how a person would go about making one."

"I guess I don't."

The boy was silent a moment. "They don't need no batteries," he said.

The elevator door opened onto the lobby and the boy showed me to a wooden telephone booth. I tipped him all the change I had, which amounted to thirty-five cents, and the would-be Huck Finn tipped his hat and smiled, showing a gap in his teeth.

I wanted it to be Aaron on the phone, but I knew better, and picking up the receiver I said, "Hello, Mom."

"Felix, you're in New York?"

It was indeed my mother's anxious voice. "Of course I am. You did phone the hotel."

"I don't need the sarcasm, Felix. I mean, did you get in all right. The flight, the cab. I was thinking about you two all night."

"Sorry. I know you worry. But everything is fine. All those detective shows you watch have convinced you it's not safe here."

"Well, it isn't safe. I've read the statistics in the paper. Let me speak to Aaron."

I paused, not because I even considered telling her that Aaron had disappeared, but in order to think of a lie. "Don't you want to talk to me?" I said lamely.

"All of a sudden you want to gossip with your mother on the phone. Where's Aaron? Is something wrong?"

"No, of course not. He's still sleeping. I guess the trip knocked him out. Do you want me to wake him up?"

"No, let him sleep. But I don't see why he should be tired. It's not as if he's flown in from Asia. There isn't even a time difference between Toronto and New York."

"Well, he didn't sleep that well. I guess he was overexcited. You know Aaron, how he gets quiet but his eyes shine just like when he was a kid."

"You stick by him, Felix. Aaron needs you. He's so unworldly, God knows what could happen to him in New York. He's always been the one I worried about."

"Really? I find that hard to believe. I was the one you made stay home from school when I had the slightest sniffle. Aaron never did."

"Because he refused to. If he had a fever I had to practically tie him to the bed. But you, Felix, you loved staying home. Even if you weren't that sick you used to whimper so much I would finally give in. If you could stay in bed and cut pictures out of magazines or write your stories or watch TV you were happy. Sometimes I'd just watch you from the door — you were in another world. And then sometimes you'd want attention from me, to play Scrabble or just keep you company. I had a hard time making dinner."

"You make me sound like Proust."

"Don't show off, you've never read Proust," she said sharply. It was true, I hadn't yet got up the nerve to tackle all those volumes, but my mother had read them years ago. I remembered she had once told me that bragging was especially deplorable in truly intelligent people. Now she said, "Aaron wasn't like you. He always had to be stoic. He didn't even like to be hugged. Once I found him in our bedroom, standing in front of the mirror and trying on your father's beat-up hat, the one he refused to throw out. I sometimes used to think that Aaron wanted to be your father, that he couldn't stand just being a boy. But you were different. Remember when I caught you trying on one of my brassieres — ?"

"Please, Mom."

"Your father was terrified you'd turn into a homosexual. That's why he bought a *Playboy* and put it in the basement cupboard for you to find."

"That's how it got there?"

"Soon after that your bedroom door was locked all the time and he knew you'd be all right."

"This is awful," I said. "If you're trying to humiliate me you're succeeding."

"Well, I'm not trying."

"Anyway, if I was the one wanting all the attention, why did you worry about Aaron so much?"

"Because wanting to be so tough all the time wasn't normal, was it? He was always working so hard at being somebody he thought he ought to be. Maybe it was because of your father's brusqueness, I don't know. He wasn't an easy parent and it's always been hard for him to express emotion."

"Except anger. And annoyance. He's very good at expressing annoyance."

My mother laughed in her familiar way, an aural version of rolling the eyes. It was strange having a conversation like this, that a mere three hundred miles could make such a difference. Despite our natural rapport, my mother and I hadn't spoken frankly in months — certainly not since I'd had the secret of Alice to keep from her. "Your father loved you both," she said now, "and he spent all his free time with us. He didn't play cards or run around."

"I know. And his anger was just a lot of steam. Underneath he was always a softer touch than you. If you didn't let me have something, I would go to him."

"You knew that but Aaron was never as perceptive about people. The truth is, the two of you were different from the day you were born. You were always the happy one, Felix. A joy — at least until adolescence. Aaron didn't hardly seem to have an adolescence. No rebelling, no girlfriend, hardly any friends at all. But you had that lovely girl, Theresa. It seemed such a shame when you broke off after all that time."

"Actually, she's the one who broke off with me."

"She said you were both unhappy but that you couldn't bear to do it so she had to be the strong one. We had a long talk about it."

"When?"

"Oh, the day after. She phoned me."

"And you never told me?"

"We girls like to keep our little secrets."

"And there I was, suffering so much I thought I would die."

"Amazingly, you survived. I remember I had to force-feed you a lot of chocolate chiffon cake. By the way, I ran into her mother the other day. Theresa's getting married next spring. At Holy Blossom."

"I can't believe she's engaged already. She must need more time than just a few months to get over me."

"Sorry, Felix, but there are no Jewish nunneries for her to lock herself away in. I hear the groom has his own business, something to do with water filtration."

"This part of the conversation is driving me crazy."

"I'm just trying to keep you up to date."

I could hear the lilt in her voice; she did enjoy teasing me. "Let's change the subject," I said. "So how is Dad taking our absence?"

"He doesn't like to mention it. Instead, all he talks about is Skylab."

"Skylab?"

"Yesterday it was the Arabs controlling the oil prices and forcing the gas lineups. This morning it's Skylab. You know, the American space station."

"I know what Skylab is, but since when does Dad care about anything not made out of concrete?"

"Since the Americans announced that the station is going to fall out of orbit and break apart over the earth. You didn't hear about it? You haven't picked up a paper?"

"I've been kind of busy since yesterday, Mom."

"It's coming down in the next few days, but NASA isn't sure when. It weighs seventy-seven tons and as it enters the atmosphere it will break up into about five hundred pieces of debris and drop all over the place. It could be on the U.S. or the Amazon jungle or India, they just don't know. They say the chance of being hit is one in six hundred billion, but your father is in a panic. The only thing he has said about you and Aaron being in New York is that you should go down into the subway where it's safe and stay there until it's over."

"Talk about sublimating your emotions. This from a man who thinks that psychology is for perverts. And are you worried we'll get conked too, Mom?"

"Don't be foolish. You've got a better chance of being stabbed with a needle by a crazed drug addict or getting caught in a race riot. Those are real things to worry about."

I sighed so she could hear me. "Try to calm Dad down. It's hardly good for his blood pressure. Tell him everything will be all right."

"I am telling him. Maybe you can get President Carter to give him a call. Or better yet, your brother. If he could only talk to Aaron —"

"I'll try." I felt as if my heart *was* being stabbed by a needle. "Listen, Mom," I said, rubbing my forehead and trying to think of how to take her mind off Aaron. "Remind me of the time when you visited New York."

"You've heard me tell that a dozen times. Since you were a kid. Now I should tell you long distance?"

"Come on. You were nineteen, right?"

"Eighteen. It was the last long weekend of the summer of 1949. My sister Rona and I went by train. It took twelve hours and we didn't sleep a wink. Our aunt picked us up at the station and we stayed with her in the Bronx. It's such a shame she died ten years ago, you would have liked her. I remember before we came we went to see that movie with Frank Sinatra and Gene Kelly and the other fellow, I can't remember his name. *On the Town*. Did you ever see it?"

"Sure. Don't you remember we watched it together on television? I was still in high school."

"Well, Rona and I wanted to do everything that those three sailors did in New York. I remember the first place we went was the top of the Empire State Building. Such a spectacular view! We shopped at the big department stores — B. Altman, Bloomingdale's, Macy's on Herald Square. We ate at Delmonico's. We even went dancing at Roseland with some young fellows who were sons of my aunt's friends. I remember Rona didn't want to stop dancing. I think she was falling in love with this boy — he was a great dancer, and your aunt Rona was a sucker for a great dancer. They had a fight just before midnight. But that wasn't my favourite part of the trip. You know what it was?"

"I know, Mom. Carnegie Hall."

"Jascha Heifetz and the New York Philharmonic. He was such an artist, and he looked it, too, with that wild hair. The audience was dressed in evening gowns and black tie the way people never do anymore. They played Liszt, Beethoven, and then Mendelssohn's Violin Concerto. I'll never forget hearing that first violin note, it was so divine. My heart swoons even now when I think of it."

"That's a great story, Mom."

"Tell me, Felix, do you really have enough money? Even though your father doesn't want me to I'll send you some if you need it. He doesn't have to know everything —"

"No, I'm all right for now. I really better go."

"I love you, Felix."

"I know, Mom."

"Watch over Aaron for me. And yourself. Remember, in New York you're not such a big shot."

# 7

## Like Warsaw

Outside, a man with a stomach like a medicine ball was hosing down the sidewalk in front of a smoke shop. In the window of a pizza takeout next door two teenage kids were playing Pac-Man and I stopped for a moment to watch the little cartoon head move through the maze on the video screen as it snapped its jaws. I could not see the pleasure in it and decided that either such mind-numbing entertainment was a passing phase or that at the age of twenty-one I was already losing touch with the generation coming up behind me. I felt like running to the nearest bookstore and buying them a copy of *Catcher in the Rye.*

A white limousine slowly drove along Thirty-ninth Street and, never having seen one so long before and wondering what Arab sheik or Broadway star or rich Texan out on the town was inside it, I didn't look where I was going. If it wasn't for the raised iron grille I ran into, I would have stepped into the hole in the sidewalk like one of the Three Stooges that Aaron had thought were so funny when we were kids. A couple of burly men were lowering cases of Budweiser into the basement of a restaurant. There was something brutally poetic about them as they ignored me and continued to argue about the Yankees.

At Forty-second Street I descended into the gloom of the subway. An IRT-Broadway train pulled in to the uptown platform, its entire length spray-painted as a snarling dragon, the open mouth poised to crush the driver in the window of the front car. Around the dragon's body were the incomprehensible words and symbols of the street gangs. I knew that Norman Mailer had written about the artistry of subway graffiti, but to me it just looked menacing. The train was almost empty when I got in, the only passenger in the car a man sleeping across a bench with his artificial leg tucked under his head, probably to prevent it from being stolen.

I regretted not having the manuscript of my story with me and could only hope that Alice was reading it at this moment. It was foolish of me to have only one copy, and back in Toronto I had meant to take it to the library and make several Xeroxes. But I kept forgetting, or leaving it at home, or finding myself with insufficient change for the copy machine. Of course Freud would have said that I wanted to forget it out of some self-destructive impulse, but thinking about it now I was more inclined towards crediting some superstitious belief (my mother held to such things too) that if the manuscript was really worth something it would end up in the proper hands. Whatever the reason, the impracticality was all too evident this morning as I made my way to Isaac Bashevis Singer's apartment house on the Upper West Side. Back in Toronto I had tried to reach him through his publisher, Farrar Straus & Giroux, and his agent too, but secretaries at both offices had given me the brush-off. I had no choice but simply to show up, and should I be so lucky as to find the great writer in, I did not have the manuscript to give him. The best I could hope for was to get him to agree to read the story and then bring it to him later.

It was a strange story I had written, different from the little family dramas or the barely fictionalized depictions of my and Theresa Zeitman's emotional and sexual despair, all of which now seemed so tedious to me. I had continued to work on it through the early summer months, late at night when I couldn't sleep for thinking about Alice. The story had not appeared to me all at once, but came slowly, one paragraph and then another forming into a seamless whole, like the way Thomas Mann describes Aschenbach writing in *Death in Venice*. For once the writing was not accompanied by the usual doubts and misgivings, and the voice was as sure and unwavering as if it belonged to someone far wiser than me.

The train was a local and stopped frequently, giving me a glimpse of chipped tile walls, iron pillars thickened by layers of paint, blackened mosaic patterns like remnants of lost civilizations. At Eighty-sixth Street I exited the station, the stale underground air giving way to the freshness of outdoors. It was strange how the New York air did seem fresh to me. Broadway was divided here by narrow green meridians, while Eighty-sixth Street was unusually wide for a cross street, with cars lurching in both directions. The buildings around me were broad but not so high, ten or fifteen stories at most. I saw arched doorways, canopies, iron balconies. And there, across the traffic of Eighty-sixth Street, stood the Belnord Apartments.

I knew that Isaac Bashevis Singer lived on the top floor of the Belnord because I had read it in a profile in *The New York Times Magazine.* It was massive, spanning the entire block from Broadway to Amsterdam Avenue, but of a simple design, white stone for the first three floors and yellow brick above that, with only a minimum of carved neoclassical adornment. I already knew all about the Belnord, how it was built in 1908 as the largest apartment house in the world, with an enormous oval courtyard in its centre that reminded Singer of his childhood Krochmalna Street in Warsaw. When he walked in the courtyard or around the streets of the Upper West Side he sometimes forgot he was in New York. Up there in his apartment he produced his stream of brilliant stories, novels, memoirs, many set in Warsaw but in recent years more in New York; a New York haunted by refugees and survivors, by forgotten Yiddish poets, love-starved widows, aging Jewish Casanovas. He was an old man of seventy-six but he had a creative fountain of youth inside him. Every time I read one of his books or stories I became almost unbearably exhilarated, my mind swarming with ideas and my breast with emotions that I couldn't separate into an orderly pattern. All my critical faculties were disarmed. His characters had hearts that refused to be ruled by reason and their yearnings became my own. Their cheap restaurants, tangled beds, noisy streets, and dingy newspaper offices were more real than the physical world I inhabited.

For several minutes I stood looking up at the Belnord in a kind of reverie, foolishly hoping that Singer might emerge from under the high carriage entrance for one of his regular lunch spots in the neighbourhood or just to take a walk. I knew — I was not delusional, after all — that it was a crazy idea to ask a Nobel Prize-winning author to read my story and almost certainly doomed to failure. But when my mother asked me to go to New York I wanted a reason of my own for being here; being Aaron's chaperon wasn't good enough. Did I really believe that even if Singer read my story he would tell me whether I was the real thing? I knew the source of this idea, Somerset Maugham's *Of Human Bondage*, which Mrs. Springbottom had assigned to our advanced English class at Yorkview High School. It was about this novel that she had used the word *Bildungsroman*, a novel of the education of a young man. I thought this word so splendid that I used to go around repeating it under my breath.

I fell under the spell of Maugham's novel, carrying it around for weeks and even dreaming that I was Philip Carey, the club-footed boy who becomes infatuated with an unappealing, asexual, dull-witted woman. Perhaps there is a clinical term for this overinvolvement in the life of fictional characters. The episode I found most engrossing had Philip in Paris trying to become a painter. Desperate to know whether he has any real talent, Philip approaches the painting master Foinet for a judgment of his work. "Do you wish me to tell you it is good? It isn't," Foinet declares. "Do you wish me to tell you what to do with it? Tear it up."

And so it was Maugham's book that put in my head the dramatic notion of asking Singer whether I had what it took to be a writer, although of course I hoped for a more positive response. I stood before the Belnord and pleasantly imagined that Singer had already read my story and was praising my talents, when from just behind me someone began to shout. It was a man with the face of a bulldog inside a newspaper kiosk. He was picking up a few coins someone had dropped on a stack of newspapers even as he scolded me for blocking the view of his customers. I apologized and took advantage of the light to cross over to the Belnord.

The building seemed even more massive as I stood against the wall, dwarfing me with its great stone base. I reached the carriage entrance — it had to be twenty feet high — and looked into the inner courtyard as if through a giant keyhole, all green shrubbery and flowers and delicate trees surrounding a fountain, the streams of water cascading over an immense stone urn. The doorman, I could see, had a little office reached through a door in the archway, and he just now appeared sweeping the courtyard pathway. He had a large jaw that seemed to dislocate itself as he chewed his gum. His hair was swept over a bald spot and looked too black, as if shoe-polished. As soon as he saw me I strode confidently up to him in order to get a full view of the courtyard. It was even larger than I had imagined, with a walking path around the perimeter and four canopied entrances, one in each corner.

"Excuse me," I said. "Can you tell me which is Mr. Singer's apartment?"

"Do you have an appointment?" His voice sounded suspicious but his eyes betrayed him; I saw them involuntarily glance at the northwest entrance.

"More of a standing invitation to drop by," I said with a smile. "When I'm in the neighbourhood."

"No one sees Mr. Singer unless he has an appointment and I'm informed of it. Besides, he isn't home."

"Oh," I said, unable to conceal my disappointment. "Perhaps I could leave a note."

"Suit yourself."

"You wouldn't happen to have any paper, would you? A couple of sheets would do."

He narrowed his eyes at me a moment, but retreated into the office and came back with two sheets of Belnord stationery. I thanked him and went out from under the arch again, sauntering back to the corner of Broadway as I took a pen from my blazer pocket. The note would have to perk Singer's interest, which was why I had asked for two sheets — I wanted to write a draft first. I leaned down to press the paper against the side of a garbage bin and began —

*Dear Mr. Singer,*
*I am a young writer who is humbly hoping that you will solve a dilemma.*

This was no good at all. A writer like Singer must be pestered by hundreds like me. I crossed the lines out and tried again.

*You have said, Mr. Singer, that a writer must never forsake his past. But what of my generation? What of we hungry young writers who have been raised in the bland security of the suburbs, who have listened to the choirs in our reform synagogues? Where does our authenticity come from? I ask you,*

> *Mr. Singer, because I have written a story. A most surprising story.*

This seemed promising; only the tone was wrong, too rhetorical and pushy. On the other hand, maybe it was a mistake to mention my story at all. Maybe I should do away with all scruples and lure him with the kind of note that sounded like one of his own stories —

> *It is urgent that I see you. Only I.B. Singer, author of* The Magician of Lublin *and other works, can understand how a man, against his better judgment and all that he believes in, lets himself be blown about by passion. I have given up everything for a woman who deceives me constantly. And yet I am satisfied and even my torment is dear to me. Perhaps you might find something useful in all this.*

My head buzzed; I needed to think this through. I stood up and gazed absently across the intersection. At the end of each Broadway meridian was a wooden bench and I could see a middle-aged couple talking while the man used a pocket knife to cut thick slices from a salami. On the opposite bench an old man, slightly stooped and wearing a hat, made noises at the pigeons flurrying around his feet as he dropped bread crumbs from a paper bag. I watched the pedestrians going into the ground-floor stores, watched the stream of lunch-hour traffic. It seemed to me that I would never be able to write about New York because I would never know it well enough, not after five days or five years.

I decided that my second draft had been the best

and wrote out a revised copy. I hoped that it was both firm and supplicating, asking for a favour but offering something of interest in return. When I looked up again the couple with the salami were gone and the old man must have emptied the last of his paper bag, as the pigeons suddenly rose in the air, their wings making a hollow whir. The old man watched them arc over the street and settle on the stone sills beneath the windows of the Belnord.

Reading my note one last time, I felt satisfied and threw the draft into the garbage. The light was red and so I stood and watched the old man slowly crossing Broadway to the Belnord side. I noticed that his suit jacket pocket was tucked in by error, exposing what looked like the paper bag, carefully folded. His pants were too long so that they dragged at the heel as he carefully began to cross.

And then I realized who he was.

I could not make myself move.

He walked with an energetic shuffle, just lifting his heels from the ground as he stared at the pavement before him, occasionally glancing up at the light. A man passing the other way greeted him and Singer paused to lift his hat, although he looked a little confused, as if he couldn't place the man's face. He looked again at the light and saw, as I did, that it had turned yellow, and now he appeared concerned as he hurried his steps to get to the other side before the traffic came barrelling towards him. I did not think he would make it, but a woman took his arm and helped him reach the curb. He turned and smiled and spoke to her, and even over the cars I could hear her piercing laugh. The woman didn't even know who held her arm, what a literary genius walked tremblingly beside her! When she let go of him he touched his hat in thanks and made his own way to the entrance of the Belnord.

And what was I doing standing there? So often did I relive the scene afterwards that I could see not only Singer but me as well, two dots on the corner of Broadway and Eighty-sixth while Manhattan swirled around us and history rushed onward. It seemed to me afterwards that the reasons for my immobility had to be complex and mysterious. Later that day I questioned myself as to whether I secretly *wanted* something awful to happen, for the Nobel laureate to stumble and fall on his face or for a taxi cab to mow him down. In other words, whether my unconscious was imposing an image of the oedipal father upon this elderly man who happened to be a great writer — whether my intense and awestruck admiration for him was tinged with the fantasy of patricide.

But in the end I couldn't see it that way. For one thing, I could not feel competitive with such a master sorcerer. My own talent, if I had any at all, was unquestionably more modest. Nor did I think a boy who grew up in Willowdale could find in his life experience the stories that might stand against a rabbi's son who had first seen the world from the vantage point of a flat on Krochmalna Street, home to pimps, prostitutes, gamblers, and poor sinners. And there was one other thing. I already had a father, Saul Roth, owner of Roth Cement and Gravel, and I did not feel inclined to replace him with another.

So why didn't I rush to help him? And to introduce myself? Perhaps the simple answer was fear. I was afraid he would dismiss me, or that I would say something stupid, or that no words would come out of my mouth. But then suddenly it was as if I woke from a trance. I sprinted to the curb, but the light had already turned against me and the traffic on Eighty-sixth Street was too heavy to dodge. I danced impatiently until the light changed and then practically flew across, only to be caught up on the sidewalk by a man from one of those dog-walking services with six yapping pedigrees straining on their leashes. I had to untangle a schnauzer from around my ankles before I could get to the Belnord's entrance.

By the time I got to the archway it was deserted, and as much of the courtyard as I could see. The only sound came from the splashing fountain. I began to walk purposely under the arch when sure enough the doorman emerged from his hobbit's hole of an office and folded his arms across his chest like he was a member of the National Guard.

"Did Mr. Singer just go in?" I said. "We were just speaking outside — it was a lucky coincidence that we met — and I forgot to mention the dinner arrangements. Must be this summer weather, it makes me forget everything. I'll just zip up after him."

I took a step forward and he put a firm hand on my shoulder. "Do you have an appointment?"

"It really won't take a minute." My voice came out as a squeak.

"Mr. Singer regrets that he can no longer see visitors without an appointment."

"Well, if I could just use the house phone to speak with him —"

"There's a pay phone at the corner. You can call him from there. *If* you know his number."

He grinned.

"All right," I said, trying to sound annoyed but unconcerned. Then I remembered the note I'd written. In my shock at seeing Singer I must have dropped it; no doubt it was being ground under the heels of New York at this very moment. I would have to write it over again.

Just then a woman came under the arch, talking sharply to the doorman even as she approached. She must have been past seventy, with thinning hair and loose wattles of skin under her chin and deep caves for eyes, but she wore high silver heels and, despite the warm weather, a fox stole around her neck, and she held her chin up defiantly. "Who are those workmen on the eighth floor?" she demanded. "Their manners are disgraceful. I don't know what's happening to this city. Cat whistles and staring — as if I was some chorus girl." The doorman, who evidently was used to such complaints, began to soothe the woman and assure her he would phone the Parkinsons, who were having their floors varnished, and let them know of the trouble. Would she mind stepping into his office for a moment?

And so I had my chance. As soon as they were through the office door I dashed into the courtyard and around the path. I skidded under the metal canopy in Charlie Chaplin style and pulled open the door. And even though I heard the doorman's shout behind me I did not stop.

# 8

# Uncle Isaac

As a child, the sensation of an elevator ride was strangely disorienting to me. The vibration in the soles of my shoes and the barely perceptible change in air pressure lifted me out of the present moment almost as if I were drifting through time and history. I used to think the elevator door might open upon an African jungle or an Indian buffalo hunt or the giant rings of Saturn. For the first time in years that odd feeling came surging back to me in the elevator of the Belnord, only this time I felt sure the door would open upon some decrepit hallway of a Lower East Side tenement in the 1920s or I would suddenly smell herring and cheap tobacco and know I was entering the Warsaw Yiddish Writers' Club. And surely there would be a young man from a Singer story or novel, some thin and bookish Asa Heshel being embraced by a married woman or helping an egotistical rabbi to write his memoirs. I thought the elevator door might open and deposit me into the very middle of *The Family Moskat.*

Instead, the door opened onto a modern mirror reflecting my own wan face, below which stood a vase of artificial flowers on a lacquered table. The carpet was new, with a pattern of pink and white roses. I looked down the hall in one direction and then the other and realized that I had no way to discover which door belonged to Singer except by knocking at each. Some annoyed tenant was bound to call the doorman or the cops before I found him. For all I knew the doorman had already phoned the police, in which case I would be making the next call to my mother from Rikers Island.

As I was hesitating, a door halfway down the hall opened and a young woman stepped out, locking it behind her. She was about my age or likely younger, not more than five feet tall, and so lovely that I simply stood and looked at her. Her hair was dark and fell in tresses — that was the right word. Her eyebrows were black like her hair. She was a biblical princess in one of those new denim skirts, below the knee and with red stitching. When she caught sight of me she did not smile; if anything her mouth and eyes expressed annoyance.

She started down the hall and appeared about to pass me without wasting another glance when I said, "Excuse me," my voice catching in my throat. "Could you tell me which is Mr. Singer's apartment?"

She stopped and looked at me, her silver earrings swaying a little. Then she looked back over her shoulder, as if to make sure no one was in the hall behind her. "What do you want with Uncle Isaac?" She had a strong, high, no-nonsense voice, with a guttural accent.

"You're his niece? Please, I just want to speak with him for a few minutes."

She didn't answer right away but bit her bottom lip instead. "You can't," she finally said. "He's resting and afterwards he has a story to finish."

"But he just came in, I saw him. If I could have two minutes —"

"Absolutely not. I regret to say."

"I really think you ought to let me see him." I tried to sound forceful but not aggressive. I didn't want her to think I was a bully, just admirably determined. "If you don't your uncle might be quite upset with you."

"Oh, I don't think so." *I doan tink zo* in her pronunciation. It was an adorable accent, and each of her words tapped a small bell hanging inside my ribcage.

"Well, there can't be any harm in knocking on the door you came out of," I said. "If Mr. Singer doesn't answer, I'll go away."

"There might be some harm. To you. I am on leave from the Israeli Army."

That made me hesitate. True, she was several inches shorter than me and a girl after all, but the Israeli Army had a ferocious reputation. I had read somewhere that all Israeli soldiers were taught how to kill with their bare hands. At the end of their gruelling boot camp they made a ritual climb to the heat-baked summit of Masada, where the Jews had committed suicide rather than be taken captive by the Romans. I decided on another approach.

"I'll make so much noise that your uncle will wake up and come out to see what the fuss is about."

"How like a child you are. Besides, my uncle has been living in New York for over forty years. Do you think he runs to look every time he hears a commotion?"

I didn't enjoy the dismissive way she turned away from me just as she dropped her keys, which she had been holding in her hand, into the woven bag that hung from her shoulder. I said, "All right. I'll go away under one condition."

"You are not in such a position as to be making conditions."

"How about I make one anyway?"

This time she smiled at me. I felt myself blush and, looking down, noticed her sandals and painted toenails. The small toe of each foot was funnily shaped, turned in like a comma. I looked up again. "The condition is that you come and talk to me about your uncle. We'll go somewhere public. A restaurant."

Her eyes shifted away from me and she bit her bottom lip. "It seems that everyone must sacrifice for Uncle Isaac. All right, I agree. But I am staying only as long as I want."

"Absolutely. I ought to introduce myself. My name is Felix. Felix Roth."

I held out my hand but she just made a face. "You are named after a cat?"

"I didn't know people watched cartoons in Israel."

"You think maybe we spend all our time planting trees? Let's be going and get it over with."

"You haven't told me your name."

"My name? I don't know if I should." She looked almost panicky.

"Just your first name, then," I said quickly. "I have to call you something."

"I suppose so. It's . . . it's Hadassah."

"That's a beautiful name. There's a Singer character named Hadassah in his story 'Yentl the Yeshiva Boy.'"

"I know, the one who marries a girl dressed as a boy. My uncle tells me that it is going to be made into a movie. A musical with Barbra Streisand."

"You're pulling my leg."

"Stranger things have happened. They already sent him a big cheque."

She banged the elevator button with the palm of her hand. We waited silently for it to arrive, Hadassah impatiently twirling a strand of her hair round a finger, and when the door opened I motioned for her to step in.

"A gentleman," she said sardonically. "You are an endangered species."

"You're staying with your uncle, then?"

"For the meantime."

"And do you like New York?"

"It is not so much a matter of liking. I miss home, but to an Israeli, New York feels very familiar. In Israel we too must push hard to get what we want. Of course it's different. No one understands what life is like for us."

"And what is it that you do want, Hadassah?"

She looked at me. "Whatever I want, it is more than to live on a kibbutz and shovel the shit of chickens."

We came out to the courtyard and took the path to the carriage entrance. The doorman was helping a woman take some parcels out of a taxi cab. He began to get all huffy when he saw me, but when he realized that I was with Hadassah he just smiled and nodded at her.

On the sidewalk, the sunlight made me squint, but Hadassah tilted her chin up towards the light, perhaps missing the unrelenting sun of her own country. "We can walk down to Eclair's," she said. "My uncle likes to take me there."

"That would be great."

"Oh, look," she said. I saw a street vendor at the corner of Broadway, a tall gangly black man with delicately chiselled features and wearing a long woven robe. He looked like an African king in melancholy exile, forced into the indignity of wearing his product on his head, a pair of bouncing wire antennae with pom-poms at their ends. I had seen sellers like him all over the city, and adults and kids wearing the antennae as if Manhattan had been invaded by imbecilic aliens.

"They are so cute," Hadassah said. "I could wear them to parties back in Israel. Nobody would have one."

"Let me buy you a pair," I offered gallantly.

"Would you?"

I was surprised by her acceptance but went to the seller and took out my wallet. For my five dollars he drew from a gym bag between his feet a cellophane-wrapped pair of antennae with green pom-poms. I could see what junk it was, worth a buck at most. I handed the package to Hadassah with a flourish and we began to walk down Broadway.

"You must be very rich, to have money like that to waste," she said and dropped the package into the same trash can in which I had thrown the drafts of my note for Singer.

"What are you doing?"

"I am not going to betray my uncle for some stupid toy."

"No, no, you're wrong about me. That isn't fair, I was just trying to do something nice."

She didn't answer but kept walking, dodging the crowd like a veteran so that I lost her for a moment and had to sprint to catch up, mumbling apologies to people I knocked against.

"I think maybe you are from somewhere like Iowa," she said as I managed to reach her side. "Or Kansas, perhaps. Like Dorothy."

"Close enough," I said. "Canada."

"I don't know very much about Canada. You have that big waterfall, don't you?"

"We have to share it with America. But Madame Tussaud's Wax Museum is on our side."

"And forests and beavers and you speak French."

"*Un peu, seulement*. Honestly, Hadassah, if you want a tourist guide to Canada you've come to the wrong guy. I know more about New York. You know what this street, Broadway, used to be called up here? Bloomingdale Road. There used to be shantytowns on the Upper West Side and packs of wild dogs. Then came the elevated train and the Dakota Hotel. You see that amazing apartment house coming into view? That's the Ansonia, designed in the beaux arts style by Graves and Duboy. Theodore Dreiser used to live there. Also Babe Ruth, Caruso, Toscanini, and Florence Ziegfeld. I really should have been born here, Hadassah. It was just some mistake, an administrative error in heaven. I was meant to be a New Yorker. Hey, why are you laughing?"

"I am just wondering about someone who knows so

much more about another place than the one he lives in. We are not very far from Eclair's."

We didn't say anything more. At Seventy-third Street we came to Verdi Square, but I didn't tell Hadassah it used to be called Needle Park. People were sitting on the benches reading newspapers and ignoring a man in a stovepipe hat standing on a box and shouting hoarsely about a conspiracy to make New York the capital of Mexico. We turned at the next block and this time Hadassah opened the door for me. I felt a blast from the air conditioner wedged above the transom. "Follow me," she said. "You can have the very great thrill of sitting in the famous author's regular spot." She took me to the last booth, the seats of cracked beige vinyl, with a poor reproduction of van Gogh's "Sunflowers" on the wall. I sat down across from her, feeling the springs sigh beneath me. "Sometimes my uncle has a baked apple or maybe rice pudding. But if you want the full experience you should order his favourite."

"All right, I will."

"Borscht with a boiled potato. Borscht is the secret of his talent."

"Sounds perfect," I said, although I didn't actually like borscht. "And please, Hadassah, have whatever you want."

"Are you still acting like J.P. Morgan? I only want a cappuccino."

The waitress arrived, a frail woman with skin like tracing paper. It took her about two minutes to return with the cappuccino for Hadassah and the bowl of brilliant red borscht for me, a potato rising from the middle like a denuded island. "I don't have the whole day," Hadassah said, pouring sugar onto the foam. "So ask your very urgent questions."

"I hardly know where to start. How long are you going to stay with your uncle?"

"That is a question about me, not him."

"Fine. Does he use a typewriter?"

"Only after. First he writes with a fountain pen. In notebooks. Sometimes his assistant types the pages for him. His favourite place to sit and write is a big chair — a bird chair, is it called?"

"I don't think so. Oh, I've got it, a winged chair."

"Yes. Sometimes he writes in bed before he gets up and sometimes even in the bathtub. Wherever he is, that's where he's writing."

"He doesn't have a study?"

"Well, sort of an office. But it's more for storing things. You should see the mess, my aunt is always pestering him to clean it up. The walls are covered with awards and honorary degrees. There are suitcases full of old stories printed in the newspaper where he first publishes them in Yiddish."

"*The Forward.*"

"The other day I looked inside and almost stepped on his Nobel Prize medal. It fell off the bookshelf. And Uncle is always upset because he can't find a certain story or some pages he wrote. He says that some demon likes to play tricks on him to remind him not to get too big for his trousers."

The waitress passed by and Hadassah called her over. "Bring me a piece of Black Forest cake," she said. We watched the waitress lift the plastic dome off the cart and bring the piece to Hadassah. She picked up her fork, took a bite, and shrugged. "Every so often

Uncle Isaac likes something sweet too. But he doesn't like anyone to see him."

I said, "Does he talk about what he's writing?"

"Sure, he doesn't keep it a secret. Sometimes he even asks my opinion. Do I like a certain ending, or do I think a woman would sleep with one kind of man and not another. Everything goes into the work, nothing is left out."

"Are you a writer too, Hadassah?"

"Another question about me. But no, I'm not. To be in a room all day like an animal in its cage, thinking and scribbling. How awful. I think that a writer must have some kind of sickness. He must prefer to imagine life than to actually live it. To me, life should be an adventure. I have no burning desire to achieve something great or to be remembered after I die. I don't need anyone to tell me I'm special, but my uncle loves attention, to be in the street light."

"Spotlight."

"You should speak Hebrew so well as I speak English. In my opinion, Uncle Isaac is made a prisoner by his talent. To me it's more important to be free."

"But when you're a writer the act of writing itself is what makes you free."

"Oh, no," she said, rolling her eyes. She took a forkful of cake, leaving a touch of chocolate icing like a fingerprint at the corner of her mouth. "That sounds like another writer talking. Or somebody who wants to be. I suppose you are dying to tell me why you want to see my uncle."

"Yes, I am, actually. I want him to read a story I've written."

"Big surprise. Everything about you gives it away. I'm sorry, but Isaac Bashevis Singer does not have time for all the young geniuses who would like his blessing."

"Forgive my selfishness, but I don't care about all the other young geniuses. I only care about this one."

"At least you are saying something honest to me. Here, have some of my cake."

I picked up a fork and the two of us went at the cake from opposite sides, a thrilling intimacy.

"Tell me something," I said.

"What do you wish to know now, my shoe size?"

"Do you have somebody in Israel? A boyfriend?"

She looked exasperated. "You are very big with putting your nose into another person's business."

"So there is someone. What's his name?"

"Yoni."

Though I wasn't surprised, my heart sank. "And he's waiting for you to come home?"

"He's stationed in the Sinai. I'm not allowed to know where. But every day he writes me."

"I can't blame him. If it were me, I would write you three times a day."

She looked at me as if I were mad. "You foreign men don't understand what it means to be one of us. It is so easy to live in America or Canada. Like a holiday all the time. Everyone has a television and a stereo and a car. You hardly have to work to make things grow out of the earth — you drop a seed and a garden blooms. We must dig in the sand and rock. We must turn seawater into fresh. You take everything from your country without ever having to give in return. Like children. But for us, to be Israeli is to carry responsibility like a load on our backs every day. We are used to it and don't complain. To die for our nation is something we don't even think about anymore. So you see, it is hard for us to take people here seriously."

"I see." I didn't know what else to say, my chances of winning her over seemed so hopeless.

"Don't look so sad. It is also important to live for the moment — that also we have learned. All right, give me your story that is so important and will change the world. I will read it and if I think it is worth wasting my uncle's time I will give it to him."

"Do you mean it? You'll really read it?"

"Isn't that what I said? Now please hand it over so I can go."

"That's great. That's fantastic, Hadassah. I can't tell you what it means to me. Unfortunately, I don't have it with me at the moment. I've only got one copy."

"You only have one copy? Why? You are treating it like the original Ten Commandments maybe."

"No, it isn't that. I'm getting the story back later today. Just give me a time and I'll bring it to you."

"If you don't have it then you will have to tell it to me."

"Pardon?"

"Tell the story to me. I am completely ears."

"Hadassah —"

"If not you have no chance. Okay, it was nice knowing you."

She began to rise but I grabbed her arm. "All right, I'll tell you. Sit down. It's called 'The Goat Bride.'"

"That is a very strange title, I think."

"You don't like it? The title could change."

"Just go on."

I took a deep breath. "It's about a man, a middle-aged accountant named Joey Pechnik. This Pechnik works downtown in a decrepit office doing the books for the neighbourhood storekeepers, the local delicatessen. But he lives in the suburbs and every morning before going to work he sits on his front porch drinking instant coffee and perusing the paper."

"Why does he not make real coffee?"

"Because he lives alone. He can't be bothered. One morning a big truck comes lumbering down the street. Usually trucks in this neighbourhood are delivering a new sofa or refrigerator, but this one is a long transport type, with slatted sides. An animal carrier. At the stop sign in front of Joey Pechnik's house it slows down and the back door swings open. Out jumps a small goat. Tan coloured, with a white nose. Small horns. The truck surges forward and the door swings shut."

"Surely the driver will notice he's missing a goat."

"That's not part of the story. So Joey Pechnik stands there — it's seven a.m., the street is deserted, the kids not yet trudging to school — and looks at the goat. The goat stands on the road and bleats once or twice. He is afraid that some car might flatten it, or some neighbour with peasant blood might pull it into a backyard and slit its throat, the blood draining into a bucket. So Pechnik, overweight, with a bad haircut and wearing a polyester dress shirt still unbuttoned at the top, walks over to the goat and tries to coax it off the road. The goat won't move. He pulls it. Nothing. But when Joey walks back to his house, the goat follows."

"A goat with a mind of its own."

"Exactly. They reach Pechnik's lawn. Pechnik says, half to himself, 'Oh, so now you decide to come. Stubborn animal.' And the goat answers —"

"The goat *speaks*?"

"Yes. The goat answers, 'Why not? Goats too can have free will.' It has a goaty, vibrating voice, but somehow sweet. Feminine. Naturally, Pechnik can hardly believe it."

"I can hardly believe it myself."

"The story makes you believe it. Pechnik leads the goat into the backyard, where it immediately begins to feed on clover growing among the grass. He says to it, 'I've got to go to work. Will you be all right until I get back?' The goat says, 'It's nice here. Don't worry. Goats are patient.' And so it goes. Every day Pechnik rushes home from work to make sure the goat is all right. She tells him that her name is Tirza. He tells her about his day, how this shopkeeper or that real estate shyster is giving him a big pain. And before long Joey Pechnik, this awkward man with thick glasses on his nose and who wears a belt he had to punch an extra hole into himself, is in love with a goat."

"So it's a love story," Hadassah said. "Go on."

"One night there's a terrific rainstorm. What can Pechnik do but bring the goat into the house? First to the kitchen, and then the bedroom. In short, man and goat become lovers."

"You describe this?"

"Not in so many words. Joey Pechnik asks, 'Is this a dream?' The goat says, 'No, my beloved,' but offers no other explanations. Joey is quiet for some time.

Then he says, 'Whatever you are, a demon or an angel or something else, I thank the Almighty that you fell off that truck.'"

I paused to calm my voice. "The people who know Pechnik begin to notice odd changes in him. At the delicatessen he stops ordering pastrami sandwiches or stuffed derma and has vegetarian dishes instead. He smiles more and could be heard to sing snatches of songs under his breath. His neighbours watch him plant lettuce, celery, and carrots in the spring. He wears a gold band on his finger; the goat wears one in its nose. It is against the municipal bylaw to keep livestock in the suburbs, but none of the neighbours has the heart to turn crazy, harmless Pechnik in. They see him talking to the goat on their walks up and down the street. He strokes it between the ears, laughs. Sometimes he even seems to be arguing with it and occasionally the two walk in silence, like a sulking husband and wife. For five years they live together, ten years, twelve. The goat grows old. Its ribs show, its beard turns white. One autumn the goat develops a cough, hoarse and painful. Then a fever. The neighbours watch Pechnik take the goat in a station wagon from one vet to another, looking for a cure. But what can a vet do for old age? The simple truth is that goats do not live as long as humans.

"Having exhausted all possibilities, Pechnik stays home to nurse the goat during her last days. The neighbours whisper about germs, disease, foot-and-mouth; one of them anonymously telephones the authorities. A car from Animal Control comes to the house. Pechnik throws a pot at them from a window and bars the door. Animal Control calls the police for reinforcements. The

SWAT team arrives in full regalia — bulletproof jackets, shields, high-powered rifles, tear gas. The street is cordoned off. Three days of standoff go by. Then, in the night, with Pechnik holding a compress between its horns and whispering in its ear, the goat dies in his bed. In the morning he calls out a request: that the goat be buried in the Jewish cemetery, with nine other men to join him in saying Kaddish. When the police agree he comes out, only to be grabbed, pushed to the ground, handcuffed.

"Pechnik is held in the Don Jail. He is allowed out to attend the burial of the goat, not in a Jewish but in a pet cemetery, in a plot next to dogs and cats. Pechnik rends his garment, sobs, and tries to throw himself into the grave. Diagnosed as paranoic, he spends nine months in a mental institution outside of London, Ontario, and is released. The neighbours never see nor hear from him again. The house goes up for sale, the grass grows long. The men joke uneasily that Pechnik is wandering the earth as a widower in search of a new bride. What next, a horse? A chicken? But the women, they think to themselves: and if we died? Would our husbands be so torn up, mourn with such heartache? They look at the long grass growing and they sigh."

I stopped speaking. I was staring unseeing at the tabletop but now I slowly raised my eyes to Hadassah. She was looking at me, her lower lip quivering.

"That is the end?" she said finally.

"Yes, that's it."

"And what happens to the man — we don't find out?"

"No."

"I . . . I don't know what to think. I can't tell if it is good or not."

"You can't tell? After all that?"

"All right, I'll show it to my uncle. Bring it to me tomorrow. I will meet you outside the Belnord at one. Now I have to go. You will please wait for a few minutes after I leave the restaurant. I don't want you to follow me."

"I'm not that kind of person."

"Yes, I know. But please wait anyway."

She rose and I did too, holding out my hand. She looked at it a moment and I silently prayed that she take it. I felt that her hand would somehow be imprinted with my own and then I really would see her again. Finally she reached out; her hand was small but strong. I watched as she walked through the restaurant, forbidding myself to silently wish for her to turn around, knowing that would be asking for too much.

# 9

# What Is Authentic?

It took almost two hours to walk the forty blocks from the Upper West Side back to midtown. The sun was warm and the shirt beneath my blazer began to cling to my skin (but I stubbornly refused to take the blazer off) while the heat from the sidewalk penetrated the soles of my running shoes. A veritable purgatory of faces passed me by: pockmarked salesmen with heavy cases, women with stiff hair whose grimaces showed from behind their painted masks. And I pitied them even as I felt levitated off that hot sidewalk by my own intoxication.

Hadassah of the sharp tongue. Hadassah of the dark eyes. I was smitten in the original sense of the word, struck by a blow. It was not just that she was beautiful, and perhaps there were others who would not even have thought so. It was that something peculiar and specific in *me* had responded to her, as if her image had been marked on my soul at my own conception and this first sight of her was actually the deepest and most profound recognition. Alice was right: I was old-fashioned and I believed in fated, eternal love, only I had tried to deny it to myself. But now it seemed to me that everything that had ever happened in the twenty-one years of my life was in long and secret preparation for this moment. I had even written "The Goat Bride" so that I might meet Hadassah; my brother's religious conversion was so that I might meet Hadassah; the affair with Alice had matured me in preparation — all of it was some divine conspiracy to bring me to her.

These thoughts, I knew, were going too far and yet I could not stop them. I felt so light-headed I might have been breathing helium. For those two hours I thought and planned how to woo her. What if I simply got down on my knee in front of the Belnord and asked her to marry me? The desire was as large and sentimental as that. Oh, I had lost my mind surely.

So carried away was I that by the time I found myself standing in front of the Gotham Book Mart on Forty-seventh Street I could not remember almost any of what I had passed to get there. But there was the famous and oddly delicate cast-iron sign — "Wise Men Fish Here" — hanging over the doorway beside the Jewelers and Dealers Exchange. I stepped inside and saw the piles of leaflets for poetry reading and stacks of the new paperbacks. The store was narrow, crowded with carts and racks of books that the walls couldn't hold, and had a dishevelled appearance, as if the place had been ransacked by desperate readers. Several people were absorbed in browsing, while a voice in the back must have been shouting into a telephone, as there was no response but only short pauses before the shouting began again.

I made my way to the fiction walls and took down a book, only to discover that a second row of books was hidden behind the first. It seemed doubtful that Isaac Bashevis Singer had ever stepped foot in this store; it had been a haven for a very different set of writers, Henry Miller and Anaïs Nin and later Delmore Schwartz and his crowd. As I moved along the wall, looking at one book and then another, a semblance of calm returned to me. How often I had lost myself in bookshops just this way, only to find that half the afternoon was gone and I had accomplished not a thing.

Slowly I worked myself over to the "S" authors to see which Singer books the store carried. I found five paperbacks and a little hardcover I had not seen before and that must have been brand new, a thin book of just thirty or so pages called *Nobel Lecture*. I held it in my hands and a different kind of excitement flooded me; I was glad to discover that my sudden feeling for Hadassah had not erased all other interests.

"You think his books are any good?" a voice said behind me.

The man was fifty or perhaps older, heavy-set, with a large head and jowls. Eyes set in deep sockets. His hair was cropped or shaved down to his knobbly scalp and scratched by the blade in several spots.

"I think they are, yes," I said cautiously, putting the book back on the wall. It might be better to buy it later. "Maybe the early novels are a bit stiff. He was trying to write too much like his brother, Israel Joshua."

"Stiff?" The man had a gargle of a laugh. With his thumb he touched his nose, cheek, then chin, possibly an obsessive tic. "Try sloppy. Singer is a short story writer and that's that. He can't sustain a novel, he doesn't have the depth. I told him that to his face."

"You know him?"

"And you know what Isaac said to me? That the public likes novels. That the great writers — Tolstoy, Hamsun — wrote novels. Can you imagine such an answer? So I said, 'You're no Tolstoy. What are you planning to write, *War and Latkes*? Stick to stories.' But he can't help himself. He wants to feel he deserved that Nobel."

"He has doubts?" I said in astonishment.

"Not that he admits to. But every writer has doubts. I'm sure that when God wrote the Torah He said to Himself, 'Is the opening snappy enough? Should I beef up the role of Eve? Put in more sex, adultery? Maybe the destruction of Sodom should be more graphic.'"

The man began to cough. His face flushed to the colour of a plum and he fished out a handkerchief from his suit pocket — actually, it appeared to be a roughly cut square of bedsheet — and spit up phlegm. I took an involuntary step back. Slowly his breath returned to him and he did the nose-cheek-chin touch.

"I need something hot, a cup of tea," he said.

"I'd be glad to buy you one."

"There's a place across the street. They know me there." He nodded, his eyes reduced to slits, a world of secrets lurking behind his words. I didn't know whether he was one of those sad, deluded people who haunted cities muttering to themselves or whether he really did know Singer. I had never spoken to anyone like him — such people did not generally wander up to the suburbs — and I was both intrigued and repulsed by him. He wore a wrinkled linen jacket over a soiled undershirt, and as he bent to pick up his battered briefcase I thought his jacket might split across the back. The briefcase, I saw, was in fact two cases bound together by black electrical tape. A string was tied to the handle of one and the other end around the man's wrist. Was he afraid of forgetting it or of being robbed? I doubted he could possess anything precious enough to require a precaution even this dubiously effective.

"Some bookstore," he sniffed. "Not one book by Nefish." He started to walk out and I followed him, wondering who Nefish was. He crossed the street without seeming to look, not even turning his head when a cab driver leaned on his horn. I hurried after and we ducked down a set of stairs into a basement restaurant. It looked like a gypsy tea room, with check cloths on the round tables and candles flickering in the dimness. The waiter, a young Asian man, was leaning against the counter and reading a martial arts comic book.

We were the only customers and took a table by the wall.

"My name is Harry Winter," the man said. "They make nice cabbage rolls here. Please, have some."

My stomach felt empty but after having borscht I didn't think I could take a plate of cabbage rolls. I asked the waiter if it was possible to have something simple, like a cheese and tomato sandwich. "Give him the black bread!" Harry Winter bellowed as the waiter went through the curtain of beads to the kitchen.

It struck me later as curious at best that I would offer to dine with a stranger who appeared quite possibly demented. He was also certainly poor, unless he was a type like Hetty Green, who died in her worn-out clothes in a Manhattan rooming house in 1916, though she was worth sixty-seven million. The waiter brought our orders on wooden platters and Harry Winter ate noisily, bits of cabbage and rice sticking to his chin. It did occur to me that I might suddenly want to bolt, and so I said, "I don't really have much time."

"Quick, slow." Harry Winter shrugged. "It's all the same to the belly."

"When was the last time you saw Isaac Bashevis Singer?"

"Eight years and three months ago. I helped him to translate a story. For rotten pay. And he didn't even give me a credit. Usually he prefers more subservient translators, preferably female. If I thought a word should change or a line be taken out I didn't hide my opinion. I questioned the motivation of his character and told him he was being too sensational. Naturally this annoyed him, but like I told Isaac, with me it isn't a matter of ego but of literature. Mind you, we never hit it off from day one. When Bellow knocked off 'Gimpel the Fool.'"

"You were there? When Saul Bellow translated 'Gimpel the Fool'?" I could not believe it. Bellow's translation of that story had finally made Singer famous when it was published in the *Partisan Review* in 1952. Harry wiped at the platter with a piece of bread. "Why were you there?" I asked.

"To lend a hand. There was me, Irving Howe, Lazer Greenberg, and Bellow in Greenberg's apartment on Nineteenth Street. Bellow wasn't such a big shot then either. He'd only published his little European-style novels, like he was planning to be the Jewish Camus. I remember how Lazer read aloud the Yiddish while Bellow sat at the typewriter hammering out the translation. His Yiddish wasn't perfect and there was a lot of discussion about this word or that, nuances and second meanings. I objected to Bellow's tone — it sounded too American, too tough-guy. He even used the word *slugger.* Can you believe that! A little joke, baseball language in a story set in a Polish shtetl. But would they listen to me? Afterwards I tried talking to Isaac about it but he didn't want to hear. And from one story he conquered the world. Because the audience is too ignorant to know otherwise. All right, I exaggerate. He's not without talent. Some passable work in earlier days. But now he writes the same two stories over and over. And all the hoopla —" He waved his hand in front of his face, as if to dispel some distasteful image — Singer accepting the Nobel Prize, maybe.

I said, "It so happens that I'm trying to get in touch with him."

"What for?"

"It's personal."

"Don't tell me. I'll read your mind." He put his hands over his eyes and rocked gently back and forth in his chair. His thumb went up: nose, cheek, chin. "I'm getting it now. You . . . you too are a writer."

"All right, yes. Or trying to be."

"I thought all the Jewish boys wanted to direct movies like Steven Spielberg now."

"I don't care for movies all that much. Only books."

"So you're a throwback, an *alte-kop.* You know what that means in Yiddish? Someone who doesn't belong to his time."

"That describes me."

"And I bet that you have brought something, a little sonnet maybe, for the master to read. You hope he'll pronounce you a genius, phone up Robert Giroux, and get you a book contract."

"It's a story. And no, I don't expect any of those things. I just want to know if I have talent."

"How old are you?"

"Twenty-one."

"A baby still in his cradle. Writing is not like playing the piano. In music a teacher can listen to a pupil and decide whether or not he has a gift. But writing works differently, it takes longer to come out. It demands maturity. A person may write merely competently for years and then in a sudden fever or over a long period produce a masterpiece. And it will turn out that all the early drivel was preparation for the real work. Besides, Isaac is just one man. He has his likes and prejudices, just like every other writer. Anything too out of the way he despises. A story must have a beginning, a middle, and an end — I've heard him say that a dozen times. And why can't a story have three beginnings and no end?"

"I understand that. But this story is different. He can tell me whether or not it's authentic."

Harry Winter made a noise like dislodging a bone caught in his nose. "And what is authentic? Is Singer's work authentic? When he writes about Warsaw or some muddy Polish town from sixty years ago does he have a perfect memory? That's what he tells the interviewers, but I know better. He invents. He puts things in that happened to him yesterday, that he read in the newspaper. Any trick he will use. And those stories about New York! As if everyone has three mistresses. He projects his fantasies, that's all. People are right to call him a magician, but if a magician turns a scarf into a bowl of prunes, is that authentic? Your question is naive."

"Perhaps. But I still want him to read it."

"Why Singer? There are plenty of other writers around. Why not phone that New England weather-vane-up-his-ass John Updike? Or maybe Joyce Carol Oates, that vampire. I get it, you want a Jewish writer. Then go knock on Stanley Elkin's door in St. Louis. He's not in such demand. I see you don't take to any of my suggestions. No less than Singer will do. By the way, Mr. Prodigy. You haven't told me your name."

"Felix Roth."

"Felix Roth? As if there aren't writers already with that name. Have you read Joseph?"

"I've read *The Radetzky March* and *Job* and a couple of others. He was born in some Galician town and fought in the Great War. Became disillusioned, went into exile in France, drank too much. Killed himself while in exile in 1944. His work has this real tenderness about it. A great writer."

I knew I was showing off. Harry Winter wiped his mouth with a paper napkin. "Waiter, bring us tea! And tell me, Felix, have you also read Henry?"

"Of course. *Call It Sleep* is a wonderful novel. It depicts the sensibility of a child growing up poor on the Lower East Side. Extraordinarily sensitive and unsentimental. The only fiction he's published. Ignored when it first came out in the 1930s but discovered thirty years later. Influenced by Joyce."

"The schmuck became a communist and his inspiration dried up. I hear he's living in New Mexico and writing again, even as an old geezer. All right then. Philip."

"That's too easy. Born in New Jersey. Exploded on the scene with *Goodbye, Columbus* in 1959. Since then a stream of novels. Wildly uneven, often excessive. Sometimes I want to throw his work in the trash, but when he's good he's very good. His last novel, *The Professor of Desire*, is probably the best so far."

The waiter dropped onto the table a battered metal teapot and a couple of thick porcelain cups. "Lemon, I need lemon," Harry Winter grumbled. The waiter brought two thin slices of lemon and Harry squeezed one into his cup before pouring in the tea. "So tell me," he said. "There's Joseph, Henry, and Philip. And with each generation the genius is watered down a little. Meanwhile the audience still left for serious books has grown tired of Jewish writers with their fancy styles and references to Kafka and Dostoevsky, their deep thoughts and depressing sex. I tell you that it's over for the Jewish writer — his day in the sun is gone. Already three Roths and here springs up another. Do you really think there's room for Felix too? A fourth Roth?"

"I don't know."

The thought did not make me happy. I tried to drink the tea, but it was too hot and almost scalded my tongue.

Harry, however, swigged it down. He said, "I've got to go. If I waste time in idle chit-chat my work will never be done."

"What exactly is your work?"

He leaned over to pat the bound-up briefcases. Then

he did his nose-cheek-chin routine, three times over. "Wouldn't you and everyone else like to know. All right, give me that story of yours and I'll read it."

"You really want to?"

"At least I'll be impartial. The only genius Isaac can recognize is his own. And I know some people who might be able to help you, though I won't name names. So give it to me so I can get out of here."

First Hadassah and now Harry Winter. "I don't have it on me."

"Then I'll write down my address. Bring it to me tomorrow morning."

"I'll need it back right away."

"Do I look like a speed reader? When I finish I finish."

"I'll bring it," I said, although in truth I wasn't sure if I wanted him to read my story. He was unpredictable and possibly disturbed. But he also seemed to have a commanding and solemn judgment when it came to books. He took a scrap of paper and a pen from inside his jacket and wrote the address with his free hand, the one not tied by the string. "Come by any time before eleven. Oh, by the way, I have something else for you."

He reached inside his jacket again and withdrew the small book, *Nobel Lecture*, that I had looked at in Gotham Book Mart. "For your precious collection," he said, sliding it across the table.

I picked it up and opened it to the title page. "How did you get it? Without paying? I can't take the book if you stole it."

"If you don't take it I'll sell it to a dealer. Everyone needs to make a living, Mr. Roth. The publishing industry is at the heart of what's wrong with this country. Don't forget to come by with your story. And another thing. If you do get to talk to Singer tell him that Harry Winter is willing to translate for him again. I forgive him for what he said to me. Tell him that I'm the best translator he ever had and he knows it."

# 10

# A Million Years of Human Development

Although I should have returned to the Schraft Hotel to check for a message from Aaron, I descended again into the subway and rode it all the way to South Ferry. Coming up, I immediately smelled the ocean. I was at the southern tip of Manhattan, a long verdant crescent of park underlined by a boardwalk above the black and oily water. How could the grass be so green, I wondered, when the other squares and triangles that made up New York's parks looked so faded? Here were the ports where ferries left for Staten Island, Ellis Island, and Liberty Island, formerly Bedloe's. On the boardwalk I leaned against the iron rail and looked out at the Statue of Liberty stiffly holding aloft her torch, turned outward to the ghosts of those crowded immigrant ships and elegant liners. Isaac Bashevis Singer had come on such a ship in 1928 when he was still in his thirties, slight of build and already almost bald. He had written one book, *Satan in Goray*, but it had not yet been published in Warsaw and when he arrived in America his fictional voice turned silent. Looking out from the side of that ship, he must have already felt his language, his very subject matter, slipping away from him as if drowning in the sea.

I had come down to South Ferry to clear my head and bring myself down to a less excited state than the one that meeting Hadassah and then Harry Winter had put me in. I walked along the boardwalk, sat on a bench, watched the gulls rise and skim and give their plaintive screams. The breeze from the ocean was refreshing despite its smell, but I could still feel all of Manhattan behind me, like a gigantic steam iron pressed against my back. Of the two it was of course Hadassah I thought of most, and her face, which continually appeared to me, but I thought of Harry also and whether I could even trust him. Perhaps Hadassah was wondering about that too — about trusting me, that is. If she was I could hardly blame her. Obviously she had not felt the same keen pain of recognition, the same pull of destiny, as I had. Did that mean I was wrong or that it was my personal trial to prove that destiny to her?

Looking out at the bay where the waters of the Hudson and the East Rivers mingled, I considered this relation between Hadassah and Singer. How was it that he had an Israeli niece? His brother, the writer I.J. Singer, had children before his early death in the forties, but as far as I knew they lived in America. I knew from Singer's memoir, *In My Father's Court*, that he had had a sister too, but not of what became of her. I had also read somewhere of Singer having a son, not with his wife but from an earlier relationship, and in fact Singer had published a story called "The Son" about a nervously anticipated meeting between a father and son who did not know one another. It also occurred to me that Hadassah was too young to be Singer's niece; instead, he had to be her great-uncle. Was it possible that her relation to Singer had heightened my feelings for Hadassah, that I had somehow transformed my admiration for him into an infatuation for his niece? But I did not know who she was when I first saw her and the first pangs I felt had occurred before we spoke. No, I did not believe my feelings for her had anything to do with wanting to reach Singer. When I asked her to go to the restaurant, Singer had been more an excuse to hold on to her company than anything else. If she had been the doorman's niece instead I would have felt the same way.

Yes, but could I say truthfully that I no longer cared whether I met Singer or not? I grappled with my turning emotions and had to admit I still wanted him to read my story. Hadassah *had* given me new hope that it might really happen. Well, why couldn't a person want two things at once? Or even a dozen? There was no limit to wanting.

A ferry gave two long blasts of its horn as it came into dock. The afternoon had slipped away in reverie. At four o'clock I was to meet Alice at the Plaza, when I would get my manuscript back from her. Strangely, I would have liked to share all these thoughts with her. The idea of telling Alice about Hadassah gave me a thrill of expectation, perhaps because I longed to speak Hadassah's name to someone else. But although I had found myself to be emotionally naive at times, I knew better than to tell an old lover about the woman I now hoped to win.

I took a last look at the dark water. Perhaps one day New York would sink into the sea and become another Atlantis. What if it began happening at this very instant, taking me and Alice and Hadassah and Harry Winter and my brother, Aaron, with it? But at twenty-one I was not afraid of death, because I could not imagine it. I understood rationally that my life was insignificant and that the universe was indifferent to my fate, but I did not believe it. Staring at the ocean had made me more calm but not less excited. At this moment even the prospect of unhappiness was exhilarating. Would Hadassah love me? If she could, I would be faithful to her to the grave. What should I say to Alice to extricate myself without hurting her? Would Isaac Bashevis Singer declare me a writer of genuine talent?

I felt like shouting my name into the sky above the ocean.

Lingering so long at Battery Park, I was panicked to discover, on asking a woman in red sunglasses the time, that it was already past four. Alice would undoubtedly read my late arrival as a sign of callousness, and while I was absolutely determined to end our romance this afternoon, I had no desire to hurt her more than necessary. I easily recalled how devastated I'd been when Theresa Zeitman had broken off with me and concluded that in an affair suffering is always unequal. Perhaps my pleading and tears with Theresa had been more annoying to her than touching because she had already removed herself emotionally, as if her own feelings had floated imperiously above us. This was a cruel aspect of love that I had not recognized before.

But I wanted to see Alice, to speak to her and, more urgently, to find out what she thought of "The Goat Bride." I ran across the park to Water Street and waved at two cabs, both of which had no passengers but did not stop. Maybe I looked too frantic and so scared them off, or something was wrong with my technique that could be corrected only by a native. However, a third did pull over and I threw myself into the back even as I announced, "The Plaza, and step on it," like I was in some Dashiell Hammett novel.

The cab took off fast enough but within moments we were stalled behind a line of honking cars. I had forgotten about rush hour. Someone on the sidewalk could have measured our progress with a ruler until the driver backed up, thumped over a curb, which sent several pedestrians leaping, and lurched onto Trinity Place. Moments later we were moving slowly but steadily up past the World Trade Center. If only I could think of an excuse to tell Alice for being late, for the coward in me did not look forward to seeing her injured and haughty expression. That I had been held up by a gunman? Or had helped a team of firemen hold a net beneath a distraught office worker balanced on the ledge of the Woolworth Building? At least the driver was proving himself a virtuoso of Manhattan traffic, shooting uptown like a steel ball ricocheting inside a pinball machine. A liberal user of his own horn, he joined the symphonic cacophony. "Ah, you see that?" he said, shaking his head. His words had to pass through the small holes in the acrylic divider separating the front and back seats. "Limousine drivers are so arrogant, man. They think they own this town."

I noticed on the dashboard a photograph of a child in a heart-shaped frame. To make conversation I said, "Is that your daughter?"

"Her mother stole her from me." I could hear the anger making him grind the words between his teeth. "Not three years I have seen her. She must be big now. That woman! When I find her again I'm going to strangle the life out of her."

I leaned back in my seat, sorry for asking. He drove even more aggressively, pounding the accelerator. If all the suppressed emotions in people were suddenly released, I thought, they would ignite a firestorm and consume the planet. The driver turned onto Fifty-ninth and cruised along the bottom of Central Park before turning into the circle in front of the Plaza. I folded a twenty-dollar bill into the little metal trough and pushed it through the divider.

"You expect me to change this, man?" he said. "My shift just started."

"But I don't have anything smaller."

"That's not my problem. Read the sign. I don't have to accept anything bigger than a ten."

"All right, keep it." I peered into my wallet at the money I had left even as the Plaza doorman opened the cab door. I bounded up the steps, straightening my tie as I went. The red carpet took me up to the revolving door and into the black and gold lobby. Through the arches I could hear a violin and piano playing Gershwin's "But Not for Me" and I followed the music into the Palm Court.

The Palm Court was all marble columns and mirrors,

the occupied tables laid with white cloths and silver teapots and little stands of cakes. It was a scene to make a person sigh for the comfort of it, only I felt sharply how Alice must have sat there stewing and had probably already left. A small crowd waited patiently by the entrance and I excused myself to get through until I stood before the maitre d', a tall man in dapper tuxedo with oiled hair and a Habsburgian moustache.

"I'm late for meeting someone here," I said.

His eye screwed up with contempt. "The lady is expecting you," he said. "She has been waiting some time." He crooked a finger at me and then made a little shooing motion to move the waiters aside so I could follow him. We crossed the Palm Court and I felt as if everyone stopped to look accusingly at me. Alice sat at a corner table, the only one who was alone. She was not reading nor even looking about but sat staring towards a potted palm. Her dress of pale rose was becoming and her new haircut made her neck and shoulders look alluringly bare. When she saw me her eyes registered my presence but she did not move when I leaned down to kiss her cheek.

"You can't believe the traffic," I said, taking the opposite seat. "And then there was this firetruck —"

But she didn't seem to be listening and my excuses faded away. After a moment she said, "I've been sitting here thinking about civilization."

"That's a pretty big subject."

"It came to me that every instant in time and place — for example, right here and now — is the accumulation of all civilization. The history of human ambition and technological development that caused this city to rise. The economic forces that made this hotel. The taste for nostalgia that draws people to this antiquated tea ceremony, the fashions we wear, the private thoughts we are experiencing, the pacemaker in that old man's chest, the antidepressants coursing through that woman's bloodstream. The busboys thinking about the train ride back to their tenements in Harlem or the Bronx, the men flashing their gold cards, the memories of affairs . . ."

"I think I see what you mean."

"Well, this is what civilization in all its glory has made. And you know what else it has made? Me. Sitting here and waiting like a fool for almost an hour."

"I'm really sorry, Alice."

"I don't blame you. As I said, I'm the fool. It's civilization I'm most disappointed in. After millions of years of human development I would have expected it to accomplish a little bit more than this. Oh, good, here's the waiter. I'm starved. We'll have tea and sandwiches and sweets, please."

She spoke brightly to the waiter, as if suddenly in the best of moods. I had seen this brittle, acerbic side of her before and it was not a good sign. "It's so nice to meet in New York," she said, still in that artificially pleasant tone she had used with the waiter. "Are you enjoying the city, Felix? Have you gone to the top of the Empire State Building or toured the United Nations? Maybe you're going to see a Broadway show. I hear *Sweeney Todd* is delightful."

"Stop it, Alice. You enjoy punishing yourself too much. You should direct your anger at me."

"But I'm the corrupter of youth, the evil crone in the

fairy story. You ought to know that, Felix. You're the literary genius —"

I reached across the table and grabbed her wrist. She tried to pull it from me but I held on firmly, pressing my fingers into her so hard that I must have been bruising her pale skin. The surge of my own greater strength sickened me but I kept holding her while she clenched her jaw. And then suddenly her arm relaxed. I let go of her wrist and gently took her hand instead. She neither resisted nor returned the pressure.

"I want things to have meaning," she said. "I can't stand it when they don't."

"They do have meaning, Alice. *We* have meaning. You've made an indelible impression on my life. It will never be the same because of you. It's better, richer, more meaningful. Even the things we don't understand."

She took her hand away from me. "I should know myself better. I'm thirty-five. I have a seven-year-old son. And I still get lost so easily. I have a difficult personality — dependent on everything around me. Maybe that's why I need Arthur. But then I have this opposing need, to risk everything, to put it in jeopardy. I start to feel I'm not alive if I don't do something reckless."

"Is that what I am? Doing something reckless?"

"You know you're more than that. Christ, I'm sorry, but this is not enough for me. Not just you. All of it."

The waiter arrived with a busboy carrying the paraphernalia for our tea — a large pot, cups and saucers, a three-tiered tray of finger sandwiches and pastries. Alice reached out, picked a sandwich without looking to see what kind, and took a bite. I took this as my signal and ate one in two bites, then another and a third.

She said, "You know what I like about New York? It shows me that there are people who are richer, happier, more famous, wilder, more extravagant than me. And people who are poorer, more desperate, crazier, destructive. In a strange way it makes me feel more free. Last night I couldn't sleep and finally went for a walk at four in the morning. I would never do that back in Toronto. It's safer at home but what would be the point? Here I walked down Fifth Avenue and there were plenty of people out. Some of them even nodded to me, like we were members in a secret society of insomniacs. Twice I was propositioned for sex, three people tried to sell me dope or crack, a woman begged me to look at the scars she had inflicted on her own stomach, and a guy who said he made art out of garbage fished from the East River asked if he could do my portrait. I did buy a joint, from a nice boy who said he was making his way through architecture school. Smoked it as I walked along. A policeman on a horse smiled at me. For a few minutes I actually forgot who I was or that I belonged to anyone or even that I had a name. Of course it didn't last long. I looked into the window of a linen shop and suddenly thought of Everett asleep in his bed back home. This morning on the phone he said he wanted me to come back right away. I wondered what I could be doing away from him like this. I must be a terrible mother."

"You know that isn't true. Besides, you have a reason for being here. You're working, remember? The Lady with the Rose."

"Yes. I do have a reason."

"Did you go to the auction house today?"

"I held her in my hands."

This was good, I thought. A calm conversation that could lead to a quiet discussion of why we could no longer be lovers. "And is she the real thing?" I said. "The one that Napoleon gave to Madame de Something-or-other?"

"Desmarets. The yellow pigment on the rose looks original. I'll have to do some tests back at the museum. The mark on the bottom is from the Limoges workshop and the right time period. But there isn't anything conclusive. Still, I think the circumstantial evidence along with its uniqueness will be enough to persuade most other experts in the field."

"And no one else has linked it to the little French general?"

"Not as far as I can tell. The assistant said that two or three other collectors have examined it. But it's in lovely condition; any collector would be pleased to own it. I don't want to raise suspicions so I won't go back until the auction and I'll bid on a few other things as well. Actually, I was hoping that you would come. It's tomorrow night at eight. I could use your moral support."

"Of course I'll come."

"Here," she said, opening her purse. "I brought you a card with the address." I took the card and slipped it into my wallet. So Alice hadn't made up the story about Napoleon's mistress after all. "Have some pastries," she said. "The little mille-feuille looks delicious. I can't stay much longer. I have to meet somebody. Somebody who's usually on time." She smiled and took a strawberry tart.

"Who?" I asked. It hadn't occurred to me that she had someone else to see in New York.

"An old professor of mine from Columbia. A specialist in Byzantine art. He's a wonderful man. We're still good friends."

"When you say old do you mean *old*?"

"No, he's not yet sixty."

"Did you have an affair with him?"

"Felix, don't ask stupid questions."

"I'm not asking out of jealousy. I'm just interested in knowing about you."

"All right. But it wasn't an affair because I wasn't married at the time."

"Was he?"

"Yes. He's married now too, only to someone else."

"And when you visit New York to see him, do you sleep together?"

Her eyes narrowed. I knew the question only made me look pathetic, but I couldn't help myself. My heart beat faster and I felt slightly ill. It was crazy to be jealous when I was trying to break off with her. Was this the usual male need to possess even what I no longer wanted? If so, Alice was right: humankind hadn't advanced much since the Stone Age.

"I apologize, Alice," I said. "It just snuck up on me."

"I wasn't trying to make you feel that way. I don't play games like that. Seeing Leonard when I'm in the city is a longstanding tradition."

"Leonard."

"Oh, that's enough. Have a chocolate eclair, Felix. They're really good."

She picked one up and held it to my mouth; what could I do but take a bite? I wondered whether Alice too understood that our relationship was changing and that during the transition we had no choice but to torment one another. She said, "Anyway, it isn't my old professor you ought to worry about. It's Arthur."

"What do you mean?"

"He found that copy of *The Spinoza of Market Street* you gave me. I suppose I shouldn't have asked you to write something in it."

"But I didn't sign my name."

"He knows your handwriting."

"Oh, Jesus."

"I was very clever. I told him that I saw you reading it when I came by the office last week and that you very gallantly gave it to me."

"Did he buy it?"

"Hard to tell. He just said that if he caught you reading during work time you'd be out on your ass. If Arthur can deny the truth to himself he will. You have to understand that under all his bluster, Arthur is as big a coward as you are."

"Thank you very much."

"The truth is, I think you're both afraid of each other. I truly hope he hasn't guessed about us because it would hurt him deeply. I would never want that. At least I hope that I don't. Also, if he thinks that you know that *he* knows then he'll feel obliged to act like a man and confront you."

"Act like a man? How act like a man? You mean challenge me to a duel or something?"

Alice sighed. "God help me."

I pushed away my plate. "I'm not hungry anymore."

"I'm not surprised, considering how much you've eaten."

We sat without speaking. The conversation had hardly gone as I expected or wanted. Now for all I knew, when I arrived back at the office of *Lowenstein's Sheet* on Wednesday morning, Arthur would be waiting with a pistol or sword in hand. Meanwhile, Alice looked disgusted. I wouldn't blame her if she wanted to run a sword through the both of us.

"I'll sign the tab so we can get out of here," she said.

"Alice, I need my story back."

"It's in the room. You can come up with me and get it."

We left the Palm Court. I ought to have insisted on paying, but I could see that my money was going to run low. Besides, we had fallen into an early pattern of Alice always picking up the tab, which I resented — it made me feel like a kid being taken for a treat in reward for good behaviour — but did nothing about.

Alice unlocked her door to let us in. My story was lying on the table beside an empty glass, the pages curling and a pink smudge that might have been lipstick under the title.

"I've got to get ready to meet Leonard," Alice said, slipping out of her heels. "I need to take a shower. This city always makes me feel so dirty. You can take your story and go if you want."

I followed her into the bedroom. "But what did you think of it? Please, Alice, you have to tell me. And be truthful. There's no point in being otherwise."

"I can't reach the top button," she said, struggling to undo her dress from behind.

"Here, let me."

"All right, I'll tell you. It made me cry."

"Really? You actually cried?"

The dress fell to her feet and the slip followed. She

always wore exquisite lingerie and now she turned to me in her satin bra and panties. She was slightly knock-kneed, which I found touching. Had Alice orchestrated this moment, or had it been me who had brought us to this place? I leaned forward and kissed her and reached behind to unclasp her bra. We separated a moment and even as I looked at her I tried to will myself to apologize and march out of the room. But Alice grabbed my tie and pulled me towards her; for a moment I thought she was going to strangle me. Instead, she drew me in close, pressed her mouth to mine, and began unbuckling my belt.

Silently, I asked Hadassah to forgive me.

Alice did not meet her old professor that night, although she eventually broke away from me long enough to leave him a message. Around ten we called room service and had them bring up a couple of steak frites and a bottle of wine, after which we took a bath together in the oval tub. The rest of the world vanished in the bubbles.

It was only after I left her some time after two, standing on Fifth Avenue with my manuscript in my blazer pocket, that I felt back in Manhattan again. The cooler air was refreshing; it brought me out of the sexual daze I'd been in. With a start I realized that we had spoken no more about "The Goat Bride." Alice had not told me what parts she liked best, whether any of the characters or passages were weak, or anything else for that matter. She hadn't actually told me whether she even liked the story. She had cried, yes, but what exactly had she cried *about*?

# 11

# French Postcards

In the morning — Sunday morning, my third day in New York — I came down to the murk and dust of the Schraft Hotel lobby to see a man in a green leotard sleeping on one of the moth-eaten sofas. Perhaps he was just resting with his eyes closed. Was he a dancer, an acrobat, an aerialist? The leotard had a hole in the foot, showing a callused heel. I felt some sympathy for the man, whose hairpiece had come slightly askew and whose impressive chest rose and fell as he breathed. Perhaps writers were something like the performers who stayed at the Schraft, entertainers whose tricks were beginning to bore an audience with an increasingly short attention span and a decreasing ability to imagine realities other than their own. We too were becoming hopelessly anachronistic.

Aaron had not been sleeping in the hotel room when I came back from seeing Alice, nor did he return during the night. I was depressed by the sight of his undisturbed bed on waking but not surprised, for I had already guessed that he was staying with his Hasidic acquaintances, who I knew had offered to put him up. It should have been my duty to track him down, but I did not know their names or where in Brooklyn they lived. Instead, I myself had decided to leave the Schraft.

Despite my grudging affection for the hotel, it felt like a mausoleum and I was too young to reside among the living dead. Also, the midtown location was getting on my nerves: too much traffic, too many people, too much sour air from the open doors of the pornographic cinemas and fast-food restaurants. But my real motivation was the desire to be near Hadassah. The closer I was to the Belnord Apartments the better chance I had of really getting to know her and winning her over. I felt a prick of concern about leaving in case Aaron decided to return, but did I not have the right to pursue my own future? And so I assured myself that leaving a forwarding address would be safe enough.

There was a telephone book in the lobby booth and after putting down my bag and checking to make sure the manuscript of "The Goat Bride" was in my inside blazer pocket, I began searching through it for somewhere cheap on the Upper West Side. After several pages I came to a small advertisement.

TIRED OF IMPERSONAL HOTELS?

Join us for a night or a week.

Clean, well-appointed rooms.

Breakfast included.

THE KEMEL BED AND BREAKFAST

The address was on West Eighty-second Street, four blocks south of the Belnord. I fished in my pocket for a dime.

"Kemel Bed and Breakfast. May I help you?" An elderly woman's rasp on the other end.

"My name is Felix Roth," I said. "I was wondering if you had a room for a couple of nights."

"You have good timing," the voice answered. A slight accent, German perhaps. "A guest left not an hour ago. We have only two rooms to let and one is taken by the month."

"I'll come right away."

"Very good, my dear. We do so enjoy company. We're on the second floor, first door on the left."

The prospect of being so close to Hadassah gave me new energy. I went to the front desk to pay my bill to the clerk, who looked like Uriah Heep's older brother and took my money without speaking. I wrote down the address and phone number of the Kemel Bed and Breakfast and asked him to refer all inquiries there. I hesitated a moment, then took out my wallet and handed him ten dollars for his troubles.

Too impatient to wait for the subway, I took a cab uptown. The driver had a shaved patch at the back of his head and a horseshoe-shaped outline of stitches in his scalp, as if he had recently undergone a little brain tune-up. I would have liked to ask him about it but decided not to risk upsetting the man. Whatever the reason for the stitches, his sense of direction was still intact and before long he left me off in front of a brownstone apartment house with oddly bulging windows. It had the sort of high stoop from which a sensitive kid could watch the life of the street and then grow up to write an unsentimental but moving autobiographical novel. My parents' house had no stoop or front porch, but only an iron gate before the pretentiously elaborate entrance, and if I had stood there from sunrise to dusk I would not have seen life unfold but only the occasional gardener's truck.

I pushed the intercom button and heard the buzz and unlatching of the door. Inside, the hall was dim and icy as a museum after closing time. I climbed the steep stairs to the second floor and knocked on the heavy door. Bolts complained as they were pulled back and the door opened.

"Please, come in."

The woman's voice, undistorted by the telephone line, was still raspy but pleasant. She had a sharp face, the nose and chin and even eyebrows pointed, and her brittle silver hair fell to her shoulders. She wore a rather stylish dress with a low neckline that exposed the bony ridges of her shoulder blades.

"I'm Hannah Kemel. Why don't you put down your bag and come sit at the dining table. I've made some Indian spice tea. And the cookies are baked yesterday. I've just made up the room. Mr. Tanenbaum is our permanent guest, but he prefers the more modest room, so the one with the view is yours. If you want it, of course, you must not decide right away. Let me pour the tea."

We had moved the few steps to the dining room, which was small and octagonal, its front windows trimmed with lace curtains. Heavy furniture crowded the room — corner armoires displaying china behind glass doors, a round table with a carved central podium. The air smelled of dried apricots. On the walls were hung small paintings, one above the other, mostly abstracts of circles and lines and patterns that hummed gently with meanings I couldn't understand.

"You are looking at the paintings," Hannah Kemel said. "That one is by Kandinsky, and those three little works are by Klee. He was a lovely man, Paul, with a child's sweetness. When I was little he used to get down on the floor so we could play with my dolls. That larger one is a Hoffman and that square there, do you recognize the style? Chagall, but very early. My husband and I gathered them up like orphans just after the war. We hardly had enough to eat and we bought paintings." She had an appealing laugh. "Some people return to us just to look at them. Do you like art, Felix?"

"Yes, but I don't know a lot about it, at least not paintings." I sipped the milky, aromatic tea. "You came from Europe?"

"In 1946. My family was Swiss. But my father moved us to Lyons, where he became partners in a hat factory five years before the war. I was engaged but my fiancé wasn't Jewish and he broke it off. My parents refused to leave France but they insisted I enter a convent for safety. I wore a habit like the nuns and prayed and fasted and scrubbed floors. We rose at five every morning. It was hard but also a kind of bliss. My parents did not survive the Nazis because they could not believe such barbarity really existed. When the war ended I met my husband in a refugee camp, where he had come in search of his own relatives. He didn't find them. He was older than I was, a German Jew who had emigrated to the United States before the war. Both of us were left alone and without illusions. We were married by an American army chaplain and came back to this country. My husband is a rare-book dealer. He has a shop just around the corner, on Amsterdam Avenue. It's a shame that you missed him by only a few minutes."

I wondered why it was a shame, given that I was a stranger, just as I was surprised at her openness. It was as if, by some paradox of nature, her experience had made her more trusting of human nature rather than less. I said, "Do you have any children?"

"We decided not to bring any more souls into this world. Of course," she smiled, "we consider everyone who stays with us to be like our family. Our guests feel that this is their home. We get many businessmen who feel lost in the city, away from their wives and children. They lose their bearings and fear that they may do something foolish. Or their troubles suddenly seem too much to bear. I cannot tell you the number of men who have leaned their heads on this table and wept. Please, Felix, take another cookie."

I gingerly removed my elbow from the table, thinking of those men with their cheeks pressed to its polished surface.

"And you?" she said. "You are not in New York just for sightseeing, I think. For one thing, few young men these days wear a jacket and tie. Although I know that you are not a painter, I sense that you are an artist of some kind, yes?"

"Of some kind, I suppose. I'm trying to be a writer."

"Ah, I knew it!" She clapped her hands with delight and laid one — it was cold — on my own for a moment. "Sam will be so pleased to meet you. But I do not mean to be presumptuous, for you have not even seen the room. Would you like to?"

"Yes, please."

She ushered me down a hall wallpapered in a velvety fleur-de-lys, which struck me as rather Victorian for collectors of modern art. "This one is your room," Hannah Kemel said and stood beside the doorway to let me see. It was small but neat, with a high canopied bed, an elegant small table and lamp, a bookcase filled with volumes in French and German. The view through the window was of the weedy yard below, a couple of sagging lawn chairs, and a deteriorating brick wall.

"I like it very much," I said. "But I just realized that I forgot on the phone to ask how much it is."

"Is twenty-five dollars a night too much? If it is I will speak to my husband about accommodating you."

"No, it's less than the hotel where I was staying. I'll take it, Mrs. Kemel."

"You must call me Hannah."

"Hannah."

"Here are keys to the street door and the apartment door. Of course you are free to come and go as you please. The bathroom is down the hall and I will put in fresh towels for you. Now I will leave you to unpack. Please don't hesitate to ask for anything."

"You're very kind."

She closed the bedroom door as she left. There was a narrow closet and I unpacked my few things. Only when I closed the closet door did I notice the four small photographs in black frames that had been hidden by the canopy over the bed. They were old French postcards of naked women, one stretched out on a divan with her legs in the air, another on an animal skin, a third stepping demurely into a bathtub, and a fourth lying on her stomach on a bed and smoking a cigarette. They were fleshier than fashionable women today and their faces looked smaller and their skin more white. They seemed seductive and innocent at the same time and somehow I was not surprised to find them in the room.

# 12

# The Mortuary

Back in Toronto, a dreamy teenager in his own room, with maybe only the muffled *hoosh* of the cleaning lady pushing the vacuum cleaner somewhere else in the background, I had read not only Isaac Bashevis Singer but many other Yiddish novelists and Irving Howe's *World of Our Fathers* and Abraham Cahan's *The Rise of David Levinsky* and the sweat-shop poets. With my door closed I had declaimed the lines of Morris Rosenfeld and Moishe Leib Halpern and especially my favourite poem by Mani Leib, first in awkward Yiddish pronunciation and then in the English translation:

> I am Mani Leib, whose name is sung —
> In Brownsville, Yehupetz and farther, they know it:
> Among cobblers, a splendid cobbler; among
> Poetical circles, a splendid poet.

I imagined the streets of the Lower East Side clamorous and choked with pushcarts, the tenement windows open for a little air, the noise of wailing babies and young women calling down and the Yiddish recriminations and moans and laughter. I saw the rows of sewing machines humming from dawn to dusk and the tired workers filing out at the end of the day. Also the marquees of the Yiddish theatres on Second Avenue and the labour organizers orating in the halls and Emma Goldman lecturing weary shopgirls about Henrik Ibsen. And the cafeterias brightly lit against the inhospitable winter night (for it was always winter I imagined, with snow piled against the sidewalks and pelting the plate-glass windows) where the writers and poets, exhausted from their long day of stitching or wallpapering but elated to be artists again, shared their camaraderie and bitter gossip.

It was foolish, of course, to think this hard life had any romance in it, but I could not resist believing that these people, the literary ancestors I wanted to claim as my own, had truly lived, not in spite of suffering but because of it. And I recalled these thoughts of mine as I walked to the subway and caught a B train for downtown. Harry Winter lived in the Lower East Side, on Eldridge Street according to the address he had written down for me, and as he had told me to come by any morning I saw no reason to put it off. I had said goodbye to Hannah Kemel (who had mildly startled me with a kiss on each cheek, continental style) and had rolled up my manuscript and slipped it into the inside pocket of my blazer.

The subway car reeked of marijuana, although none of the other riders were smoking. Two men in caps argued in some Slavic language while a handsome black boy in a private-school tie was using his briefcase, like a little businessman, as a lap desk to do his math homework. Across from me a woman dandled on her knee the ugliest baby I had ever seen. It looked like its mother, only with a wider mouth and a high forehead and red tufts of hair, and it reminded me of the pig-faced baby in *Alice in Wonderland*. This child, nicely dressed in little striped overalls and soft shoes, had the hiccups and every time it hiccupped it laughed and threw back its head to look at its mother. And the mother cooed and leaned down to nuzzle the baby's cheek, offering it an uncompromised love the likes of which it — and the rest of us — would never find again.

I hoped that Harry would read my story while I waited so that I could get his opinion and still take the manuscript to Hadassah this afternoon. I knew that my reason for going to see him was not only to receive his judgment but also because I was attracted to his eccentricity — although that was the wrong word, I thought, too sweet and toothless. It was true that Harry's slovenly appearance made me feel some revulsion, but even this reaction was of interest to me. It seemed only right that he lived in the Lower East Side, which I knew was no longer much of a Jewish neighbourhood and had become even more decrepit, crime- and drug-ridden. I thought that Harry would be a dose of the real, for which I had only an increased hunger, like a loud growl in my stomach.

I came up from the subway at East Broadway and Rutgers Street, surrounded by the rising tenement buildings. Having some time, I decided to take a little tour and so looked into the bookshops on Canal between Ludlow and Essex, crammed with religious volumes. I saw a synagogue with shattered windows and boarded-up doorway, graffiti scrawled across its brick front. Two young Hispanic men played checkers on the steps with a homemade board and buttons for playing pieces. On Hester Street stood barrels swollen with pickles in brine, shops selling tefillin and prayer shawls. Peering through an open door, I spied a bearded man bent over a slanted desk with a quill pen in his hand. A Torah scribe. He might have been in ancient Persia or in some alleyway in the Lodz ghetto.

I came to Harry's apartment house on Eldridge, an iron stairway zigzagging up its nine stories of measled brick. A tree grew from the sidewalk in front but all the branches had been twisted off, as if by the hand of a golem. Someone had "decorated" the trunk by hammering hundreds of nails into it. Harry's apartment was below-ground, next to a liquor store and with the trash cans chained under his front window. The window itself was striped with bars, and I had a momentary illusion that the bars were not to keep intruders out but to keep Harry in.

The door looked so heavy I doubted that it could be penetrated by any sound, but I pounded on it with the flat of my hand. After a moment I heard Harry's muffled voice.

"Who's there?"

"Felix Roth. Remember, we met yesterday?"

"What do you want?"

"I've brought you my story."

"Leave it on the mat."

"Can't I just give it to you?"

"I don't open the door for anyone, not even Elijah."

"But it's my only copy."

"It's not my fault if you're a fool. Besides, a short story by an unknown writer is the one thing my neighbours won't steal."

"This is crazy," I muttered. Crazier still was that I did as he said, leaving the manuscript, whose title page was beginning to tear away from the staple. When my foot was on the first iron step leading back up to the sidewalk I heard the door open behind me.

Harry Winter looked at me through the three inches of space that the door could open while still on its chain.

"You're alone?"

Who did he expect me to be with, a couple of G-men, maybe? "Yes, I'm alone."

He closed the door and I heard the chain fall. Then he opened it again and picked up the manuscript, leaning down with difficulty because of his bulk and what seemed to be bad knees. He motioned for me to come inside, not looking at me but letting his eyes slide from side to side along the sidewalk.

Harry locked, bolted, and chained the door behind me. There were no lights on but only the dusty haze from the barred window. I had half expected the apartment to be filled with junk — discarded sofas, broken radios, pictures from magazines taped to the walls — but instead it was as spartan as a monk's cell, with only a threadbare Persian rug, a couple of armchairs, their seats neatly patched, a coffee table made from a battered steamer trunk on which rested a pile of the *New York Times* with various articles marked in blue or red ink. The tape-bound briefcases stood beside the trunk. Only the Murphy bed was untidy, and Harry straightened the sheets before pushing it upright into the wall with a grunt. He was wearing what must have been his sleeping attire, a pair of longjohns, the kind with the button flap at the rear.

What I did not see at first, because they were against the wall behind me, was the most notable feature of the apartment: rows of wooden crates wired together and stacked almost to the ceiling. The crates — there must have been close to a hundred — were rough and splintery, salvaged from some vegetable depot or chicken slaughterhouse, and must have been anchored to the wall as they did not lean forward. Each was filled with files, papers, photographs. Also old books, some without covers, others held together with the same black tape that bound the briefcases, and most with titles on their spines in languages I could not read.

"So, sit down," Harry said, as if annoyed that I was looking at the crates. I took an armchair and he settled into the other, putting his large feet up on the trunk so that I could hardly help staring at his purplish toes. My manuscript was in his hand but he seemed to have forgotten about it. "I didn't expect you to show up. Did you have lunch? I was going to make some salami and eggs. The trick is to cut the salami thin. And let the slices simmer in the pan. You don't need any oil — there's plenty of fat in the salami. The smell is exquisite. Sometimes I put it in a sandwich but I'm out of rye."

"I'm really not hungry, thanks."

"You don't eat this sort of food? You like only quiche Lorraine, maybe? Tell me, when is the last time you ever saw somebody eat a nice piece of challah smeared with chicken schmaltz? It's like they passed a law against it. Let me see." He rolled my manuscript into a tube, then scrutinized me as if through a telescope. "So this is the great work, the magnum opus." He let the pages unfurl in his lap. "What's it called? 'The Goat Bride.' I don't like the title."

"I've been thinking of changing it."

"Wait, wait. No need to rush anything. It's a good thing you brought this to me. I'm a better critic than Isaac Bashevis Singer, more impartial. The only genius Isaac can recognize is his own."

"I was wondering if you'd mind reading it while I wait."

"What? You think I need an audience to read? Maybe you want to see if I move my lips."

"No, it's just that I've got to get it to someone —"

"Someone more important than Harry Winter? Then take the damn thing." He tossed it at me and as I grabbed it the title page tore off. "I don't like to be rushed. Besides, I've got to get to work at the Jewish Museum by noon."

"You're a curator?"

"They should be so lucky to have someone of my ability as a curator. I just do a little cataloguing in the rare-books department. They don't like me but nobody has my depth of knowledge. This is only occasional work. Also I do proofreading for a publisher of worthless books. A little translating. I've been a dishwasher and a mail sorter too, whatever I can stand for a while."

"You left out book thief," I said, remembering the little Singer volume.

"If necessity demands. There are bookstalls that will pay one-third the cover price for a new title. You think this bothers my conscience? Perhaps you know the term *luftmensch*. A man who lives on air, on nothing. Singer likes to fancy himself a *luftmensch* but he's been making good money for years, publishing his stories in *The New Yorker* and *The Saturday Evening Post* and even between the titties in *Playboy*. For him the Nobel was just icing on the cake."

I did not want him to see my disappointment over his not reading my story. "How is it that you know Yiddish?" I asked. "Were you born in Europe?"

"Not in that graveyard. I've never even been. My parents came before the war. I was born in Louisiana."

"You're kidding me. I didn't know there were Jews in Louisiana."

"There are Jews in India, in China, why wouldn't there be in the South? My father had a cigar store in some backwater town. But we moved every six months or year. The only thing he was really good at was bankruptcy. And languages, a natural aptitude, better even than my own. He taught himself Urdu though he never met a single person who spoke it. Whenever we left a place just about the only thing we took with us were books."

"My parents don't speak Yiddish that well," I said. "It's all mixed with English. And they only used it when they didn't want my brother and me to understand."

"The usual story," he said with a shrug.

"I've tried to study it on my own from a textbook but I didn't get very far. I'd really like to learn."

"Why, so you can talk to your bubbie? Soon she'll

be dead, just like the language. Better to learn how to program a computer — that's the sorry future."

"Not for people like us."

"Oh, so now we're a club."

"Well, if you don't want to read my story I guess I better go."

As I got up his hand went up to his face and his thumb did its little dance — nose, cheek, chin. He too got up. "Don't be such a hot-head. Who said I didn't want to read it? Do yourself a favour and leave it with me for a day."

He held out a hand and I gave him back the manuscript, minus the title page. "And what about you, Harry," I asked. "Do you write too?"

"Me? I know better than that. I'm a lesser being, a mere scholar." As he said the word he waved towards the wall of crates. It was an odd gesture, both grandiose and dismissive.

I said, "So that's your research."

"Ten years of it. I estimate another ten at least."

"And what is it about?"

He looked at me hard and I noticed what I hadn't seen before, or perhaps had avoided seeing: a skin ailment, a scaly encrustation under his right ear. "I don't talk about my life's work to every Tom, Dick, and Harry. Not after the attempts to destroy it. Four years ago a fire in my apartment on Henry Street, last year the IRS, and now a blacklist circulated among the publishers. Oh, don't bother to ask anyone — they'll all deny it. But it exists nonetheless. So I keep mum. But when the work is ready the public will hear, you can be sure of that."

He could not resist running a hand lovingly along

the edge of a crate. "About you I feel different, Felix. Worthy of trust. Perhaps a few select people ought to know, in the event something happens to me. All right, go ahead. Look for yourself. The system is alphabetical. When my work is published nobody in the literary establishment will thank me. Harry Winter will never win the Nobel Prize. In fact, I expect to be denounced. I count on it."

He folded his hands as if already triumphant and I knew that I was in the presence of the sort of shining-eyed fanatic that I had only read about in Dostoevsky novels. But such fanatics were sometimes tellers of truth. Yet despite my burning curiosity to know what was in those shelves, I kept my hands at my sides. Perhaps I was simply afraid of discovering that he was no visionary but a mere crackpot who spent his days filling pages with nonsense words or the five Books of Moses in mirror writing. However, with Harry standing expectantly beside me I had no choice but to tentatively pull out a folder from one of the crates.

"Which one did you get?" Harry said, unable to hold back. He let my own manuscript drop from his hand to the floor. I read what was printed on the folder's tab: "Kissak, Zsigmond." Inside were sheets filled to the edges with a minute handwriting that almost required a magnifying glass to read. Also several photocopied pages of type in an Eastern European language and a photograph of a long-faced man in a wool suit standing in front of the empty wicker chairs of a street café.

"Is this Kissak?" I said. "Who was he?"

"A writer of parables," Harry said, thumbing his nose, cheek, and chin three times in succession.

"Brilliant, lucid, heartbreaking paragraphs in a splendid Hungarian. Kafka adored him. But is there a country in the world where Kissak's books remain in print? Where he is read and discussed and revered? Not one. Only once was he translated into English — not even a good translation — and that book went out of print twenty years ago. And look here —"

He pulled a file from another crate. "Let's see who this is. Raymond Larra. A Spaniard who died in 1957, hit by a bus in Barcelona on his way to visit a prostitute with whom he was obsessed. He wrote poems to her of almost perverse lyric beauty. Even the Spaniards don't know who he is. And see here, this one will interest you."

He handed me another file and I read the name: "Nefish, Yitzak." Even as I opened it Harry began talking again, shuffling from one foot to the other. "Yitzak Nefish was born in Lublin the same year as Singer. He was the son of a butcher but his father's profession was an abomination to him. When he was a young man he decided to become a writer and walked on foot to Warsaw. He tried to meet authors at the Writers' Club but they ignored him. Even Singer, who was a nobody, ignored him. Nefish came to America on the same boat as Singer. Here he began to write his stories, long, twisted, vitriolic condemnations of human hypocrisy. His hero is always the same, without a name, a man who has committed a murder that he refuses to speak of and who lives on in rage and pity. Nefish himself was the most shy and gentle of souls. No one would touch his work and he had to publish it at his own expense, on the cheapest paper. They were reviewed only to be denounced and he died heartbroken in

Madison, Wisconsin. Most of the copies have already turned to dust."

Harry had laid each successive folder on the floor around our feet and he did so with the Nefish before taking out another. "And look here. 'Slutsky, Josef.' And this one. 'Colonna, Fabrizio.' Each of these crates is devoted to someone else and I have hardly scratched the surface of Europe and America. You know what I call this wall? The Mortuary of Forgotten Writers. Each one suffered for his art, suffered agony and heartbreak and disappointment. Why did they not become famous? Win awards? Receive heaps of praise in the newspapers and magazines? I used to suspect that it was a conspiracy, not just of publishers but of Washington and Moscow and the movie studios and organized religion. But it is not that. It is mere human indifference. These writers drew their own blood to write with and what they had to say is of no interest to mankind. They sang or whispered or shouted or screamed and they were not heard. But I hear them. I take them to my bosom and love them. I give their crumbling books a home, I honour their names. Every so often I try to interest a publisher in reprinting one of their works but I never succeed. I have translated Yitzak Nefish's best stories but the publishers won't even look at them unless I can get an introduction from the only Yiddish writer who sells books, your Mr. Singer. I've written to Singer a dozen times but he refuses to answer."

"Perhaps he never saw the letters. He must have a secretary for all that mail."

"Not read a letter from Harry Winter? No, it is a deliberate insult. But no matter, I am a patient man.

For years I have been building a secret fund, a little at a time. The name of the bank I keep to myself. There are people out there who have been sent to swindle me out of the money with bogus stock tips and pyramid schemes. But I resist. And at the proper time I will publish my book on these forgotten writers, bringing their names back into the light again. I will show that our beloved literature is a tragedy and a farce —"

He stopped, breathless, his face blotchy and damp. A fan of folders was arrayed around our feet. Now he stepped carefully over them and went to his brief-cases, from which he took an inhaler. He put his lips around it and sucked in.

"Sit down, Harry," I said. "Can I do anything for you?"

He did sit back down, closing his eyes for a moment. "No, I'm all right. I get a little excited, that's all. You have to forgive me."

"Should I call the Jewish Museum? You'll be late for work."

"Let them wait. They don't own me. Sometimes I have dreams that those crates will come toppling down onto me in bed, pinning me down, squeezing the air out of my lungs. I am not unbalanced, Felix. I am moved by the fate of these writers. And I understand clearly what it has cost me. So," he said, and groaning he leaned down to pick up my manuscript from the rug, "do you still want to leave your story with me?"

"Yes, if I can get it back tomorrow."

"All right. Where are you staying?"

"On the Upper West Side."

"I am evaluating a private library not far from the

Natural History Museum. These old bastards always want me to put a higher price on their boring collections so they can donate them to the alma mater and take a big tax deduction. Let's say we meet at the museum at eleven a.m. I'll give you my opinion then. And don't expect kindness."

"I don't want it," I said. He was staring at the first page of my story, as if I had already left. I made my way out of the apartment as soundlessly as I could.

# 13

# Central Park Promenade

I was glad to get away from Harry Winter, to feel the warm New York sun after the gloom of his apartment, even if it was only for a few minutes before reaching East Houston and Second Avenue to take the concrete stairs down into the subway. With each day in the city it seemed that circumstances caused me to travel farther underground, and now I headed diagonally across the island to get back to the Belnord Apartments and meet Hadassah. All right, Harry was odd. All right, he was at least mildly hostile and certainly suffered from persecution anxiety. Possibly also from megalomania. But the names of the writers on his files rang in my ears. Maybe Yitzak Nefish and the others really were unfairly forgotten and Harry was a kind of saint keeping their memories alive. Except that saint was the wrong word; there seemed something peculiarly Jewish in the act, like saying Kaddish or lighting a candle for *yahrzeit*. Perhaps the best that I could hope for was that one day some future Harry Winter would have a file labelled "Roth, Felix" containing my own sad history.

Only I couldn't see it that way, for I was too young and full of belief in myself. No, not in myself exactly, but in the life that would come to me — that was coming to me this very moment as the express train rushed faster through the flickering darkness. Wasn't I on my way to meet Hadassah? Didn't I have a chance to meet Isaac Bashevis Singer and show him my story — assuming I could get it back from Harry Winter? Wasn't Alice expecting me at the auction tonight? *My* life was no sad history. If anything, it was like one of those Jewish novels of ambitious young men, *The Apprenticeship of Felix Roth* or *The Rise of Felix Roth* or *The Adventures of Felix Roth* or even *What Makes Felix Run?* only with a more lovable protagonist and a happy ending.

But still I was oppressed by the remembrance of Harry in his longjohns, surrounded by his files, and I was only too willing to turn my thoughts to Hadassah. I did not have my story to give her as promised, but on the other hand that might provide the very excuse I needed for seeing her yet again. I was slightly disconcerted only by the fact that I could not precisely see her face in my memory, but only in soft-focus, like a movie from the thirties. If anything, this made me more eager to see her and I practically bounced with impatience on the hard subway seat.

Needing distraction, I studied the woman across from me, painfully thin and with a veiny nose too large for her face. She had two clips in her hair, as if the style was unchanged from childhood, and wore a high-necked dress too warm for summer. I had read somewhere that you could tell people's economic situation by their shoes and I noticed that her low heels looked shaved down at an angle from too many miles of walking. She sat reading a paperback called *Love's Tender Fury*, the book close to her face and her lips moving slightly. On the cover a brawny male with open shirt was clasping a resisting female in antebellum dress while behind them a flash of lightning struck the porch of a white porticoed estate. Usually I dismissed such junk, but I saw the woman's eyes widen for a moment and a flush come to her hollow cheeks, as if something tremendously exciting was happening in the story. Oh, what I would have given to overhear her thoughts at that moment! Surely it was inexcusably condescending not to appreciate a reader's need to escape from her own crappy life. Some people didn't want books that portrayed reality — they got enough of it every lousy day. Maybe for a privileged kid like me the gloomy tragedy of a Hardy novel or the ineffable sadness of Chekhov was just an escape of another kind.

The train shuddered to a stop and three boys got in with a basketball and a thumping boombox. The kids took seats across from one another and started whizzing the ball back and forth, but the woman with her big nose in her book remained oblivious. She reminded me of all those unhealthy-looking women in Singer's stories who were so ravenous for passion. Like the woman in "Teibele and Her Demon," about a widow in a Polish town who is fooled into believing that a man who comes into her bed every night after dark is a demon, a ruler over darkness. The man tells her all sorts of wild stories about his devil wives and the punishments of hell, and because he treats her tenderly her fear of him turns into love. When her demon becomes ill, with a racking cough and high fever, she cannot help herself from praying to God to look after him. It was a heartbreaking story and I wished that I could know if it would satisfy this romance reader as much as it had me.

When the subway reached Eighty-sixth Street I leapt out the door, through the turnstile, up the stairs, and sprinted as the light turned yellow. I was breathless more from the expectation of seeing Hadassah again than from running as I walked along the Belnord's high white wall towards the carriage archway where I knew she would emerge. But when the doorman appeared to pick up a cigarette butt from the edge of the archway and flick it into the street I swivelled away just as he turned in my direction. Although he had seen me with Hadassah, I suspected that he might still have it in for me on account of my bolting past him that first time. It was a peculiar and lowly position this doorman held, reducing the world to a few square yards of sidewalk. It required deference to residents — hustling for doors and cabs, gratitude for the annual Christmas tip. Yet it also draped him in the uniform of authority, like some Latin American generalissimo, and allowed for the sternest treatment of delivery boys and service men swinging paint cans and ladders. It conferred the power to exclude entry, the possession of keys and secrets.

On the other hand, the man was just trying to earn a living for the wife and kids, and every night his feet probably swelled from standing so many hours so that he had to soak them in epsom salts. I heard his voice now — "You have a good one, Miss" — and saw Hadassah come out from under the arch, half-turned to smile back at him. I waited two beats for the doorman to retreat into his sentry post before approaching her. When she saw me she made a face, which I decided to take as a good sign. Her tresses were tied at the back and she wore a jean jacket, a peasant skirt that left her pretty knees bare, and cowboy boots so shiny they must have just come out of the box. It was the sort of outfit a foreigner might concoct after looking through American fashion magazines, everything correct and somehow wrong at the same time.

"Hello, Hadassah."

"Ah, so you are here."

"You didn't believe me?"

"Do you believe everyone you just meet? Well, since you are here perhaps you wouldn't mind walking with me."

"It would be my pleasure."

"If there are any puddles you don't have to lie down for me to walk on you."

"And you don't have to push me into one."

She smiled. "We are not seven years old, Felix."

"You said my name. I didn't think you'd remember it."

"All I have to do is think of the cartoon cat."

We fell into step together and walked towards Amsterdam Avenue. "Ow," Hadassah said sharply. "These boots are pinching my toes."

"Do you want to go back and change?"

"The salesman said I had to break them in. When we were kids my brothers and I played cowboys and

Indians. They always made me an Indian girl and I liked being one except that I wanted to wear cowboy boots. Are there still cowboys and Indians in Canada, Felix?"

"Indians, yes. A few cowboys too, I suppose, although not where I live. How many brothers do you have?"

"Four. All older than me. Two still live on the kibbutz where we grew up, one is a television director in Tel Aviv, and another is a plumber in Haifa. Someone told me that there are no Jewish plumbers in America. In America, Jews have to call a Gentile to fix the sink."

"Not my father. He can fix anything." I neglected to mention my own disinclination to learn such things. "How is Uncle Isaac today?"

"With his head in the clouds as usual. When I left he was sitting in his big chair writing and didn't even hear me say goodbye. But when one of his lady admirers rings him on the telephone he always has time to speak. Well, it doesn't bother me. I'm not in competition for his favours."

When we crossed Columbus I could see the canopies of trees ahead of us. "Look, there's Central Park," I said.

"Of course. I have walked across the park every day of my visit. Now you really do sound like a kid. Maybe you would like to ride the carousel."

"You want to know the truth? I'd love to. I could draw you a map of the entire park, from Heckscher Playground to the Block House. I could tell you about the Hooverville shacks in the Depression. Did you know they planned the park so the rich could parade in their carriages? The truth is, it didn't occur to me to actually go into the park, there's so much else to do. But now I can't wait."

"You will have to. I can't run in these boots."

But Hadassah did walk quickly and we crossed over to the park, where a stone wall opened to a dusty path. We were hardly the only ones taking the path and as I watched the fathers loaded with coolers and picnic supplies, the mothers hoisting babies and diaper bags, the entwined couples and baseball-uniformed kids and skateboarders, I realized that Sunday was the park's busiest day of the week. Still, for me stepping on that hardened earth was like touching sacred ground. In only a few steps the sound of traffic began to recede and we were on a green plain, the grass burned to brown in spots and dotted with sunbathers. A circle of young black men and women, neatly dressed, were singing a hymn with hands joined, their voices rising into the air. I could smell earth, trees, grass, horse dung. Bicyclists rang their bells to pass.

"Hadassah," I said, "has your uncle ever gone back to Warsaw? To see the old neighbourhood and Krochmalna Street where he grew up?"

"I don't think so. The Jews and the buildings are both gone. Destroyed in the war. The communists made concrete apartment houses in their place. Sometimes I think that the old Warsaw existed only in Uncle Isaac's head."

"How old are you, Hadassah?"

"Is that important?"

"I just want to know more about you."

"Again, me. I am nineteen."

"You seem older. I don't mean you look older, maybe you even look younger. But there's something about you. I suppose it comes from living in Israel. And of course you have a boyfriend already."

"Nineteen is hardly young for that. Zuzi is my third boyfriend."

"I thought his name was Yoni."

She blushed, not just her cheeks but her neck turning crimson. "Zuzi is my nickname for him. I never told anyone before. It is funny, America is a country where everything is about sex. The commercials on the subway, the movies, the fashions. But the country seems so — I don't know how to describe it — proper. Making judgments all the time on people's lives. In Israel we are more relaxed about these things. It is the European and the socialist influence. If people want to make love they make love. When Zuzi comes to visit he stays in my room. Why should it be different? But here sex is such a big deal. So much noise is made about it. Either do it or don't do it, but why talk about it so much?"

She caught the toe of her boot on a root, but fended off my arm when I tried to help. Was Hadassah slyly talking about me? After all, hadn't I wanted to possess her almost from the first moment, to have her for myself, in marriage even, a signatory to a contractual obligation that would keep us bound until death? Perhaps I believed that marriage was a guarantee not just of present but of future happiness, ensuring that love, excitement, pleasure, and devotion would endure.

Under the low branches of a nearby tree I noticed a man crouching as he arranged various things — sofa cushion, stringless guitar, lampshade, ski pole, life jacket. He had woolly hair and a matted beard and filthy rags like some Neanderthal, though for all I knew he'd once been a professor of mathematics or a flamenco guitarist playing in Spanish restaurants. He might have even been married and had kids. From where I stood I could smell him. There were few visible homeless people back in Toronto and it was terrible seeing him; it turned my stomach. Also, it gave me a sudden jolt of unease. Perhaps the solidity of our identities was an illusion and one or two bad turns could reduce any of us to the same feral existence.

Hadassah too was looking at him. "Maybe we should do something for him," she said. I wondered if this was another test, like pretending to want the bouncing antennae, and if so what was the right answer? But I had learned my lesson and realized that I could never be right by trying to second-guess her. I remembered my brother giving change to the legless man in the subway entrance and what he had said about the charitable impulse.

"Yes, we should," I said and pulled out my wallet, although when I looked inside I was shocked how little I had to spare. Still, I took out a ten-dollar bill and, holding it before me, I made a few tentative steps towards the man.

"Say something," Hadassah said.

"Here," I called out, my voice breaking a little. "Take this."

The man turned around. He looked at me and the money. Then he picked up the ski pole and lunged forward.

We ran.

And did not stop until we saw before us a vision. A wide, silent expanse of water, a lake surrounded by a chain-link fence. It was the reservoir. A group of joggers appeared and followed the path by the fence around the water's curve. Behind the still surface rose a lush wall of trees and above that the apartments of the Upper East Side. I hadn't expected the sight to be so lovely.

"Ah, my toes are getting the third degree," Hadassah said. "Let's sit on that bench for a moment, okay? And now it is your turn to tell your history, Felix Roth. About your girlfriends and everything else."

She pronounced the word *geerlfriends*. The bench was set back from the path beneath a large plane tree. It wasn't exactly private, as every few moments someone else strolled or jogged past us, but most did not turn their heads. I immediately broke my rule about not second-guessing and tried to decide what was most likely to raise Hadassah's interest in me: telling her the truth about Alice or keeping my mouth shut. True to my nature, I tried to do both at once, telling her about the affair but implying that it was over and not mentioning the small detail of Alice's presence in New York. As I did not wish to appear selfish or predatory I spoke eloquently of my hesitation in becoming involved with a married woman, my regret for Arthur Lowenstein, and the personal suffering that I experienced even at this moment.

As I spoke my voice trembled and slowly gained strength. I occasionally glanced at Hadassah but mostly I stared out at the passersby on the path. My speech took a good fifteen minutes and when I was finished Hadassah remained silent for a moment before speaking.

"I feel sorry for that woman," she said.

"Why is that?"

"You were such a reluctant lover. Think of the risks she took. She had everything to lose and you had nothing. And what did she want? Passion, an earthquake. This is not to say that I do not believe in loyalty and faithfulness. These can be very beautiful. But sometimes other things happen. The woman wanted to be desired not because it was right — she knew better than you how wrong it was — but because it could not be resisted. And what did you give her? Guilt. Sighs. Worry. Ah, I feel sorry for her."

She sighed herself and undid the tie in her hair, letting the tresses fall.

"I've given you the wrong impression," I said hastily. "I was passionate. I was extreme. I'm telling you, I was an earthquake, a volcano even."

She tried to pull off her boot. This was not coming out the way I had intended. Hadassah struggled with the boot, her leg held in the air.

"Here, let me help." And standing before her I grasped the boot at the heel.

"Here is John Wayne to the rescue," Hadassah said. She held on to the wooden slats of the bench seat as I pulled hard, but still it wouldn't budge.

"It is . . . stubborn . . . like . . . you," I grunted and then the boot came free and, exaggerating just a little, I let the force throw me to the ground.

"How ridiculous," she said, but laughed. I hadn't really heard her laugh before; it was surprisingly deep, Garboesque. She hopped over on one foot to offer me a hand, and I took it, careful not to pull her over.

"Those are dangerous boots," I said.

"They are to protect me from notorious bad guys in Central Park."

"Well, I'm not a bad guy, Hadassah. So teach me how to say something in Hebrew."

We were back at the bench and Hadassah was rubbing the side of her foot. "What do you want to say?" she asked.

"I don't know." I pretended to muse on the subject. "Teach me to say, 'I love you.'"

She looked at me. "Why?"

"Who knows, it might come in handy one day."

"Oh, yes, very useful. Better I should teach you to ask where is the toilet."

"No, you teach me what I want."

"If you insist." But she didn't speak. She slipped her foot into the boot and stamped on the ground.

"Have you forgotten your own language already?"

"Very funny. All right. *Oz mich looz.*"

"That isn't very romantic sounding. You're sure you're not pulling my leg?"

"I am definitely sure. That's it. *Oz mich looz.*"

"All right, I'll try it. *Oz mich looz.*"

"Your pronunciation is like listening to a broken accordion. Didn't you take Hebrew lessons in the synagogue basement like other good Jewish boys?"

"I wasn't a very attentive student. My mind was elsewhere."

"Yes, probably on the girl who sat in front of you."

"I'd like to learn Hebrew now." Even as I said it I remembered telling Harry Winter the same thing about Yiddish. "I could take lessons from you, Hadassah."

"What a tempting offer. But unfortunately I am no teacher."

"What are you, then?"

"I make jewellery."

"You mean you design it?"

"No, someone else designs it. I stamp out the parts

and string the beads on the chains. Sometimes I do the packaging."

"It sounds like honest work."

"You are disappointed."

"I'm not, not at all."

"I don't like studying so I don't want to go to university. Not everyone has great ambitions like you and Uncle Isaac. Some people just want to live."

"That's the best thing, absolutely. To live because, well, because you want to live. Honestly, Hadassah, I'm suspicious of my own ambitions. I wish I could tear them out of me."

"What nonsense," she said, although she didn't sound annoyed. "Last summer I took care of children. A daycare, yes? This is a very progressive policy in Israel. Everyone should have the right to leave her child and go to work. But I saw how the mothers suffered. And the children were so hungry for love. All the time they wanted hugging, soothing. I thought that one day they would eat me up. These days a woman is supposed to want other things, and I do want other things, but I also want to be a mother. And then I will stay home with my children."

"I want to have children someday too. But I worry about being a good father."

"That means you will be."

"You sound just like my mother."

"Yes? I would like to meet her. My mother died when I was three years old. On a Jerusalem bus."

"That's so terrible. I don't even know what to say."

"It's such a long time ago. I think I remember her face. Come, we can't sit here all day. Let's walk."

We didn't talk for a while as we continued along

the path, the reservoir vanishing from view and reappearing again. As we passed under a rusting iron bridge she asked me if I had really come to New York only to meet her uncle. I told her about Aaron hiding out somewhere in Brooklyn and she said, "Your brother is a fool," and told me of the harm that she believed had been done to Israeli politics by fundamentalist Jews.

"You might be right," I said, "but I can't help feeling at least some sympathy for Aaron's need to find something more in life."

"Sympathy can be harmful too," she said softly. "But I understand. He is your brother. You love him."

I felt a sting of remorse for not having tried to find him these last two days, pursuing my own interests instead. How long could I lie to my mother? I would have to find Aaron as soon as possible. I told Hadassah of this guilt — I confessed it, and a lot of other things that, whenever I remembered them later, made my face burn. I presented to her my weaknesses and faults the way a dog submissively presents its neck to a larger beast in the hope of being accepted instead of bitten. I wanted Hadassah to learn everything about me in a matter of minutes instead of days or weeks, but I understood afterwards that this need for confession was a form of hysteria that rose when I was afraid of losing something, of being abandoned. It was the same compulsion that had made me speak insultingly to Aaron the night before he disappeared. And so I told her what I had moments ago hidden, that Alice was in New York and that I had been too much of a coward to break it off. That I was afraid of Arthur when I got back. That I had lost sight of Aaron and my parents would never forgive me. That when I saw her I felt something that I had never experienced before, an overwhelming emotion and a hope that I might be saved —

"Shhh, enough," she said, placing her hands on my chest as if to calm the beating of my heart. "You are going to make yourself sick. I never met someone who needed to say so much. You must slow down, Felix. You can't make everything happen right now just because you want to. You understand?"

"Yes." I had been hyperventilating and I tried to calm my breathing.

"You must have patience. In everything."

"I'll try, Hadassah."

We were on the other side of the reservoir now and walked a little farther until we could see Fifth Avenue through the trees and the inverted shell of the Guggenheim Museum.

"I'm sorry, I have to go," she said. "I'm glad we took this walk. You can give me your story now. I will read it and give it to Uncle Isaac."

"I'd love to give it to you but I don't have it with me."

"I am beginning to think there is no story."

"No, there is. A man named Harry Winter has it. It's too complicated to explain. Meet me tomorrow and I promise to bring it. If I don't, then you never have to see me again."

"Such drama. All right, but I'm not sure when I can see you. Perhaps tomorrow evening."

"Give me your number and I'll call you."

"Uncle Isaac won't let me give it out. Leave a note at the Belnord. Leave it for Miss Sussman. That's the name we use to keep people from bothering Uncle. Such craziness."

I didn't know what she thought was crazy, living with her uncle or arranging to meet me. But before I had a chance to ask she turned her face up and kissed me quickly, catching the corner of my mouth. "Until tomorrow," she said and ran down the steps to Fifth Avenue.

# 14

## Zugzwang

That little kiss, so quick and tender, lingered on my mouth as I walked back across the park. When I closed my eyes I could see her face reaching up to mine, her eyelids briefly closing. If it had been possible to suspend time, I think I would have kept myself in the moment that her lips touched me for eternity. But alas time was already drawing it away from me, so that all I could do was live in expectation of another.

At eight o'clock I was to meet Alice at the auction house and as I could feel a weariness beneath my excitement I decided to return to the Kemel Bed and Breakfast for a rest. I walked back through the park alone, emerging onto the Upper West Side again, and headed down Amsterdam Avenue. But I was soon arrested by a dirty shopfront window wedged between one of those new video rental stores and a pharmacy. The window must have once belonged to a diner; the words "Breakfast Special 99 Cents" were faintly legible on the glass. But there was a new sign, amateurishly scrawled on a rectangle of cardboard and taped to the window's inside corner. "UPTOWN CHESS CLUB" it read, and underneath, "New Members Welcome."

In fact I saw the sign only after I noticed the chess players inside, so many that they were almost pressed against the window. There were tables lined along the narrow space and observers crowding around the players. Not one face even glanced through the window at me on the sidewalk, for their concentration was all on the games. The players themselves appeared to grimace or smile or mutter to themselves, although of course I could hear nothing through the glass so that the impression I had was of watching a display of lunatics. A businessman in a Burberry raincoat sat opposite a teenage boy in an army jacket; a Manhattan garbage collector still in his uniform faced a man who kept rubbing his bald head anxiously as if in hope that a chess genie might emerge out of his ear. There were no women. Each player I imagined as someone just barely able to hang on to normal life in the city, prevented from total breakdown by this oasis, this narrow room thick with cigarette smoke and the delirium of highbrow mental exertion. This was not a little piece of the Upper West Side, or New York City, or even the United States of America. It was chess and only chess, with its peculiar language and laws and acts of victory and shame.

The sight of all those intense faces could not fail to make me think of Aaron, who had been our high-school chess champion. Aaron had played in dozens of provincial and national youth tournaments and even a handful of international ones, and his official national ranking for his age group was in the top thirty. A late starter, he hadn't begun to play until he was eleven, but by thirteen he knew intimately the careers of such famous players as Capablanca, Alekhine, and Fischer. By fifteen he considered himself a disciple of Nimzowitch, who had refined Tarrash's ideas on containment and central board control.

Unlike Aaron, I was not a natural player. My mind refused to concentrate for long periods, nor could I force myself to project beyond two or three moves. I didn't even feel much urge to win. But Aaron's latent competitive nature emerged when he played chess. Although he was generally a defensive player, preferring to gradually improve his position while whittling away at his opponent's pieces, he could attack ruthlessly when the opportunity arose and make daring sacrifices for the sake of strategy and surprise. I tried to keep up with him as best I could, and when we played he would offer me a handicap, removing his bishop or knight from the board, later his queen, still later his queen and a couple of other pieces. He would move a piece and say, "This is the Falkbeer countergambit," or "Steinitz used this defence against Pillsbury in St. Petersburg." He chided me for being impulsive and not thinking through the implications of a move. He said that rather than honouring its traditions, I played as if the game had just been invented.

Being the high-school chess champion conferred on Aaron a kind of cult celebrity. Not like the kids who won starring roles in the annual musical, or the football quarterback, but celebrity nevertheless. During lunch period he would sit at a table and play one challenger after another, knocking most off in a matter of minutes. In his last high-school year, which happened to be my first, he raised fifty dollars for the United Way by playing ten games simultaneously.

It was after that display that I received the nickname Brother of the Brain, which stuck to me even after Aaron went on to university. When my mother heard she worried that I would resent it, but I was proud to be Aaron's brother, although I wondered about this odd position of his in the school mythology. What concerned me was the way Aaron stood outside of the hierarchies and cliques, belonging to nothing but himself. I could not tell how much of this pedestal he stood on he had built himself and how much had been thrust beneath his feet. However it had been built, he stood there, or so it seemed to me, both defiant and forlorn.

It was during his first undergraduate year that Aaron's play began to fall apart. Only slowly had I realized the pressure he felt during a tournament and how devastated he was on losing, although I could not understand precisely why. The tournaments were usually held in some school gymnasium or Holiday Inn ballroom, and although I kept attending them out of loyalty it became awful to watch him play. Before matches he started to get ill, throwing up in the toilet. My father and I (my mother could not bear to watch) would try to persuade him to withdraw but he would refuse. He would still shake his opponent's hand before the match, would still stare at the board with concentration, but his fingers would shake as he picked up a bishop or pawn and hold it uncertainly over the board, as if afraid to make a decision. Inevitably he would lose, sometimes in the first thirty moves, and his ranking started to fall.

One night after a particularly disastrous tournament an exhausted Aaron went to bed early and I sat with my parents at the kitchen table, drinking tea and saying little. Then my mother began to tell me that although I had been too young to remember, Aaron had experienced similar episodes as a young boy. He had started to become ill each morning before school but cried if they tried to keep him home. They took Aaron to a psychiatrist, unusual for children back then, but the man didn't do much good. All they could discover was that a new boy in class had started to compete with Aaron for the highest marks, bragging when his were better. Aaron didn't want to compete, he wanted to be left alone, but he could not resist. It seemed to my mother that his very sense of self, of worthiness, was threatened by this boy. The problem ended only when the boy's family moved again and he left the school.

Aaron lost his last eight tournament games, although in two of them he was arguably ahead when he resigned. Then he quit altogether. Though he continued to subscribe to several chess newsletters, he would play nobody but me. I knew that my parents were worried when he entered law school, where the pressure and competition were notorious. And Aaron did lose weight and become sick before every examination and trial, but he managed to survive to graduation. Now he had an articling position with Kalman and Schwartz due to start in September. It was hard not to wonder whether his sudden need to visit the Kovner Rebbe in Brooklyn was the result of his career suddenly looming before him.

Most of our chess games were already a blur in my

memory, but I was unlikely to forget the game we had played a week before leaving for New York. Actually, Aaron had given up even our games long before then but he had caught a summer cold and was staying in bed. When I came home from the office of *Lowenstein's Sheet* I looked in on him and found him moving pieces on his portable set as he lay propped up in bed. He asked me if I would play a game just to pass the time. Even with his head stuffed up he confounded my attempts to surround his king and during the endgame he moved a rook and said, "Zugzwang." What did he mean, zugzwang? Aaron blew his nose — lately he had started to give a prolonged honk when he blew, just like our father — and explained that I was trapped in such a manner that any move I made would only make my position worse. "Chess is like life," he sniffed. "If you aren't careful you'll find yourself cornered."

I wanted to tell him he was wrong, that life wasn't like chess at all, with its arbitrary rules and severely prescribed limitations. That life had far more possibilities. Except that I thought I knew what he was talking about and felt my face burn with shame.

During Aaron's second year at law school he had surprised us by bringing a girl home for the weekend. She was not a student but worked in the law-school cafeteria, dishing out chicken cutlets and shepherd's pie. She was from Sault Ste. Marie of all places, had dirty blond hair cut in a straight bang, a flat oval face, and wore home-knit sweaters and tartan skirts. My mother and father and I were astonished to see her follow Aaron into the kitchen; as far as we knew he had never had a single date, never mind bringing a girl home. And then we tripped over ourselves to show her attention, offering her cold drinks, a place to sit, asking her a hundred questions to show our sympathetic interest. She spoke slowly, as if she wasn't used to conversation, but we managed to piece together that her father was a porter for Canadian National Railway, she and her five siblings were raised as Baptists (she wore a little gold cross around her neck), and that she was the first of her kin to make it to the big city.

Her name was Patricia but Patty was what she liked to be called. So Patty slept in the guest room, which had been intended for a maid until my mother discovered she couldn't stand having a servant live in the house. She and Aaron didn't do anything special for the weekend; they played Monopoly, watched television, walked to the mall for ice cream. My father seemed to like her despite himself, or perhaps he just couldn't bring himself to act anything but graciously to a woman. But my mother was clearly appalled. She spoke to Patty with exaggerated politeness and in a simplified language, as if addressing a visitor from a foreign country. She offered Patty extra helpings at dinner because she was so "skinny" and one afternoon came down the stairs with a handful of clothes she didn't want anymore for Patty to try on.

I held back longer than my mother but could not help admitting to myself that I disliked this Patty. While I had not yet broken up with Theresa Zeitman, we both knew the end was only a few miserable months away; perhaps I was sexually jealous. It was also simple snobbishness; in this too, perhaps, I was my mother's son.

One night during that weekend I woke up and lay

in bed for some time. As I occasionally did when unable to sleep, I went out onto the balcony that ran along the back of the house overlooking the lawn and swimming pool. I heard splashing first and then, as my eyes adjusted to the dark, I saw the two of them swimming side by side, until they reached the deep end. When they climbed out I saw that they were both naked, Patty thin and pale in the moonlight but for her dark patch. She dove in first, entering the water almost soundlessly, and Aaron went in after. When they came up again he must have grabbed her, for I heard her laugh.

The weekend ended and my parents said nothing more about her. But a few days later, just before going to bed, I went into Aaron's room and found him working at his desk. I knew he had a last moot trial to perform. "Aaron," I said, "do you really think Patty's smart enough for you?" That was all. Aaron didn't answer, he never even looked up, and I went back to my own room.

Of course it was foolish, even egotistical, to believe that my single remark was the reason Aaron never brought Patty home again. I did not have the same influence on him that he had on me. Besides, he was hardly the first young man in history who needed to overcome a little family resistance to the girl he favoured. But Aaron never even mentioned her name after that. Perhaps it had nothing to do with my mother and me. Perhaps Patty had decided to go back to the Sault, or realized that Aaron wasn't the one for her, or feared that her family would disapprove of *him*. But even if my words hadn't been the reason, they were mean-spirited and I must have lost some of my brother's respect. So when he said that life could corner a person, I could not help thinking he was referring to his own life and that in my own small way I had helped to corner him.

I opened the door of the Uptown Chess Club and went inside. Although Aaron had brought his portable set, it was highly unlikely he would play any games here, despite the fact that New York was rife with grandmasters, that some canny players made a living as chess hustlers in Washington Square Park, and that Aaron and I used to eagerly discuss the rumour that Bobby Fischer sometimes emerged from hiding to play a game in one of the clubs. My motivation was not clear to me, although it had something to do with the faces of the players, which reminded me of Aaron when he used to compete. With one breath my lungs filled with smoke.

At the front was a small counter behind which sat a walrus of a man, reading *Chess Life* through half-glasses. Looking over his lenses he said, "You a member? I don't recognize you."

"No, I'm not. Actually I'm looking for someone. He might have come in to play in the last day or two. Aaron Roth is his name."

"You've mistaken us for the Missing Persons Bureau."

"He's my brother."

"I've got a brother too, only I haven't seen him in twenty years and he can rot in hell for what he used to take out on me. All right, hang on a second and I'll check the sheet." He pulled a clipboard from under the counter and ran his finger down a dozen pages of names. "Nope. You check all the other clubs in the city?"

"No, I haven't," I admitted. I realized what a ridiculous idea it had been even to ask and that I was simply pretending to do something to find Aaron in order to feel less guilty.

"So, you want to play?" the man said. He wasn't looking at me but underlining something in the magazine with a stubby pencil. "I can give you a temporary membership for five bucks."

"I don't know. I guess so."

"You guess so." He drew out a form from under the counter. "Put down your name and New York address here," he said. "I hope you have less trouble deciding how to move your pawn."

I filled in the form and handed over the five dollars. What was I doing, signing up to play chess? I'd played one game in the last nine months. The smoke in the air was making my eyes tear.

"What do I do to get a game?"

"We're a casual place. When you see a chair become free, that's a loser getting up. Just sit down and take his place."

I nodded thanks, but the man was already reading his magazine. And that was when I saw the Hasid. How could I have missed him, shoulders hunched in a black kaftan, tangled beard creeping up his cheeks? A big man, balding, he had placed his blocky hat on a hook in the wall but still wore a yarmulke. Like most of the others he was smoking, the ash drooping from the end of his cigarette.

To reach him I had to sidle my way between tables and onlookers, past boards caught in the gridlock of middle game or with only a handful of pieces left. I reached the little circle of spectators watching the

Hasid playing a man in a plaid jacket who kept wiping his damp face with a handkerchief, but it wasn't long before the man tipped over his king and rose from his chair, pushing past me in his hurry to flee the scene of humiliation. Before anyone else moved into the empty chair I took it. The Hasid looked at me and nodded in acknowledgement of my existence before setting up the white pieces again. I scrambled to put the black into place, for a moment unable to remember which square the queen went on. How old was the man: forty, almost fifty? His face was already lined and his eyes had dark half-moons beneath them. But his hands were slim and well manicured. Were Orthodox Jews allowed in such a club or was he transgressing? At least he wasn't mixing with the opposite sex.

"You're ready?" he asked.

"Yes, I'm ready."

He tapped the double-faced time clock, moved his queen's pawn, and tapped the clock again. Now my time was running and I should have moved immediately to save every second, but I hesitated, trying to remember what my brother had taught me. A queen opening allowed him to move his pieces out faster but was more risky defensively, so he was probably an aggressive player. I moved my king's knight, he followed immediately with his queen's bishop pawn. And so it went, my fingers fluttering indecisively over the board before putting down a piece, his hand swooping with assurance. We traded pawns but two moves later he captured one of my bishops, destroying my feeble attempt to build an offence and strengthening his own line of assault. Not having any better ideas, I castled; at least now my king could huddle in the corner.

For several moves we both worked at improving our positions, until without warning his queen crossed the board and picked off one of my knights. "Check," the man said. The most obvious move was to bring the rook back as a block. He took my other bishop. After that he concentrated on ridding the board of several of my pawns while I frantically tried to keep out of his way. Clearly I was down too many pieces to win, but I still hoped that a draw might be possible if I could shore up my defence. And then I saw it.

In his eagerness to annihilate my protection around my king, he had left his own king vulnerable to a check. All I had to do was slide my queen down the board and take the pawn two squares ahead of it. I couldn't see how to mate, but decided to worry about that after I'd put him on the defensive. Picking up my queen, I glanced up and saw the circle of faces watching us. Several of them smiled encouragement at me.

"Check," I said.

The Hasid sighed. "Sloppy, very sloppy. You cannot just lunge without planning. How can you mate from that position? Instead, you've opened a hole in your defence." He brought back his own queen so that it stood between mine and his king; it took me a moment to realize that my own queen was trapped. The best I could do was exchange mine for his, but I was down so many pieces that I couldn't afford the loss. I ought to have conceded defeat but some stubbornness made me force the game to the end. It wasn't long in coming. In three moves he had mate. When I looked up again the watchers were grinning even wider.

The Hasid stroked his beard. "Why don't you try a

game with that fellow in the corner? He's closer to your level."

"Listen, can I ask you something?"

"Ask."

"I'm looking for my brother, his name is Aaron Roth. All I know is that he has contacts with a family in the court of the Kovner Rebbe."

"Reb Samuelson? He lives in Williamsburg."

"It's urgent I speak to my brother. You see" — I managed to catch a sob in my throat — "our father is deathly ill. I'm hoping to break the news to him in person."

The man looked at me, squinting slightly with one eye as if to better judge my character. I didn't like lying about my father but couldn't see any other way. He wrapped a curl from his beard round his finger. "Perhaps you think there is a central number to call, an Orthodox hot-line. Well, there isn't. However, it so happens that a cousin of mine is married to a woman who has relatives in the Kovner court. I don't know if they can help, but since your father is so ill . . ."

He let the sentence hang so that I could tell he didn't believe me. Still, he must have thought I had a good reason, or was willing to give me the benefit of the doubt, for he got up and went to the counter to use the phone. I stood up, but thinking it better to give him privacy, stayed by the table. I watched him dial, saw his lips move as he spoke. He hung up and dialled a second number, spoke for a moment or two and even seemed to be arguing. Then he hung up and dialled a third number. During this conversation he wrote something down on a scrap of paper. Then he put the phone down and motioned to me to approach.

"Your brother is staying on Bedford Avenue," he said. "This is the address. It will be arranged for him to meet you there tomorrow afternoon at five o'clock. Wait across the street until he comes out. Please do not attempt to enter the house."

"Thank you," I said. He gave me the paper and then made his way back to the table. A new opponent was already waiting for him.

# 15

# The Erotic Impulse

No one was home when I arrived at the Kemel Bed and Breakfast and, feeling overcome with fatigue, I lay down in my clothes. My last thought before sleep was that it was important for me to decide what to say to Aaron when I saw him tomorrow.

When my eyes opened again the light in the room had grown softer and I could hear voices in the apartment. My waking had been too sudden, like a diver being hauled up from the ocean floor without a chance to decompress, and my head felt as if it would burst. A half-waking dream came to me, of Aaron in a flowing white robe about to jump from the top of the Chrysler Building. I stretched out my arms to catch him while Isaac Bashevis Singer stood beside me and wrote in a little notebook. There were sirens wailing and people shouting and weeping, but even with all the noise I could hear Singer whispering to me. “If you miss catching him, it makes for a better ending. Even better, you should miss on purpose."

A gentle knock on the door.

"Felix?" It was Hannah Kemel. "There was a phone call for you while you were out. Your mother. Perhaps you would care to join us for dinner. It would be a pleasure."

I *was* hungry. "Yes, thank you," I managed to pronounce throatily and then wondered if my mother had made inquiries about whether I looked as if I were eating enough. I got up and brushed my hair, straightened my tie in the oval mirror above the bookcase, found the washroom at the end of the hall with its standing tub and ivory handles at the sink. Cold water on the face helped to clear my head.

Two men sat at the dining-room table as Hannah came in carrying a tureen.

"I hope you like lamb couscous," she said. "Felix, this is my husband, Sam, and our boarder, Hershel Tanenbaum. They've been looking forward to meeting you."

Indeed they did look pleased, although for the life of me I didn't know why. Each in turn rose to shake my hand and express his delight, the boarder Hershel pumping my arm enthusiastically and Sam Kemel, owing perhaps to a more reserved Germanic background, with a hand that was unappealingly limp. He was a handsome seventy, with a dapper moustache and thinning black hair, most likely dyed. A monocle in his eye would not have looked out of place.

"What a treat to have you aboard," he said, his accent reduced to an unnatural clarity of English speech.

Hershel Tanenbaum heaped salad onto his plate.

"We always enjoy fresh company," he said. "Lord knows these two get sick enough of me." The Kemels protested and he laughed good-naturedly. His hosts' formal dinner attire — Sam wore a dark suit and tie, Hannah a faded silk evening gown — made no impression on Hershel in his Adidas track suit. His sharply trimmed Vandyke provided compensation for his bald scalp, high-shined as if by a boy with a felt rag.

Hannah served the couscous, Hershel cut the baguette at the sideboard, Sam poured the Burgundy. When we were all sitting down Hannah raised her crystal glass and said, "To our new guest and success for his visit."

"This wine would have been better in another six months," Sam mused.

"Felix," Hershel said, "before you came in Sam was telling us he sold a first edition of *Justine* today."

"The Lawrence Durrell novel."

"No," Sam said, brushing his moustache with a fingertip. "The Marquis de Sade. In a contemporary binding of red Morocco and an intricate design in gold tooling made from an interlocking series of whips."

Hannah shook her head. "I still don't think you should have anything to do with that criminal's books." To me she said, "Sam specializes in erotic literature. But to me there is a limit."

"*Chacun à son gout,*" said Hershel, shrugging.

"Yes, to an extent. But are there no boundaries at all? Coercion, force, cruelty? Let people take enjoyment in whatever form they will as long as there is consent."

"Hannah has a point, my friend," Hershel said.

Sam sighed. He delicately lifted a forkful of couscous and slipped it into his mouth. After swallowing, he said, "Consent, certainly. But in the matter of a work of fiction the consent does not belong to the characters but to the reader. Besides, can a dealer in rare books, the proprietor of a bookshop containing work that is virtually all banned somewhere in the world, act as a censor? The contradiction is too obvious. We are all familiar with the legal battles that went on for years over *Ulysses* and *Lady Chatterley's Lover* before they could be published in this country. I do not claim any authority for judging which books deserve to be defended and which do not. And if you will forgive me, Hannah, my love, I might suggest that your argument lacks sophistication. After all, we must distinguish between the written word, which is always a kind of dream, and reality. The French imprisoned de Sade for his very real crimes and perhaps they were right to do so. But he wrote his books while incarcerated, to satisfy his imagination, and for this he deserved no punishment. I think that we must read his work as an elaborate fantasy, if we care to read him at all."

"That is too subtle by half." Hannah made a face — she had a long, elastic mouth — and picked up her wine glass. Age had made her hands bony and liver-spotted, but there was a grace about the way she moved. "Imagination itself can be a dangerous thing, like a Pandora's box. It is my belief that something once imagined is always at risk of becoming true. Of course, if writers cared only for being socially responsible there would be no great books. But there are limits, just as in a free society there must be limits to acceptable behaviour. A private thought has no restrictions, but when it is written down and published, when it is made public, surely then the social good demands at least some minimal standard. Otherwise we will descend into barbarism, as happened in Nazi Germany —"

"Oh, I really must object," Sam said, but without raising his voice. "You forget the Nazi book burnings. Felix, you must support me on this."

I had dipped a piece of bread in the couscous broth and was holding it to my mouth when I saw the three of them looking at me. "I — I see both points of view," I said. "It does seem dangerous to give anyone the power to determine what can and can't be published. I mean, doesn't every body of power seek in the end to protect itself? So the danger of abuse of that power is at least as potentially harmful as the material in question."

"Good, good! You hear?" Sam said.

"At the same time," I went on, "I don't agree that there is such a clear separation between imagination and reality. Surely words don't exist in a realm apart from actuality. If they did, books would not mean so much to us. We couldn't feel so passionately about them. They are somehow life and not-life at the same time. Does that make sense? And because I don't think books are so likely to corrupt us doesn't mean they have no influence at all. I think they influence us — or maybe *affect* is a better word — they affect us in the best and most generous way. Even then, a book doesn't affect each of us in the same manner. Reading isn't passive. It's active, and what we get out of it depends on what we bring. And yet at the same time it is true that we often do feel the same way about a certain book. Because there are commonly felt emotions and universal experience. That's part of what makes us both individuals and a community. But I've moved away from your discussion and have given you no answer at all. Forgive my confused ramblings. I don't think I've hardly begun to understand these things."

I felt myself blush for how my own words had gotten away from me, like some fervent character in *The Magic Mountain*. But the three of them were beaming.

"We can still put our faith in the young," Hannah said. "Sam, pour Felix some more wine."

Hershel said, "Hannah tells us you are a writer and now I believe it."

"I don't know that I have a right to call myself one. I haven't produced much that I'm happy with. One story, maybe."

"One story is a start," Hannah said. "Did you bring it to New York?"

"I did, actually. I was hoping to show it to someone."

"And who is this someone?" Sam asked.

I wasn't sure that I wanted to say, but there didn't seem any polite way not to. Besides, the temptation to make myself sound a little more important was too irresistible.

"Isaac Bashevis Singer."

"A brilliant writer," Hannah exclaimed. "We've read many of his books."

"Occasionally I find a copy of one of his books for a client," Sam said. "It's not truly erotica, of course, but the erotic impulse is the prime motivation of his characters. In my opinion, it's a shame he holds back so much. He doesn't show the intimate scenes. This is where you can tell that he is a rabbi's son."

"Felix, you will have to excuse Sam," Hannah said. "His one criterion for judging a writer's worth is whether or not he could write erotica. Zola would have been good, Virginia Woolf not. It is quite a joke in our house."

"Sam is to be commended for his high standards," Hershel said.

"You are right, my friend," Sam said, wagging his finger at us all. "Too much junk has been published, it gives the form a bad name. Few writers can produce genuine erotica. I can count the true masterpieces on my two hands. Remember, I am not speaking about pornography but something far superior."

"Please, Sam, let's speak of real art," Hannah said. "We should ask whether Felix would read his story to us. I just adore listening to an author read from his work."

"That's a marvellous idea," Hershel said. "I'd love to hear it."

"Unfortunately, I don't have the story with me." I was suddenly glad to have left it with Harry Winter.

"What about tomorrow, then?" Hannah asked. "We could have a little soirée at teatime. Say three o'clock?"

"If you really want me to."

"We'd be honoured." Sam smiled benignly.

"Then it's settled," Hannah said. "Now, who would like more couscous? Felix?"

"No, I'm full. And I'm expected somewhere soon. It was so kind of you to invite me."

"Well, you must have coffee at least."

"That would be nice." As I picked up my napkin, I knocked a spoon from the table, and reaching down for it, saw that Hannah had slipped her foot out of her shoe. With her toes she was rubbing, or rather caressing, Hershel Tanenbaum's ankle below the elastic cuff of his track suit. I came up again, my face flushed with embarrassment, to see Hannah reach over to stroke her husband's cheek.

"We are so looking forward to hearing your story," she said.

By the time I got outside it was past eight o'clock and the sky was a shimmering silver. But there was a darkening line of cloud to the north, its curling edge giving the unnerving sensation of being still and moving at the same time. Two men on the opposite stoop were tipping cans of beer to their lips and looking satisfied as only labouring men can after the long day is over. One was a black man, his hair turned absolutely white and his chest and arms knotty with muscle beneath a fishnet top. The other was white, taller and more bulky as if from bad diet, his big jaw in need of a shave. From what I could hear they were talking about car engines — overhead camshafts and torque converters — and I felt how little good I was at this sort of male discourse, even among men of my own background and class. There was a closeness and comfort to be derived from the comradely sharing of information and even friendly disagreement over, for example, the qualities of a certain ballplayer. But I had no interest in such subjects and sometimes felt keenly my difference from other men. Aaron was the same, only he seemed not to care. One year in high school I memorized the names of every player on the Toronto Maple Leafs so as not to seem ignorant, but I could never get their positions straight, whether right or left wing, centre or defence. The only player who interested me at all was the aging Jacques Plante, for his brooding position at the goal gave him the air of the distant and watchful artist.

I spied a telephone booth at the corner of Broadway and decided to call home. The Kemels would have gladly let me use their phone, but I preferred not to have my half of the conversation overheard. I was already a few minutes late meeting Alice at the auction house, but it would have been cruel not to call home, knowing how my mother wouldn't budge from the house until I did.

The door of the booth was jammed and I had to kick it several times with my heel, hoping the glass wouldn't break. Inside I was enveloped by the odour of stale beer. The metal shell of the phone itself had been ripped off, exposing the wires and gizmos beneath. Nevertheless, when I picked up the receiver, slightly sticky so that I had to hold it away from my ear, a dial tone sounded. I dialled the operator and had her place the call collect. I could hear my mother's anxious voice at the other end as she eagerly accepted the charges.

"Hello, Mom."

"Felix, why did you move from the hotel? Did something happen?"

"Nothing happened. I just found a nicer place, that's all. The owners are treating us like family."

"I'm glad for that. I hated the idea of you not knowing anyone there. Make sure you ask them which streets in the neighbourhood aren't safe to walk on. Is Aaron with you? I still haven't spoken to him. Put him on for a minute."

"Actually, he's not here. He's visiting that friend he made, the one who lives in Brooklyn. Don't worry, he's fine."

"How can I not worry? When Aaron gets an idea in his head he can be so stubborn. But at the same time he's suggestible. If he gets in with the wrong crowd —"

"Mom, a family of Hasidic Jews isn't exactly a street gang. I think we have no choice but to give him a little space."

"I'm giving him space, whatever that means." She sighed heavily. "I'm sure you think I'm fussing too much. But I hardly slept last night, I spend every second wondering what the two of you are up to, and your father is driving me crazy. At least if he would just come out and say he's worried. Instead, he gets home from work and heads right for the pool. For an hour he does laps. He's so tired by the end I'm afraid he's going to drown. Then he spends all of dinner telling me how the Skylab is going to take forty hours to break up in the atmosphere, that the lead storage vault will probably come down in one piece and weighs four thousand pounds, and that it could happen as soon as tomorrow or the next day. He says people who get hurt should sue the American government for a billion dollars. You know what he's doing right now? He's driving to Toronto General to visit Ben Weiss, who's recovering from back surgery. Your father hates Ben Weiss. He's hated him for forty years and all of a sudden he has to rush out and bring him chocolates. So I think I have a right to sound a little anxious."

"Of course you do, Mom. I'm completely sympathetic. And I know how aggravating Dad can be."

"I don't like when you talk about your father that way."

"I'm just repeating what you said."

"I never said he was aggravating. He's a wonderful man."

"Mom, of course he is. But you have to admit he can be difficult. I guess I wouldn't say this if I wasn't at the other end of a long-distance call, but I can hardly remember a time when he said something nice to you. I don't think I've ever seen him hold your hand or kiss you in public, never mind him saying that he loves you."

Even as I spoke I knew my words were a mistake. But the way he treated my mother had long been a sore point with me. She was silent at the other end of the phone; I imagined her rubbing her temples to alleviate the tension headache she always got when under stress.

"Your father just isn't like that," she said finally. "The way he grew up, boys didn't show those kinds of emotions. His own parents did nothing but bicker in the store from morning to night, so they hardly set an admirable example. But there are different ways to show how you feel, Felix. Not everyone is a Casanova like you."

"I'm no Casanova."

"Don't interrupt — who's paying for this call? Some men can say 'I love you' twenty times a day and meanwhile they're running around with the salesgirl or the secretary. You think words mean too much, Felix. Sometimes they don't mean anything at all. Your father doesn't have to say it for me to know. In his own way he treats me like I'm the most precious person on earth. If you want to know the truth, I worry that he's too dependent on me, and I don't mean for making meals or doing the laundry. I'm afraid of what would happen to him if I went first. I shouldn't even tell you this but sometimes I pray to be allowed to live just one day longer than your father, so I'll be there to look after him."

"I was wrong. I shouldn't have said anything."

"Also, you think you know everything about us. But what goes on with a couple behind closed doors is their own business, even when they've been married for twenty-seven years. All I'll say is that we've never had any trouble in that department. Your father still shows me how he feels."

"I'm glad, Mom. And I didn't mean to be nosy."

"You've always been nosy, that's the writer in you. Of course, since you're my son I have no choice but to be generous in my opinion."

"I appreciate it. I'm not sure if I deserve it, but I appreciate it. I really ought to get going now."

"It feels like we just got on. Listen, Felix, I have a surprise for you and Aaron. Yesterday I went to Lichtman's and bought a copy of the *New York Times*, I guess so that I could feel closer to you both. And I saw that the New Jersey Symphony Orchestra is playing at Carnegie Hall tomorrow night. And do you know what they're playing? Mendelssohn's Violin Concerto. The same one I saw performed at Carnegie Hall in 1949. I was so excited that I phoned the box office long distance and bought two tickets with my Visa card. They're holding them for you."

"But, Mom, the *New Jersey* Symphony?"

"I'm sure they're very good. The guest violinist is a young Oriental girl named Stephanie Chan. They used to all be Jewish, Russian, and now they're Japanese. Please, Felix, do it for me. Seeing Jascha Heifetz play was the highlight of my life before you boys were born. It would give me such pleasure if you went. And at least for two hours tomorrow night I'll know where you are."

"All right. I'll go, but I can't promise for Aaron. He hasn't shown much interest in music lately."

"Ask him for me. Thank you, Felix. And enjoy yourself. Being young doesn't last long. Take advantage of it while you can."

# 16

# The Lady with the Rose

How right she was, my mother: being young didn't last long. And unlike most people of my age, I already had — or rather I suddenly felt, standing at the corner of Broadway and Eighty-second — a poignant sense of the mortality of my youth. Perhaps Harry Winter was right and I was an *alte-kop*, born into the wrong time and living as much in some imagined past as in the present, but still this was my only youth and I wasn't keen to give it up. Yet I knew that this was the beginning of the end, and as the cabs rolled by and the sky darkened from the clouds drifting in and lights began brightening the high windows, I already felt nostalgic for these few New York days, as if saying to myself *I will never be in this moment again, or this, or this.*

Among the sea of cabs only one had its roof light on and I hailed it, got in, and leaned forward to talk to the driver.

"Can you take me to the auction house, Hines and McCutcheon?"

"Where's that?" the driver said. I couldn't see his face, but he had a fat neck and rounded shoulders and I could easily imagine that he lived permanently behind the wheel. "All I know is Sotheby's. You sure you don't want Sotheby's? That's where the chi-chi people go."

I took out the card that Alice had given me. "The address is on Spring Street, number 145."

"Down in SoHo. I'll take Riverside Drive. It's a nice view."

This seemed a little out of the way, since Riverside Drive was farther west, almost to the Hudson, but I decided the driver must know what he was doing. He started singing and I recognized the tune as "Luck Be a Lady" from *Guys and Dolls* only because Theresa Zeitman's father was a fan of musicals and I sometimes asked him to put on a record just to get on his good side. The cab hit three potholes in a row, each deeper than the last, so that I was bounced into the air. "You can blame the Democrats for that," the driver said. Then he began singing again, this time "Big Spender" from *Sweet Charity*. We drove along the green swath of Riverside Drive, beyond which lay the dark expanse of river, and then the old deserted Penn Railroad yards. I had always disliked automobiles, which I associated with riding in the back seat of my father's sedan, the windows closed and the air conditioning going full blast. As a kid I had felt separated from the life going on in the street, like some pasha being carried high above the riff-raff. Later, as a teenager, when the rich kids at school were getting sporty Mustangs for their sixteenth birthdays, I vowed never to own an automobile but to live a life of Ghandian simplicity, my Smith-Corona typewriter as spinning wheel. But here in New York I had to admit a certain growing pleasure in cab rides, perhaps because they seemed just another intricate note that harmonized into the Manhattan hum, perhaps just because my mother and father weren't in the front seat.

From the west side through Chelsea and Greenwich Village I heard selections from *Anything Goes*, *Oklahoma!*, *The Pajama Game*, *A Funny Thing Happened on the Way to the Forum*, *A Little Night Music*, and *Band Wagon*. While I had little feeling for musical theatre, I did have some interest in the history of Tin Pan Alley, which was part of the fabric of New York with its large talent for manufacturing the popular. Besides, the taxi driver had a rather handsome baritone voice and a nice sense of timing.

We crossed West Houston, which meant that we had entered SoHo, and drove more slowly after turning onto Spring Street, stopping in front of a cast-iron building with large plate-glass windows and iron half-columns thickened with uncountable layers of paint.

"Twelve bucks," the driver said.

"Wait a minute. The meter says six dollars."

"That's before six o'clock. Then it doubles."

"No, it doesn't. You're trying to cheat me." I found it hard to believe that a man who loved musicals would try to fleece a passenger.

"Listen," he said, "I got a kid who needs a new kidney."

"Really?"

"That isn't a thing you joke about."

No, but it was a good line for someone trying to lift six extra dollars out of my pocket. However, I paid. The ground floor of 145 Spring Street was taken by an art gallery, but there was a doorway illuminated by a small bulb with the names of several businesses on it — an art consultant, a wig maker, a chiropodist, and Hines and McCutcheon, Auctioneers. I went up the ammonia-smelling staircase to the second floor. The narrow hall was whitely lit with fluorescent bulbs and I passed several businesses before I came to Hines and McCutcheon, whose door was easy to spot as it was made of reinforced steel, the metal scratched and dented as if by that same golem who had torn the branches off the tree in front of Harry Winter's apartment.

No sound came from inside and if I hadn't known otherwise I would have assumed that the place was closed, but when I opened the door a strange world awaited me. The auction was already in progress and people milled about: assistants in white shirts and aprons, bidders getting up and sitting down again. The auctioneer on the platform at the other end of the room spoke into a microphone so that his voice filled the place. Right away I saw Alice sitting in the second-last row of folding chairs. What surprised me was how shabby the place was, without a hint of glamour. The ceiling was low and several acoustical tiles were missing, and the numbered paddles that the bidders held up were split at the edges. Nor was there anything impressive about the bidders who occupied about half of the folding chairs. A man in the front wore a raincoat with large grease stains on it. Several others wore the sort of cheap dress shirts and polyester pants that reminded me of the small-time builders who sometimes came to the door to plead with my father for more credit. One or two women were dressed up but garishly, with big jewellery and loud-print dresses. Most of them were dealers, I guessed, who hoped to resell what they bought at a profit. Even from the back, Alice didn't look as if she belonged.

The auctioneer was young and pasty-skinned and his hair stood up like the bristles of a toothbrush. His face did not hide his disgust at the low bidding for the object he held up, an aggressively large brooch in the shape of a seahorse.

"Ladies and gentlemen, you embarrass me. These bids are an insult to the memory of the dear departed who has given up her property for a better world. This is a very dramatic piece of genuine silver. I can honestly say I have never had occasion to offer one quite like it. Surely you can do better."

The bidders hardly seemed to be listening, but every so often someone would flash a paddle and I realized that their jaundiced indifference was a ruse. In all likelihood they were following the bids intensely and judging the interest of their fellow dealers. When the hammer came down I sidled down the aisle to the vacant seat next to Alice, who gave me an unguarded smile and grasped my hand. "I thought you weren't coming," she said.

"Has your Lady with the Rose come up yet?"

"There's still a couple of items to go. I'm worried that the regulars have spotted me as an outsider. Or maybe word has leaked. When I tried for a Tiffany lamp the bidding suddenly jumped. They think I know something that they don't. See that man in the battered hat? He's been buying most of the porcelain. And that woman in the front row seems to like anything that will fit on a mantelpiece. I just have to hope they don't have very deep pockets."

"They hardly look like it."

"You can't tell from how they dress. A lot of money can go through a dealer's hands, even if not much of it sticks. God, I'm nervous."

"Don't be. I'm sure you'll get it."

The seahorse brooch had been dispatched to the back for the necessary paperwork and an assistant had run up with the next item, a Russian sabre purportedly once belonging to the royal family. Alice's hand trembled in mine, dispelling any last suspicion that the Napoleon connection was an excuse for her coming to New York. Still, it seemed incredible that the real Lady with the Rose could end up at a third-rate auction house like this one. Maybe Alice was simply wrong and the figurine had graced the front parlour of some Parisian butcher's wife, or maybe Alice had convinced herself of its authenticity because of an unconscious desire to come to New York. And did it even matter if it was the real thing?

I said, "How high has the museum authorized you to bid?"

"They haven't, actually."

"What do you mean?"

"I couldn't quite convince them that I'm right. So I'm going to buy it myself and after I authenticate it I'll sell it to them for what it cost me. At least that's my plan."

"Are you sure this is a good idea? How high will you go?"

"I talked it over with Arthur. I'll go as high as six

thousand. I promised not to go higher. But it should go for considerably less, so I'm not worried."

"Well, I'm glad you're not. Tell me, if I sneeze or scratch my ear will the guy think I'm making a bid?"

"That only happens in the movies. Oh, look, it's coming up. They must have withdrawn the previous item. Kiss me, quick, Felix."

I had vowed not to allow any other kiss to erase Hadassah's, but what could I do, spoil the moment for Alice? So we kissed — not quick but lingering — and her lips were hot, as if the excitement had made her feverish. By accident my hand brushed her bare thigh just below the hem of her short dress.

"Lot 184," said the auctioneer. "A late seventeenth-century French porcelain figurine from the Limoges workshop. A seated woman holding a yellow rose. This is a real beauty, ladies and gentlemen, a valuable collector's item, particularly well painted and in flawless condition. I must start the bidding at five hundred dollars. Who will begin?"

The man in the hat raised his paddle. "I have five hundred," said the auctioneer. "Five twenty-five? Yes. Five-fifty, six, six-fifty . . . " The bidding rose steadily, too quickly for me to catch sight of the bidders, of whom there seemed to be at least half a dozen. The auctioneer began to raise the bid by a hundred at a time. Perhaps it was my own sense of excitement, but the usual shifting about the room seemed to cease. Alice had not even raised her paddle and the bidding passed one thousand dollars. The auctioneer looked as if he was starting to enjoy himself.

"I better get in," Alice said. "If I wait too long I might spark a new round." Even now, Alice's raising of her paddle started a flurry of bidding so that the price flew past the three-thousand mark. Alice kept her eyes on the auctioneer and I would not have dared to speak to her now. One or two bidders dropped out but still the bidding went on, past four thousand. More bidders shook their heads. At five thousand only the man in the hat and Alice were left and I prayed for him to get a sudden cramp in his arm.

"Six thousand dollars from the gentleman in front," the auctioneer said with a grin, and I knew it was over. Poor Alice would be heartbroken.

She raised her paddle.

"Alice?"

"I don't care," she said quietly. "I'm going to get it."

With only two bidders left the auction went at what seemed to me an excruciatingly slow pace. The audience no longer pretended not to be interested; everyone had stopped to watch, even the assistants. From the man in the hat to Alice the bid went back and forth while the auctioneer kept up his annoying patter. Past eight thousand, past nine. I could hardly stand to watch. At $9,900 the man hesitated. The auctioneer held the gavel up but just before he brought it down the man raised his paddle. Ten thousand dollars. Alice raised hers, the man his. This time Alice hesitated but not as long.

"The bid stands at $10,300," the auctioneer said. "Will you bid, sir? This is your last chance. All right?" He brought down the gavel. "Thank you very much. Sold to the lady at the back. Lot number 184."

Alice stared at the auctioneer as if she no longer saw him, breathing so hard that her breasts rose and fell rapidly beneath the binding of the dress. I tried to understand what she felt, but all I could sense was how alive she was at that moment.

"Alice," I said, "that's a lot of money."

Without turning to me she said, "Let's go celebrate."

# 17

# Little Tragedies

The night was charged with the suspense of rain, the air warm and caressingly moist. We walked along Spring Street to West Broadway, where the high-ceilinged restaurants were full and roisterous, their doors constantly swinging as men and women went in and out, laughing and cupping their palms to light cigarettes and running their hands over each other. What an electrically sexual town New York was, its high energy intensifying the lust already beating in the human heart.

As we walked Alice giddily replayed the auction. "Here," she said and thrust into my arms the box containing the Lady with the Rose. I had watched the assistants wrap about a mile of tissue paper around it and suggest that they have it delivered to her hotel, but Alice insisted on taking it with us. The box felt disconcertingly light in my hands, as if it might float up into the humid night sky. Inside it was a statue that the Emperor of France and Conqueror of Europe had personally ordered. He had undressed his mistress in its presence, had cried out at the height of his *petit mort*. And at any moment I might trip over some broken curb step and dash the thing against the ground. But would Napoleon himself have been afraid to hold a mere box? So I carried it as protectively as a baby in my arms.

"All these restaurants are too crowded," Alice said. "I used to like going to restaurants everyone wanted to get into. Arthur was good at slipping a tip to the host and getting us a table. He always enjoyed the power of being able to do that. But now I can't stand these places where everybody wants to be seen by everybody else. Oh, here's a nice spot."

We had come to a bar that appeared to have no name. Through the window I could see the slender stools along the marble bar and the dark, twinkly lighting. Only a few people sat at tables along the brick wall. Alice went in first, not even holding the door open for me so that I had to catch it with my foot while guarding the box. When she looked back and smiled I realized that she had done it on purpose, a risky joke. She perched on a stool, and as I put the box on the bar I could not help admiring her slender legs. I wanted to remain faithful to Hadassah, but Alice, who did not even know Hadassah existed, was certainly making it difficult for me. The bartender was putting away some wine glasses. He looked too young; he wasn't yet sour-eyed from hearing so many hard-luck stories.

"Two scotches," Alice said. "Put lots of ice in his."

We watched him take two glasses, scoop the ice, pour the shots, and slide the drinks to us.

"Let's make a toast," I said and raised my glass. "To the Lady with the Rose."

"No. I hate toasts. Let's not drink to anything. Let's just drink."

And she did, emptying half her glass. "Before you got there, I had this strange moment back at the auction house," she said. "I was just waiting for the lot to come up and I thought I was all right when suddenly I had this very black feeling. And all these *things* — these lamps and pocket watches and tea services and art nouveau clocks — they were just debris floating about after a shipwreck. And that's what the past was to me just then, a kind of shipwreck, and either a person went down dancing to the orchestra or screaming or even in her sleep, but one way or another everyone went down. And here were these objects that once belonged to them. Why would we possibly want them? Why even know about them? It's morbid when you think of it, like keeping the lock of a dead child's hair or the bones of some tortured saint under glass in an Italian church. We pretend to like these things, we say they're pretty or fascinating or a good investment, but really we're lying to ourselves. It's death that we want even though we're afraid of it. And these things we care about don't belong to us any more than they did to the people who once owned them but are now dead and rotting. So that's what I thought, but then you came in and cheered me up."

She pulled a packet of Lucky Strikes from her purse, tilted a cigarette upwards from her lips, and touched the spearhead flame of her lighter to its end. Her cheeks concaved as she drew in. When she talked like this I realized that our lives had never really merged but had only overlapped for a moment, like shadows falling over one another. Reaching for my drink, though I hated scotch which was too potent for me, I looked at the box resting on the bar and had a sudden impression that it was filled with funerary ashes. Her look of happiness after the auction turned out to be short-lived, the sadness not really gone but only hidden for a moment.

"There's something I've been wondering about for a long time," I said. "Your interest in porcelain. You could have made painting your expertise, or architecture, something —"

"Important?"

"That's not exactly what I meant. But, yes, a major rather than a minor art."

She drew on the cigarette and then blew the smoke languorously upwards so that it formed a haze above her. "You're not the first to ask me that question. My father thought I was wasting my talent, but then he always insisted I was supernaturally gifted, given that I had inherited half my DNA from him. I used to have this very reasoned response — how the decorative arts reveal more about a culture than the so-called high arts, especially about the place of women. Or I'd go on about the history of labour practices and the rise of bourgeois taste. But I never told anybody where my interest really came from."

"Why not?"

"I guess I thought they would laugh."

"I won't laugh."

She stubbed out the cigarette in a glass ashtray. "When I was a kid my father went to Japan for one of his medical conventions. He brought back this porcelain figurine of a geisha. She was about a foot tall and the most beautiful thing in the world. A chalk-white face, red lips. Only the head and hands and feet were actually porcelain. The body was cloth and dressed in a perfect little silk kimono. The organizers of the convention had given it to my father, but my mother didn't like it much so she put it on the counter of the powder room — that's what she called the guest washroom. Whenever I had to go — I was five or six at the time — I would run to the powder room just so I could see her. I would sit on the toilet with my stockings around my ankles and talk to the geisha. And she would talk to me."

"She talked to you?"

"Uh-huh. She would turn to me and smile and bend down to pick a flower — there were flowers on her stand — and say, 'How are you today, dear Alice?' And I would tell her what was making me miserable and she would listen without telling me to cheer up or be happy, which grownups always did when they saw me. She told me that I was very brave and that life wasn't easy for her either and she would tell me about Japan. She told me that in Japan people slept on beds so small that if they turned over they would fall off. Also that when Japanese women peed it smelled like flower petals. These conversations seemed perfectly normal to me. I never thought anything was unusual about them."

She pointed to her drink and the bartender poured her another shot. When he motioned to me I put my hand over the glass. The scotch had already made me slightly woozy.

"So what happened?" I said.

"One day my parents held a dinner party. They held one almost every week, it was certainly preferable to having to speak to each other. Usually they sent me to my grandmother's or had the maid serve me dinner early and then keep me upstairs, but every so often they liked to show me off to company. I would wear a beautiful dress and have my hair brushed until it shone and of course I was taught to have perfect manners. I never had a terribly good time, not because the guests weren't nice but because I couldn't bear to see my parents acting towards each other in a way they never did when we were alone. This night was no exception. After the main course I needed to go to the washroom, and when my mother excused me I went to the powder room and had a nice conversation with the geisha woman. I must have been a bit long because when I came back my mother asked me if I had been talking to my 'friend' and then told everyone about my talks. Of course they all chuckled and said how sweet it was, but I can't tell you how deeply offended I was by this condescension and intrusion on my privacy. I was so mad that I got up and marched upstairs to my room and wouldn't come out again. My mother must have understood something of what I felt because they didn't punish me afterwards. But the geisha woman never spoke to me again. I would go to the powder room and sit there and talk to her but she never answered back."

She took a sip of her scotch.

"That's so awful," I said. "It's really a tragic little story, Alice."

"Ah well, life's full of little tragedies for fortunate young girls. Maybe I was getting too old and she would have stopped anyway."

"Do you still have the geisha?"

"No, I don't know what happened to her. I thought of putting her in Everett's room when he was little. I know it's silly but I thought she might talk to him. But it wasn't in my parents' house, not in the attic or basement. When I asked my parents it took them a few moments even to remember her. Probably she ended up at the Salvation Army with a lot of other stuff they didn't want anymore."

"Well, now you've got your Lady with the Rose."

"Yes, but I don't expect her to start speaking French to me. I don't think I told you, Felix. I'm flying home tomorrow morning."

"No, you didn't."

"I don't have an excuse for staying longer. Besides, my son needs me. And Arthur too, I suppose. He sounded rather distraught on the phone this morning. If I really don't want to lose him then I better go and pay him some attention."

I was surprised by my disappointment. Having Alice in New York was a complication that I must have wanted and I found it hard to imagine being here without her somewhere in the city. Suddenly my compulsive need to confess came over me and I sat silently trying to resist it, knowing that I would give in. Surely people who could keep their mouths shut had an advantage over loquacious fools like myself. I said, "Alice, I want to tell you something. I've — I've met somebody."

Alice smiled, but it was a bitter smile. "Well, I knew. I didn't know it had already happened but I knew it would. I suppose it's a good thing. What's her name?"

"Do you really want to know?"

"Of course I do."

"Her name is Hadassah."

"And she's just your age?"

"Younger."

"Pretty?"

"Yes, but that's not all it's about —"

"I didn't mean to suggest it was. I suppose you've slept with her. That does hurt, even if I'm hardly one to complain about infidelity."

"No, Alice, I haven't slept with her. Nothing has happened. I'm not even sure if she likes me."

"Are you serious?" She turned towards me on her stool and laid her hand on my cheek. "You poor boy, suffering no doubt. That bartender better give us both another drink."

Almost before I had a chance to refuse, or perhaps because I didn't want to refuse her, the new glasses stood before us.

Alice said, "This girl. She's back in Toronto, I suppose."

"No, she's here in New York. I just met her the day before yesterday."

"Really?" She laughed quietly. "You came to New York and found love, just like in a fairy story. And I believe it because it's you, Felix. I don't have any doubt that you'll charm her just the way you won me over."

"I didn't do it consciously."

"No, but perhaps unconsciously."

"Anyway, not everyone is so susceptible to this charm you say I possess."

"Maybe I can give you a few pointers. You are clumsy in some ways, you know. And you do tend to say more than necessary. You have to leave her room to respond. Let her decide for herself to fall in love with you."

"You're right. I try too hard."

She opened her purse. "Finish your drink. My behind can't stand this stool another minute."

"No, let me pay," I said and took out my wallet. There were only three bills left and I took out a ten to leave on the bar. As soon as I got up I found myself a little unsteady, but I took the box in my arms again and followed Alice outside.

"Do you mind if we walk a little?" she said. "It's a strange feeling I have, like I might never come back to New York. Or as if you'll never return to Toronto. Probably it's just the feeling of something being over."

I didn't know what to say. As soon as we started to walk a drop of rain tapped my nose. Then I felt another.

"At least it's warm," Alice said. "But we better not let the box get wet. Come under here."

We ducked beneath an awning over a window heaped to the ceiling with shoes. I couldn't tell whether it was a work of conceptual art, some sort of anti-war or poverty statement, or just an abandoned factory.

"Look," Alice said, and before I saw it I heard the clatter of a horse's hooves on the street. A hansom cab was coming up West Broadway, the shining carriage swaying a little behind a droop-bellied palomino wearing leather blinkers and with an undignified feather swaying between its ears. "I've always wanted to ride in one. And it'll keep us out of the rain."

"But it's such a tourist gimmick," I said. "We could take a regular cab."

"Don't be so practical. This is my celebration, isn't it?" She hailed the driver, a grizzle-bearded man in a battered top hat and rather incongruous short pants that revealed unusually hairy legs. He swung open the little door and as we climbed in I slid the box under the seat.

"Where'd you like to go?" he asked.

"Uptown," Alice said. "And we'd like a couple of those blankets you've got up there."

"Yes, Miss."

He handed the blankets to us. The seat was wide and padded and the rhythmic bouncing almost pleasant. Although the cab was open, a weatherbeaten leather canopy sheltered us from most of the rain as it came down harder. Alice spread the blankets over us. It was natural to move close and in a moment we were leaning warmly against one another and I could feel her thigh pressed against my own leg, our heads tilting until they touched. My body had an instinctive and not easily controllable response of its own, and the thought came to me that there could be no harm in one last moment of intimacy together. I had a feeling that Alice was thinking the same thing, but if so she must also have known what a little falsehood it was, and we just kept sitting close to one another as the rain played on the canopy above us and that old sway-backed horse, whose memories of green fields must have seemed like a dream, pulled us through the dark streets of Manhattan.

When the horse plodded up to the entrance of the Plaza Hotel, I kissed Alice before descending, leaving her to pay the exorbitant fare. The rain was falling lightly now, washing away the city's accumulation of sins and giving us all another chance. My foot had fallen asleep from the awkward position in the cab, but as my money was dangerously low I began to limp back to the Upper West Side.

The Kemel Bed and Breakfast was dark when I opened the door. I went into my room, took off my wet clothes, and hung them on the back of the chair and the footboard of the bed in the hope that they would be dry in the morning. In my underwear I crept to the bathroom to wash up, trying to avoid making the floorboards squeak. In front of the boarder Hershel Tanenbaum's room I heard a noise and stopped.

From behind the door came a whispering and then something like a half-moan, half-sigh. It sounded like Hannah Kemel.

# 18

## The Genuine Article

I slept well and dreamlessly that night, perhaps because my life had simplified a little with the end of the affair with Alice. And telling her about Hadassah had helped too, both because it allowed me to speak her name aloud and because it ended an uncomfortable lie. I understood more clearly now that whatever faults I had, a facility for deception was not one of them and I would be better off leaving such underhanded doings to the characters in the novels I hoped some day to write.

And so I awoke refreshed to Monday morning, my fourth day in New York and also the second last, as Aaron's and my plane reservations had been set for Tuesday at noon. My meeting with Aaron was arranged for late this afternoon and I hardly knew what to expect, only that it was my duty to make sure he agreed to get on that plane tomorrow. But before Aaron I would see Harry Winter, who had my story, and in the evening

Hadassah, who I hoped would come with me to Carnegie Hall. This morning I would have to leave a note for her at the Belnord as she requested. And if Hadassah could arrange a meeting with her uncle Isaac, that too would have to be managed. It was going to be a complicated day, but I had the energy for it all.

The dining room was laid out for breakfast: hard European rolls, croissants, butter and raspberry jam in little crystal bowls, thin slices of havarti, a French press steeping black coffee. Hershel Tanenbaum had already left for the office but Hannah was bustling about between the kitchen and the dining room while her husband, Sam, sat at the table reading the *Times* and sipping his coffee carefully so as not to dip his moustache. He wore a striped vest beneath his suit jacket, a wilted rose in his lapel, and he looked too content with his life to know that his wife had been with Hershel last night.

"Please, sit down, Felix," he said, making a flourish with his hand. "Everything is fresh. Can I pour you a cup of coffee?"

"I don't mind doing it myself."

"But then you would deprive me of the pleasure. Hannah makes it marvellously strong. So tell me, what are you doing this morning?"

"I have to meet somebody," I said, deciding against mentioning Harry Winter by name, "but that isn't until eleven o'clock."

"Then you have a bit of time on your hands. Perhaps you would like to come and see my bookshop. I have a small proposition for you. Although I haven't read any of your work — by the way, we all look forward to your reading this evening — as I say, I haven't read anything but my instinct tells me you are the genuine article. Perhaps you would like to earn a little money."

"How much?" I asked, trying not to sound too eager. The bills in my wallet added up to only six dollars. I did not want to ask my mother to wire me some money, but even if I could survive until tomorrow on six dollars, which was doubtful, I would not have anything left to pay the Kemels for my board or even enough for a bus ticket to the airport.

"Let's say two hundred dollars."

"I think I could spare the time."

"Excellent. We can go to the shop right after breakfast. But please don't rush. I'm not in the slightest hurry."

Finding myself once again wolfishly hungry, I consumed three rolls, a croissant, two pieces of cheese, and several cups of coffee. I hadn't taken seriously the request for a reading of "The Goat Bride," but I could see they did not plan to forget it. Well, somehow everything would be done. Sam continued to peruse the paper, humming something Mozartian under his breath. I was a little wary of a proposition the details of which I couldn't begin to imagine, but the Kemels struck me as honourable, if unusual, people and I was willing to take a chance. When I announced my readiness to get up Sam said, "Splendid," and refolded the newspaper so exactly that it appeared unread.

"You don't mind walking, do you?" he asked. "The shop is only a block away and the rain is over. In fact, the paper reports that the day is going to be a bit of a scorcher."

Hannah came out of the kitchen to see us off. Did

Sam not know that she left his bed in the night for Hershel Tanenbaum's? I was astonished that she could still act the part of the doting wife. Yet she seemed absolutely sincere in her feelings as she placed her hand delicately on the back of Sam's head and kissed him warmly on the cheek.

Sam ushered me down the stairs and we entered the new day, the air damp from the night's rain and ripe with the smells of exhaust, garbage, cologne. We headed towards Columbus Avenue — for an old man, Sam was a sprightly walker, planting his cane briskly with each step — and then north half a block to a florist's shop.

"This way," Sam said, holding the door for me. The shop was low-ceilinged and poorly lit so that the flowers in buckets on the peeling linoleum floor appeared drained of colour. An elderly Asian woman with cropped hair and wearing a Mao jacket greeted us with, "Good morning, Mr. Sam," and replaced the wilted rose in his lapel with a fresh one. He thanked her with a half-bow and then continued through the store, past refrigerators of hyacinths and gardenias, to a door in the wall next to the basin. The door was marked "PRIVATE" with a small handwritten card, and Sam took out his keys to let us in and turn on the lights.

I could hardly believe what I saw. We were not in a mere room or office, but a large and sumptuous library that I had imagined existed only in the houses of the Morgans and Gettys of this world. It rose two stories, with a domed ceiling that peaked to a small round skylight. The shelves rose so high that a filigreed balcony circled the room above our heads, with a little staircase to reach it. The shelves were of a highly polished oak, with small details in the corners that I didn't at first take notice of: exquisitely carved phalluses and Amazonian breasts and naked buttocks. Above my head the dome was painted as if Michelangelo had been hired to adorn the Sistine Chapel with an orgy scene. I wanted to run into the florist shop and back again just to make sure it was real.

Sam walked to the only piece of furniture in the room, a slender rococo desk, with a few books and papers on it and a bronze inkwell held aloft by a naked girl in art nouveau style.

He patted the girl affectionately and said, "A pleasant environment for browsing, don't you think? I dreamed about such a place for many years, in the worst times. It kept me going. Of course no rare-book dealer could pay for such a place — I had to sell some of our paintings. Hannah was very understanding. But let me show you a few things."

He turned to the wall and pulled from the shelf a large portfolio tied with a ribbon. "These are Japanese shunga prints, from the early 1800s. They were inspired by the 'floating world,' the pleasure districts in the cities. For each colour a separate block had to be carved. Notice the warrior-like faces of the men and the placid features of the women. And see how exaggerated are the size of the penis and vulva. These are first-rate examples."

As he turned over the prints I made suitably complimentary remarks, though in truth the exaggerations made them grotesque to me.

"Of course I have various editions of the classics," Sam said. "Casanova's *Memoirs*, Burton's translation of *The Perfumed Garden*, *Fanny Hill*, *Venus in Furs*.

Not to everyone's liking, that last one, but I have many clients with very specific tastes. Up there is the anti-clerical literature, monks deflowering young girls, lesbian nuns, that sort of thing. I have no less than three ex-priests who collect in that area. There's a fellow in Philadelphia, a banker, who will buy anything on the theme of the derrière and a woman judge in New Orleans who's mad about spanking. Sometimes I imagine introducing them to one another. Ah, Felix, if I could find the exact book for every predilection I would be a satisfied bookseller."

Sam handed me one book after another, some in elaborate bindings of inlaid leather and gold tooling, others in plain wrappers meant to pass through customs without being confiscated. He held up a mottled page to the light so that I could see the watermark of a seventeenth-century Italian papermaker. I turned pages and wondered about the nature of a lust that might be aroused by holding such volumes; whether it was not only the descriptions and images but also the rarity that stoked desire. Did a collector believe that the beauty and expense of such books gave a legitimacy to his peculiar likings, or was there some additional thrill, like asking a prostitute to dress in Chanel gown and pearls? And what about Sam? Perhaps he experienced a subtle arousal as he acted as a procurer for his clients. Did his occupation make the liaison between his wife and Hershel Tanenbaum, if he knew about it, easier to accept? Possibly he had even instigated it.

He showed me more: a complete run of *The Boudoir*, first editions from the Obelisk Press, Viennese engravings. A new thought came to me, that Sam's calling had some connection to losing his family in the war. Perhaps he wanted to save these books precisely because others would like to see them destroyed; he saw them as the lost children of literature. But even if this was true, I felt something disquieting and forlorn about the books he passed to me. Because in the end they were fantasies for the solitary and only confirmed how alone a person could feel. Also, I knew that I was a romantic who yearned for sex to move through or beyond pleasure to something higher, a true uniting of souls.

"Would you care to hear about my proposition?" Sam asked. He was coming down the stairs from the balcony and I noticed a slight tremor in his hand. "Let's go into the office." He moved to the wall of shelves and opened an invisible door of the kind I had read about in Hardy Boys books. The room we entered was of regular height and strictly functional, with two modern office desks, an IBM Selectric typewriter, a table arrayed with kraft paper, boxes, twine, and other shipping supplies. On a metal bookshelf were stacked back issues of a journal, each with a black cover and the title embossed in gold. *Ars Amatoria*. "Please examine one," Sam said. "It is my indulgence and, if I might sound an immodest note, my contribution to the literature. I have subscribers all over the globe. Each issue contains three or four short works, classics reprinted from my collection. But I also include a single new story. Unfortunately, it is very difficult to find good new writing. Few writers have a talent for genuine erotica. My readers are discriminating and they are hungry for exciting contemporary stories or discoveries of forgotten works. But I am hard pressed to satisfy them. That is why I have brought you here, Felix. I need a new story for the next issue. Already I have commissioned work from two authors — you would recognize their names — and have rejected them, although I have paid the fee. However, I believe in hunches. Would you like to try writing something for me?"

"I don't know if I'll be any more successful than the others."

"I will pay in cash."

"It couldn't hurt to try."

"Here, sit down at the typewriter. Get comfortable. There's plenty of paper. I have some cataloguing to do in the library. If you need anything just give me a shout. Otherwise I will be as quiet as a mouse so as not to disturb the writer's inspiration."

"But I haven't even thought of a setting or character."

"Perhaps I might make a suggestion. I know from our dinner conversation that you are an admirer of Isaac Bashevis Singer. I have often fantasized about a Singer story, filled with his usual passionate characters but that did not hold back in its depiction of the intimate scenes."

"A Singer story with sex?"

"Exactly. Just imagine you are Singer. Well, I leave it to you."

He closed the door and I was alone. Some writer, I thought, picking up a sheet of paper and scrolling it into the typewriter. As I heard the typewriter's thrum, lower and more powerful than I expected, I remembered what Stephen Dedalus said in *A Portrait of the Artist as a Young Man*: that any writing that sexually aroused the reader was not real art. But I tried not to feel so bad; after all, this could hardly be a greater debasement than what I had already produced for *Lowenstein's Sheet.* Besides, I needed the money. Well, if it was to be a Singer story, then so be it. What about a young man, just off the boat from Warsaw, a would-be writer even, who finds his landlady knocking on the door of his room one afternoon. Married, of course. Nor did she have to be his only lover; in Singer's fiction his protagonist was usually balancing two or three affairs at once. There could be the landlady's niece, a young beauty, innocent in appearance but wildly desirous of experience. And then in a cafeteria he might meet a woman, the daughter of a famous Yiddishist, and instantly fall in love. But at first she would refuse his advances . . .

Before I knew it I was already writing. The voice of the young man came to me effortlessly. I was dimly aware that, despite the 1920s New York setting, the young man was based on me as much as Singer, the landlady on Alice, the niece on Theresa Zeitman, and the author's daughter on Hadassah, but I didn't allow myself to stop and think about what I was doing. For the first two I had at least real experience to draw on, even if Theresa Zeitman had not been as passionate as I was making her fictional counterpart, but as the story went on and the author's daughter finally gave in to her own great desire I had to rely solely on my imagination. Inventing the intimate scenes between them, I wondered if I was somehow violating my own possible future happiness. Nevertheless, I did not hold back. As for the young man, I did not deprive him of a single possible humiliation or ecstasy, fear or hope.

I typed without rest for two hours. When I was done my fingers ached and my heart pounded from the emotional exertion. I pulled the last page from the typewriter and then put my hands over my face and closed my eyes.

As if by intuition or telepathy, Sam knew that I was finished, for I heard the office door open. (Of course he had simply heard the typewriter's clacking cease, but I was too rattled to realize it.)

"Are you finished?" he said in a hushed voice. "Please, let me see. A very good length, three thousand words at least. If you don't mind waiting I'll just sit in the other chair and read it."

He tapped the pages into a neat pile and took them to the chair, crossing his legs in an almost womanly fashion. If only it was this easy to get my real story read by an editor, I thought. Sam took a pipe from his jacket pocket, though he did not light it as he read. I felt drained of any feeling as I watched his expression change with the rise of an eyebrow or the slight upturn of one corner of his mouth. He read for twenty minutes or more and then, after straightening the pages once again, filled his pipe with tobacco, tamped it down, and drew on the stem as he dipped the flame of a match to the bowl.

"Congratulations, Felix. It's really first rate. My pulse was racing the whole time. It hardly feels like a story but like life itself. If anything, almost too much happens. But I don't mean that as a fault, not at all. Perhaps some readers will find it a touch painful, but that only adds to the eroticism. Clearly you are a writer capable of pleasing yourself and the reader at the same time. If you do not object, I'd like to present it as an early work by a writer now famous, newly discovered and translated. We won't mention any names, of course. We'll let our better-read subscribers guess who the author might be. I knew that you could do it, Felix. You really are the genuine article. And now let me give you what you deserve."

He took out his billfold and counted ten twenty-dollar bills. But I did not reach out to take them.

"The genuine article?" I said. "The genuine fraud is more like it."

Sam folded the bills and pushed them into my blazer pocket. "Felix," he said and patted my shoulder, "don't look so glum. Think of it this way: you are about to become a published fiction writer. All art is illusion, even great art. Besides, writers too must make a living. There really is no such thing as a pure life."

# 19

# Eating Words

The concrete business, my father once said to me, is nothing to laugh about. Civilization was built on it, from the Romans up, and no matter what fancy new materials and structural ideas the scientists came up with, the builders always returned to concrete. It was cheap, strong, non-corroding. The ingredients were available virtually everywhere on the planet. You could build houses out of it, multistorey buildings, bridges, water tanks, even boats. He was proud that Toronto was home to the world's tallest tower, almost two thousand feet of poured concrete reaching upwards like the pointer used for reading the Torah that he remembered from the little *shul* of his father. He was only sorry that his sons had been too old to want to go down to the site and take measure of its progress.

For some reason it was my father I thought about as I left Sam Kemel's bookshop with those crisp twenties in my pocket. My anxiety about money was gone, but something worse had taken its place, a moral ache, a dark suspicion that at the age of twenty-one I had already sold out. What had happened, when only hours ago I felt that my life had been renewed? Whether it was Sam Kemel or Arthur Lowenstein, it seemed that I would write whatever the man waving the money wanted, in any style or voice. If this was my true talent, I would rather have been born ordinary, without any ambition beyond finding an honourable means of earning my living, a faithful marriage, kids.

My father had never been ashamed of his lack of a higher education. He was proud of how he helped to build his part of the world. I remembered him walking me as a young boy around the quarry and picking up handfuls of lime, gravel, and silica as he spoke of the importance of getting the proportions right to achieve the proper durability, strength, and give for the job. He explained to me the concepts of creep and curing, and I tried desperately to memorize everything he told me so as not to let him down. Just because concrete was simple, my father said, didn't mean it could be treated casually. Poor judgment could result in tragedy, and to prove it he kept in his office a scrapbook of newspaper accounts of structures that had collapsed. There were grainy pictures of apartment buildings with whole sides torn away to reveal living rooms and toilets, of gigantic water tanks cracked like eggs. Usually these disasters had occurred in distant countries like Brazil or Rumania, and my father said that such failures gave concrete an undeserved bad name. The fault would surely be found not in the concrete but in the builders: in incompetence and graft.

I knew what graft meant from a young age because

my father often raged about it. Graft meant that the supplier with the lowest bid did not necessarily get the job. It meant bribes and kickbacks and politicians who made deals on government projects in return for party donations or swimming pools in their backyards. It meant developers in cahoots with organized criminals.

My father was never afraid of such people; about that I never doubted. There was a story told by his brother Morris about how my father's office was once invaded by some thugs who locked the door, pushed my father against a filing cabinet, and held a pistol to his temple. If he did not submit a high bid on a certain government tender for a half-dozen new hockey rinks, they would see to it that he never got to enjoy the fruits of his labour. That was the expression my uncle said they used, "the fruits of your labour," and I had to admit being impressed by such pompous formality coming from the mouth of a man who knew how to break legs. What happened after that was disputed by various members of the family. According to Morris, my father pulled a gun of his own from under his desk and told them to get the hell out of his office. Never having found this gun, however (I looked for it sometimes when I visited), I doubted this version. According to Aunt Rhea the thugs left of their own volition, vowing to return the next week, but they were all gunned down in a Montreal nightclub on the weekend. From everything I had heard about Montreal this made sense. Both accounts concluded with Roth Cement and Gravel pouring the floors of those ice rinks.

Walking the three blocks to the Belnord Apartments, I felt the sun beat down on me at each intersection when I came out from under the shadow of a building.

Even when not in the sun I felt hot. Perhaps at this moment my father was standing in his quarry pit and squinting up at the sky, expecting to see Skylab breaking up in the atmosphere. In my teens, the simplicity of his moral outlook made me feel a haughty contempt, but at this moment I recognized how much more admirable it was than my own. He worked hard, he loved his wife without thought for any other, he provided for his children. Each year he made substantial contributions to the Cancer Society, the United Jewish Appeal, and other worthy and uncontroversial causes. But as for his youngest son — I had wanted more, a sophistication in my intellectual and moral life that he couldn't possibly sympathize with or understand. Now it seemed to me that my sophistication was no more than arrogance. And yet how was it possible to return to emotions less complicated and more honest?

As I came up to the Belnord, I drew a pen from my pocket and a sheet of notepaper that I had taken from the Kemels'. I held the paper to a flat stone in the Belnord's high wall.

*Dear Hadassah,*
*Meet me tonight in front of Carnegie Hall, at a quarter to eight. I have two tickets for the symphony. I promise to bring my story; if I don't you can call me a liar and never see me again.*
*Felix*

I folded the paper and walked with deliberate assurance to the carriage entrance. Just as I got there, the doorman, sweeping his broom across the sidewalk, flicked a load of dust towards me. He looked up with an expression of innocent apology.

"Excuse me," I said, holding out the folded paper. "Would you please give this to Hadassah."

"Who?" he said, leaning on the broom. He said the word neutrally but I could see that he did not like me and wanted me to know it.

"The girl I was with yesterday — I mean, Miss Sussman."

"Oh, *her*," he said and smiled broadly, as if he knew that she was just toying with my emotions.

But I didn't pass the note over, not yet. In a humble voice I said, "It really is important. I know you have a lot of responsibility and I appreciate the favour." From my blazer I offered him one of the twenty-dollar bills. He hesitated and then took it, although he looked more insulted than grateful.

"I need her to get it today, as early as possible."

"I said that I'd give it to her, didn't I? Any other requests?"

"No, that's all." I backed off, suppressing the urge to salute him as I retreated. Then I walked quickly away, feeling that this unpleasant encounter left me anything but assured of Hadassah receiving my note. On the other hand, a doorman had his duties to perform despite any personal feelings. She'll get it, I told myself, although the words didn't make me any more confident.

To reach the entrance of the Museum of Natural History on West Seventy-seventh, I walked down Columbus Avenue. It was an odd place for Harry Winter to suggest we meet, despite us both being on the Upper West

Side this morning, and I considered whether the choice might reveal something more about his peculiar personality. Harry Winter might have been born in Louisiana but I could not imagine him living — or even surviving — anywhere else but New York. I felt a conflicting desire to hurry and to slow down, mimicking my feelings about Harry himself. What if he thought my story was no good, that I didn't have an ounce of the talent of Yitzak Nefish or any of the other writers in his mortuary? But who was Yitzak Nefish anyway? A literary small fry, a minnow even in the little pond of Yiddish literature. On the other hand, if he should approve of my story I was not likely to reject his opinion so readily. I remembered an occasion in high school when Mrs. Springbottom had read to the class a short story of mine about an abandoned dog being taken to the pound. In the final scene the dog was given a lethal injection; I called the story "And Darkness Fell on the Animals." Mrs. Springbottom had raved about its symbolism and imagery. At dinner that night I had excitedly repeated her praise and my parents had glowed with pleasure. But Aaron had listened with annoying calm and when I finished said that praise itself needed to be judged dispassionately. Mrs. Springbottom was always overenthusiastic when she identified a keen student, he said. Did I really believe my story to be so good? My mother scolded him for trying to ruin my moment, and even my father thought he was being overly harsh. I didn't think he expected an answer so I didn't offer one except for a scowl, but the truth was I thought my brother was right. The story was heavy-handed and pretentious; I had been too conscious of laying on the symbolism even as I wrote it.

The Museum of Natural History was a massive and formidable castle, like some northern citadel facing icy Scandinavian winds. I knew that each girder holding up its weighty floors had been hauled up from Fifty-fifth Street in a wagon pulled by twelve horses. At the moment this colossus was softened by a group of kids in camp shirts and caps running up and down the vast south stairs.

I came around to the Central Park entrance and saw the gigantic bronze statue of Teddy Roosevelt in buckskin astride a stately horse and with an Indian on each side. From around the pedestal someone peeked at me, but I couldn't be sure it was Harry Winter until I went closer. Yes, it was Harry, without a hat this time so that the hot sun glinted on his high forehead. He stepped out now and I saw he was wearing khaki shorts, exposing spindly legs beneath his belly. I waved as I got nearer, but instead of returning the greeting Harry just looked at me. Something was in his hand; it appeared to be my manuscript. He let his eyes slide to the left and right and then backed up the stairs towards the entrance. I was about to call out a jovial greeting when he scampered up the last steps and disappeared through a revolving door.

What sort of game was this? There was no reason to be alarmed, I told myself; Harry was simply an unconventional person. Perhaps he had imagined that unseen enemies of his great project were watching him. I went in through the same door and found myself in the cavernous rotunda. A small line of people stood waiting to purchase tickets while others lingered by a dinosaur skeleton that looked in need of a good feather-dusting. I spotted Harry giving his ticket to a guard and passing between two marble columns before darting to the right. Having no choice but to join the line, I waited impatiently for my turn to buy a ticket before hurrying after him, down to a set of steep stairs. All I could do was guess that he had gone down instead of up and so I went too, stepping through an entrance marked "Mammals of North America" and passing brightly lit dioramas of bison and moose and grizzlies. How Aaron and I would have loved this place when we were kids, only I didn't have time to think about that now. The hall was crowded enough that I had to make my way around groups of tourists as I went, and twice I had to apologize for bumping an elbow or stepping on a foot.

Only when I reached the North West Coast Indians did I glimpse Harry again. I sprinted past the ceremonial masks and totem poles and human models in glass cases as if they'd been stuffed like the animals. A guard grasped my arm and pulled me to a stop.

"No running," he said sternly.

"Of course," I apologized and kept going, but when I saw Harry circling a long Haida canoe I hurried after him. Had he gone up the stairs? No, I decided, and continued past a succession of dull school exhibits on the water cycle and farm seasons. Then I saw him, bent over and trying to catch his breath beside a section of a giant redwood tree.

"Harry," I called.

He looked up at me and then, dragging himself forward, went through a door.

I went through after him, into the weird blue light of "Ocean Life." And there, suspended over a gaping space, was the tremendous blue whale, life size, arched as if about to dive to the floor below. Its tiny eye stared skeptically at both of us on the balcony suspended around it, Harry leaning down and frantically tying his shoe. He looked up and saw me, but instead of trying to get away again he merely finished and stood up with a groan, the manuscript tucked beneath his arm.

"Harry, what are you doing?" I said. My voice sounded thin in the vastness of the space.

He shifted the manuscript to his hand. "I thought you might decide not to follow me."

"Why? Of course I would. That's the only copy of my story."

"I know. That's the point, Felix."

"What's the point? Did you read it?"

"Yes, I read it."

"So?"

"Did you really write it?"

"Harry, you know I wrote it. This is crazy. I regret having asked you for your opinion, the way you're acting."

"Fine. Then I won't give it."

I had a sudden thought that the great whale might suddenly sway and fall, crushing us both in a farcical version of *Moby Dick*. "All right, I give in," I said. "Tell me what you think."

Harry looked away and his thumb did its routine — nose, cheek, chin — a half-dozen times. "It's a precocious work," he growled. "Advanced for someone your age. I won't deny it. A beautifully tragic atmosphere. The story doesn't drag either. You want my advice?"

"Yes."

"Tear it up and throw the pieces in the trash."

"But why, if it's so good?"

"Who said it was good?"

"Well, what's wrong with it, then?"

"If I told you now you wouldn't understand."

"That isn't good enough, Harry. I think in some strange way you really do care, and if that's true then you have to tell me."

Harry let the manuscript unscroll in his hands and we both stared at it. Harry said, "Listen to me, Felix. You are chasing a false god. You are young. You would sacrifice anything to be a great writer. Faust making his pact with the devil has its appeal for you. But you don't understand what it will really cost you. Your life. Hear me, Felix. Writing will not bring you happiness. It is a sad delusion. You still have a chance to change direction, before it's too late. Find a nice, satisfying job around other people instead of holing yourself up in an attic somewhere to spend the days and nights spitting your blood on paper. If not you'll discover — all right, not tomorrow, but in ten years, twenty — that your imagined life has ruined all possibility of a real one. And it will be too late to get it back." He looked up from the manuscript and with his other hand touched his nose, cheek, chin.

I said, "Thank you for the advice. Now please give me back my story."

But as I reached for it he pulled the story away. "Let me do it for you, Felix. Let me destroy it."

"Give it to me, Harry." I tried to grab the manuscript from him but managed only to tear the first page. Harry raised his hands and pushed me hard against my chest. More out of surprise than anything else I fell backwards and landed on my ass. Harry ran along the balcony.

Or tried to run, for it was more a half-skip, the manuscript grasped in his fist. The last person to have knocked me down was a twelve-year-old schoolyard bully named Marvin Teplitzky and just like then I was too stunned for a minute to get up. How was it no guard happened to see us? I got up, my coccyx sore, and headed after Harry.

I didn't think he could go much farther — I, too, was beginning to feel winded — but he kept moving, through the door at the other end of the ocean exhibit, around a corner (somehow we were at the Haida canoe again), down halls and up stairs. If two guards hadn't been standing and chatting I could have caught him in "African Peoples"; instead, I had to slow down and just keep him in sight as we went through narrower passages until suddenly we were among the elephants.

It was a full elephant herd, looking so absolutely alive that it might have started moving. They were on a raised platform made to look like an African plain, one elephant facing me but the others "walking" in the other direction, the largest a true giant, its trunk raised in the air. This room was the most crowded, with groups of visitors standing before the smaller wall displays of antelopes, zebras, and gorillas, and I lost sight of Harry. Slowly I began to walk among them, looking down for a glimpse of Harry's naked legs.

In front of the lions a girl of five or six was refusing to turn with her parents and look at them. "But there *is* a man," she insisted. "Mommy, a man's hiding behind that elephant."

I looked where she was pointing but saw only the

elephants silently following one another trunk to tail. Then something caught my eye and I saw Harry crouching behind a baby pachyderm. When he saw me looking he darted behind an adult foot.

I walked up to the platform and spoke in a low voice so as not to attract any guards. "Harry, come down from there."

"No."

"Don't make me come up."

"I'm not scared of you."

Actually, it sounded like *I'nn no sare uf oo*, as if Harry had something in his mouth. He poked his head out again to see where I was and I saw him chewing something white. It took me a moment to realize what it was.

Harry Winter was eating my story.

My brother had taught me to respect museums as sacred repositories of knowledge, and besides, I was not a lawbreaker by nature. But there was nothing for me to do but haul myself onto the platform after him. As he saw me coming up, Harry bolted from behind the foot and began a ridiculous dodging run down through the herd, all the while tearing off and stuffing another piece of manuscript into his mouth. I ran after him on the uneven ground, keeping just outside of the elephants until I had caught up and then crossing through the herd towards him. He must have simply panicked, for he got down on his hands and knees and began to crawl beneath the stomach of one of them. From behind I grabbed the waist of his shorts and yanked him back again, his knees scraping against the fake African plain.

By now a sizable crowd had gathered at the base of

the display and they shouted and scolded us so that I could just hear the voice of a guard calling for us to come down. "Harry," I said, still holding on to the back of his shorts while he struggled to get free, "give me the damn story."

"You know what, Felix? It tastes better than it reads."

Even while on all fours he started to rip off another piece. I lunged for the pages but he grabbed my wrist with his big hand. I tried to pull away but his grip was strong and he almost pulled me down head first. With my other hand I grabbed his shoulder to shake him but tore his collar instead. We pushed, he tried to bang the side of my head with his other hand, I shoved him in the ribs, he kicked out my foot and I fell on top of him.

"Let go, Harry!"

"No, you let go!"

We both paused, breathless. The hall was strangely quiet. I saw my story pinned beneath Harry's fingers and decided to make a lunge for it when a deep voice of authority made me freeze.

"*Get the fuck down from there.*"

I turned my head and saw one of New York City's finest standing with his nightstick in one hand and his other on his holster.

Not one but four policemen surrounded the platform, each with nightstick poised. I feel no need to describe in detail the experience of being handcuffed behind the back, marched to an elevator, and then taken through the delivery entrance and into the back seat of a police cruiser. I will only note that it was unnecessary for the officer in charge to push down on my head with quite so much force as he guided me into the car. Another officer had taken the manuscript of my story and I had the unpleasant experience of sitting silently, uncomfortably cuffed and with Harry Winter slouched morosely beside me, while the officer who was not driving began reading it aloud, commenting to his partner that we had been fighting over "a load of artsy crap." A representative of the museum accompanied the other officers in their car and we drove the short distance to the Twentieth Precinct on Eighty-second Street.

The station was dismal grey brick topped by a concrete box with slit windows. In the vestibule I saw three plaques commemorating officers killed in the line of duty, and on the hideous orange tile walls were taped up posters of murderers. A policeman pushed Harry and me through a door marked "Detectives" and then made us wait an hour in a dreary room that smelled of sweat, although the same officer who disparaged my story was decent enough to bring us a couple of Cokes. The museum representative reported to the detective that we had done no damage but that the potential harm to such an irreplaceable exhibit was incalculable. The detective noted that as I was not an American citizen he had the right to throw me out of the country for good. Or he could hold me until trial. However, as two of the police officers were about to go on their summer holidays he felt reluctant to tie them up in paperwork. I quickly offered my abject apologies, pronounced our behaviour inexcusable, and promised not to set foot in the Museum of Natural

History for the rest of my life. As well, I offered to make a donation of $160 — almost all that I had left from Sam Kemel — to the Museum Restoration Fund. Harry, although more resentful of authority and grudging in his remorse, also agreed to stay away. He could not help adding, however, that if the detective really wanted to do some good he would confiscate my manuscript.

Fortunately, he did not. Another half-hour's wait or so and we were out on the street again, the manuscript missing half of its first page but safely tucked into my inside blazer pocket. I remembered the missing words well enough to scribble them on the back of the last page as I stood outside the station. Harry only shook his head. The day was punishingly hot now, the brownstones baking in the sun, and I gave in and took off my blazer. Even so I perspired as I finished writing while fumes from the traffic thickened the air.

Harry said, "I tried my best and now I'm through with you."

"And I with you, Harry."

"One day you'll think of me differently."

"I don't know what to think of you. I've got one question. Do you really think that the greatest writers have been forgotten?"

"Not just forgotten. Deliberately erased because what they lay bare we don't wish to see."

He took out his handkerchief, rubbed his face vigorously, and started shambling down the sidewalk. My own forehead was damp from standing in the sun, my scalp prickly, but I didn't move until he disappeared into the crowd on Columbus Avenue.

# 20

## We're All So Excited

By the time I reached the Kemels' brownstone my shirt was plastered to my chest and perspiration ran past my ears. The physical and emotional exertion of grappling with Harry Winter, not to mention the police station ordeal afterwards, had left me exhausted. All I could think of was lying down. When I opened the apartment door the blinds were drawn and the front rooms dark, likely to keep out the heat. I assumed the shadowy living room was deserted until a voice startled me.

"There's a package for you, Felix."

It was Hershel Tanenbaum. He turned on a lamp and I saw him in the corner armchair, a short cigar between his lips and the smoke languorous about his head. His thin fringe of hair looked wet, as if he had just taken a shower, and his little beard glistened. He smiled in a friendly way and pointed with his cigar at a box on the table wrapped in gold paper and tied with ribbon. "A delivery boy brought it a couple of hours ago. He didn't say who it was from."

"I can't imagine," I said, draping my jacket on a chair. It took me a moment to slip off the ribbon and peel the packing tape from the box under the paper. Inside, surrounded by layers of paper and straw, nestled the porcelain figurine of the Lady with the Rose. I pulled her out and set her on the table.

"Very pretty," Hershel said. "From the looks of it that's no cheap knock-off. You must have an admirer."

"No, just a friend," I said. At the bottom of the box was a small card.

*My Dearest Felix,*
*Well, she turned out to be a fake after all. But a rather nice fake, so I thought you might want her as a remembrance. By the time you get this I will already be gone.*

*Love,*
*Alice*

I could not help sighing and Hershel said, "Why don't you take a seat? For a young man you seem to have your share of problems."

I really wanted nothing more than to lie down in my room, but I did as he suggested. "It's that obvious, is it?" I said.

The dim light was soothing and the cigar smoke, though harsh to my nose, had the pleasant effect of softening the edges of the room. Hershel said, "When you're young you think you have the ability to control your life. But as you get older you realize that there are forces, mysterious or accidental, which are far more powerful than you are and which will blow you about like a leaf. When I was your age, back in the paleolithic era, I thought that I was destined to be the next John D. Rockefeller. In the fifties when I started working the possibility of money seemed everywhere. People had come out of the Depression and the war to believe some great, mysterious reward awaited them for enduring all that hardship. But what was it? Crowds used to form in front of the first discount appliance store — I went specially to witness this for myself — because people believed maybe they could buy a better life. I made a fortune, lost it, made another, and lost that too. It turned out I wasn't smart enough to swim against the trend but only to ride with it, up or down. And here I am back where I started, selling mutual funds, which is a young man's game."

"Did you ever marry?"

"Twice. I've got three kids from each, grandchildren too. Both my wives remarried but I still send them gifts on our anniversaries. They seem to like me better now than when we were together. Perhaps I was too selfish or didn't express myself properly. But I accept the way things have worked out."

"Excuse me for saying it, but it does seem strange, your living as a boarder. I hear those funds make a lot of money for people."

"It's true I do well enough, although not like some of those young hustlers. I don't have the same drive anymore. I could afford a house in New Jersey if I wanted another mortgage around my neck. But what do I need it for? At the end of the day I shut my brief-case, refuse all invitations from my colleagues to join them for a drink, and the money world vanishes. Here at the Kemels I have nothing to worry about. I don't even have to cook. It turns out that a person doesn't have to climb a mountaintop to find the simple life."

He took a luxurious drag from the cigar and blew the smoke towards the plaster swirls on the ceiling. "You're a writer," he said. "Maybe this will interest you. My other reason for staying."

"You're having an affair with Hannah."

"I thought you had noticed. In fact, that's the reason I wanted to have this little chat. Most guests don't. But for some reason we've been incautious around you."

"Is it recent?"

"It began eight years ago, not long after I moved in. I don't think either Hannah or I intended it. From the start both Sam and Hannah treated me like family. I felt immediately that I'd found my real home. And despite a certain attraction that I admit to having felt for her, I wasn't concerned. After all, Hannah's considerably older than I am. She'll be seventy next month. Singer has a story called 'Old Love.' Do you know it?"

"Yes."

"Well, one weekend Sam went off to a book fair in Chicago. Hannah and I had dinner as always, then sat in this room and listened to a recording of *Lucia di Lammermoor*. When it came time for bed it just seemed the natural thing to do. But I was surprised by Hannah's passion. We were up half the night. Only after Sam came home did we consider what had happened."

"And how have you managed to keep it a secret from him all these years?"

"It isn't — not anymore."

"I see."

"Only I'm not supposed to know that he knows. And he's not supposed to know that I know he knows. We're never too old for games, it seems. Without them we couldn't go on. As it is, Sam and I have a most cordial friendship. But when he is alone with Hannah he calls her terrible names. She needs this. Sam wouldn't do it otherwise, he has a very gentle nature. In every other way we lead orderly and even conservative lives."

"And the three of you are happy?"

"Oh, that's harder to say. There is at least as much suffering as pleasure for any of us. Sometimes I think we would all like to stop but cannot live without it any more. Once, four or five years ago, I tried to. I even made arrangements for other accommodations. But Sam came to me one evening when Hannah was out and begged me to stay. He said that he had grown as fond of me as a brother and couldn't bear the thought of me leaving. He was able to say that out of love for her. So I stayed and here we are. Well" — he drew on his cigar — "this afternoon is our literary salon. You ought to rest up, Felix. We certainly look forward to hearing your story."

He didn't seem to expect me to say anything more and so I rose from the chair. As I nodded to him before leaving I had the impression that he was made of nothing but smoke.

Hannah Kemel's voice woke me. I could hear whispering in the hall outside my door even as I struggled into consciousness, my head feeling like a sack of water. What time was it? I groped for my watch on the night table and saw that it was almost three. It was hard to believe the afternoon was only half over, considering all that had already happened today. I could not even remember taking off my clothes, but now I got up, put on my last clean shirt, jeans, jacket, and tie, and opened the door to go to the washroom down the hall.

"Oh, you're awake, Felix," Hannah said. "I've just made some coffee. Come have a little something before your reading. We're all so excited."

She squeezed my arm with her fingers. I went to the washroom and relieved myself before splashing water on my face. My hair was flattened on one side from being pressed against the pillow and I made a few futile passes of my comb through it.

Once again I realized that I had missed a meal and that my stomach ached from being so empty. I joined Sam Kemel and Hershel Tanenbaum at the dining-room table and ate two pieces of pound cake, a linzer tart, an orange, and drank two cups of coffee. Both men had dressed for the occasion, Sam in a bow tie and paisley vest, the more casual Hershel in a corduroy jacket and cravat. Despite the heat and airlessness from the hot weather, Hannah had lit candles in the sitting room — on the mantel, endtables, even on the arms of chairs — so that the atmosphere was more appropriate for a séance. When Hannah returned I saw that she had changed into a long gown with thin straps that revealed her bony shoulders and the soft flesh of her arms.

"Ah, here is our writer," she said and, taking my arm, she brought me to the centre of the sitting room while Sam and Hershel took opposite ends of the velvet sofa. "Isn't this exciting?" Hannah said. "We're so delighted you've agreed to read for us. Today," she pronounced, turning to the men, "we have a guest who needs no introduction. Felix Roth is a rising young literary star and the protegé of none other than Isaac Bashevis Singer."

"No, no," I protested. "I haven't even met him."

"Well, I'm sure he would adore your work. Felix is going to read us his very latest story. So without further ado, I present . . . Felix Roth."

I felt ludicrous standing there but at the same time I found myself so nervous that my stomach rose to my mouth and I thought I might faint or vomit. Fortunately, Hannah had put a glass of water on the side table and I took a long drink. Then I pulled the tattered manuscript from inside my blazer, drew in a deep breath, and was about to begin reading when Sam Kemel asked, "What's it called?"

"'The Goat Bride.'"

"Fascinating title," Hannah whispered.

"Shhh." That was Sam or Hershel, I couldn't tell which, as I was staring down at the page. And so I began to read. I read of the middle-aged accountant named Joey Pechnik and of his sad little life as he commuted between his shabby office and his house in the suburbs. Of standing on his front porch one morning and seeing a goat jump out of the back of a truck. The words sounded foreign and disembodied to me, as if coming from a record player elsewhere in the room. But as I spoke the goat's first words — "'Why not? Goats too can have free will'" — the animal herself seemed to be speaking rather than me. And then the rhythm of the prose took over and the sentences flowed from my tongue. How the accountant fell in love with the goat, how the two lived together blissfully for years. I even felt confident enough to glance up and see Hannah in rapture, her fingers reaching up to touch her lip. As the goat grew old and developed a fever my voice became both deeper and softer. Then came Pechnik throwing a pot at Animal Control, the arrival of the SWAT team and the three-day standoff. And when the goat died and Joey Pechnik tried to throw himself into the grave a sob wrenched my words. The rest came out as a dark threnody or dirge, and when it was over I stood there with the soiled pages in my hands, having forgotten where I was but feeling as if I myself had lost a loved one.

What brought me back was the applause — three pairs of hands and also the noise of Hannah's sniffles. She wiped her eyes with a handkerchief while Sam hurried over to shake my hand.

"I congratulate you," he said. "You are a true artist. Such nuance, such sensibility. The story is believable and yet fantastic at the same time. I thought you were the genuine article and now my judgment is only confirmed."

Hershel was behind him. He hugged me and said, "It is a rare opportunity to catch a writer at the beginning of his rise to fame." Hannah had pulled herself together sufficiently to kiss me warmly on each cheek, the tears still hot on her face. From somewhere Sam brought out a bottle of champagne and popped the cork. He handed out glasses and then raised his own.

"To 'The Goat Bride,'" Hannah said. "A story almost too wonderful for praise."

We clinked glasses and I tasted the champagne as tiny sparks in my mouth.

Sam savoured a mouthful and then swallowed. He said, "I was wondering about one small thing, Felix. The moment of the wedding night, when you literally close the door on the man and the goat. Why be so reserved? I know for a fact that you are capable of describing the acts of physical love. Nowadays a reader doesn't want to imagine such scenes, he wants to see them presented without inhibition."

"Forgive me, my friend," Hershel said, laying his hand on Sam Kemel's shoulder, "but you are speaking nonsense. The story has admirable delicacy and tact. If anything it is perhaps just a little too formal in its diction. I found that rather off-putting. As a young writer you shouldn't be reserved about writing in a contemporary voice, energetic and up-to-date —"

Hannah interrupted. "Don't listen to them, Felix. They'll only ruin your story. Every word is already perfect. Let me kiss you again." She did so. "You're another Peretz or even Singer. It did occur to me that the story would be very interesting from the female point of view."

"But the female is a goat," I said.

"Is that a problem? After all, she's a talking goat."

"But you must be careful," Sam cautioned, "so that the reader doesn't delve into the matter of speech from an animal. Physiologically speaking, a goat could never pronounce human speech. The larynx isn't developed for anything beyond a bleat."

And yet they all professed to love the story and proclaimed it a masterpiece. In only a short time I had become strangely fond of the three of them, yet the more they praised the story while suggesting alternative beginnings, middles, and endings, the more I doubted their opinions. Perhaps their wildly diverging interpretations — the story was a political allegory, an indictment of class restriction, a work of high spiritualism — were a sign not of the story's strength but of its weakness.

Suddenly I remembered my meeting with Aaron and looked at my watch. It was already past four; I would have to hurry if I didn't want to be late. I thanked them for listening when the telephone rang and Hannah went to the kitchen to answer it.

"It's for you, Felix," she said, looking in through the doorway. "Your mother."

I couldn't imagine what to say to her. That the highlight of my day had been riding in the back of a police car? Surely it would be better to call her after I had seen Aaron and could let her know everything was all right.

"Tell her that I've already left for Carnegie Hall," I said, slipping the manuscript into my inside blazer pocket.

"But it's much too early for a concert."

"Tell her I wanted to make sure that I wouldn't get lost."

# 21

# Brooklyn Rhapsody

Brooklyn was also a part of the mythology of New York that I carried around with me, if more as a place to escape from than head towards. Even so, the name itself had a tarnished glamour, as there was even in the Bronx and Queens, tough places to grow up in but rich in material for fiction: the neighbours screaming bloody murder, the smart-mouthed kids opening fire hydrants in the heat. I thought of Malamud's *The Assistant* and its dime-store heartbreak, a novel so beautifully grim and freighted with moral tragedy that it was almost Russian.

But I didn't know what sort of rhapsody I could make of the Williamsburg Bridge. I would have preferred to enter on the famous Brooklyn Bridge to the south, but it was in the Williamsburg section that Aaron was staying. The foot of the bridge did not slope gently down onto Manhattan's Delancey Street, but appeared broken off, an amputated stump of deteriorating concrete. On the stump leaned a ramp so that trucks spewing black smoke could lurch their way up. The pavement around was strewn with paper cups and packaging debris from the nearby discount stores. To get onto the bridge I had to climb a set of filthy yellow stairs until I was suddenly and disconcertingly high above the ground. A chain-link fence ran along either side, through which I could see the nearby tenement roofs and hear shouts from a schoolyard below. The wooden slats on which I hesitantly placed one foot after another vibrated from the subway train galloping underneath.

As the edge of the island approached, the roar of traffic died away and the wooden slats under my feet turned to cement and stone, twinkling with shards of shattered bottles, and then metal sheets welded crudely together with gaps showing empty space beneath. Around me strained girders and chain-link and guy wire, a brutal latticework through which the heavenly sky was visible as if I were looking out of a cage. Already I had entered a different New York, one of raw strength and contempt for refinement. The slightest breeze tempered the heat that had not yet begun to fade. Down below I could see a strip of green along the shore, and in a few more steps I was above the moving water. On the other, the Brooklyn side, squatted a sugar refinery, ports, a pyramid of sand, cranes, smokestacks.

To cross any of the seventeen bridges into Manhattan was a hopeful rite of passage, but my brother wanted to reverse the story, just as he wished to reverse time and return to some medieval life of faith. I was anxious to see Aaron but also afraid that he might not be the same person who had been my best and sometimes only friend growing up, the first one (so my mother told me) who ever made me smile, at the late age of two months. It came to me that maybe the only thing I really had in common with Isaac Bashevis Singer was an awe for an idealized older brother. When Singer had arrived in America his brother Israel Joshua was already here, a famous Yiddish novelist, playwright, and journalist. Only after his older brother died did Isaac Bashevis find his own voice again. I supposed that I ought to have been glad that Aaron was not a writer.

Aaron did not only lack the artistic sensibility; he also lacked my own hunger for praise. This need of mine was like rain to a spring tulip, and my mother eagerly provided the watering. Possibly my fixation on writing from an early age had something to do with the hope of a lifetime of praise from the larger world. I could remember as a boy having looked to another, more immediate source, quite improbably to me now but of the greatest importance then: the Boy Scouts. In our neighbourhood there was a troop with a Jewish scout master and I was dying to belong and earn those beautiful badges that marked one as accomplished in fire building, knot tying, and other skills I had no need or desire for. My parents agreed to let me go but only if Aaron also wanted to join, for the meetings were on the same night as their bridge game and they did not have time to be chauffeuring us to different locations. Of course Aaron refused. He was like Bartleby in the Melville story, the scrivener in a Wall Street lawyer's office who one day announces, "I prefer not to." It might have been Aaron's motto, emblazoned on a crest in place of those Boy Scout badges he felt contempt for.

In the end my mother took me alone. I hoped that Aaron would regret his decision once he saw me in my uniform and heard our parents express their delight in my latest badge, but he never even took notice. At scout meetings I fumbled those complicated knots, burned my thighs trying to climb a rope, choked on the Boy Scout pledge as if the words were stones in my mouth. Within a month I was bored out of my mind and began thinking up excuses so I didn't have to go. I earned only one badge — for cleanliness — which I stuck at the back of my underwear drawer before my mother had a chance to sew it on. After three months my parents let me drop out.

The last stretch of the bridge lowered me towards the shore while the traffic noise of Brooklyn rose to meet me. The subway trains, which had begun beneath my feet, now pounded over my head. I went down a concrete staircase and found myself under the end of the bridge. I began walking down Bedford Avenue. There was no breeze here and the heat made the air so dense that my lungs had to work painfully hard. I passed five- and six-storey walkups with fire escapes, a row of used refrigerators in front of a repair shop, a Puerto Rican flag hanging limply from an open window. Beside a white stucco church a group of men lounged outside a Spanish store drinking beer from cans while a dog lay splayed in the heat.

And then came the first sign that a Jewish neighbourhood was beginning, a kosher bakery. In the doorway stood a man in a black yarmulke and white shirt and apron, his wide beard speckled with flour. I could not tell whether the man was a Lubavitch, whose Rebbe was the most famous of all Hasidic leaders. Not long before I had seen a photograph of the Rebbe shaking the hand of President Carter, who had come to see *him*. It was just like my brother not to be drawn to the Lubavitchers, whose proselytizers waylaid assimilated Jews on every university campus as part of their worldwide campaign for reconversion to the faith. My brother had managed to do it the hard way, finding a court that didn't even want converts. For Aaron, only a sect that had no interest in him could be authentic.

I had been the first in the family to find out about Aaron's secret. One February morning I went to the bathroom and noticed Aaron's light. I looked in his room but he wasn't there, so I wandered downstairs thinking that he might already be at breakfast. He wasn't in the kitchen, and when I noticed the door to the basement open I went down the carpeted stairs. I saw him standing beside the billiards table in his pyjamas, struggling to put on tefillin. He was having trouble winding the narrow leather strap around his arm even as the other one, a loop that went around the head, kept slipping so that the small black box attached to it dangled between his eyes. An open prayer book was balanced on the edge of the billiards table and he knocked it with his elbow, lunging to catch it and letting the arm strap unravel.

I backed away and went up the stairs before Aaron saw me. What on earth was he doing? Only once had I ever worn tefillin, when my father had taken me to the synagogue on the Friday before my bar mitzvah. An old man had put the boxes and straps on me with such rapid movements that I could never have repeated the process. Since then I had seen a roomful of men at the shiva for my mother's uncle Ned, wearing yarmulkes and tefillin and tallitim, swaying as they prayed. In their regular lives they were junk dealers, dentists, real estate agents, but in that shrouded living room they were transformed into eternal Jews. Afterwards, unwinding straps and putting the tefillin back into their velvet sacks, they sighed and joked and talked business, once more becoming junk dealers, dentists, and real estate agents.

Not long after that morning, Aaron began leaving the house after dinner to attend evening services at a small synagogue in Bathurst Manor. My parents didn't know what to make of this behaviour. As a family we belonged to a large conservative synagogue but attended only on the high holidays. My mother confided to me her mixture of discomfort and guilt. After all, they had tried to instill in us a pride of Jewishness, so how could they complain that Aaron was going too far? As usual, my father had less trouble speaking his mind. On the night that Aaron announced his intention of visiting a Rebbe in Brooklyn (we were sitting in the family room with the television on), my father said, "What, a pilgrimage? Next thing I know you'll want to see where Moses was circumcised." Did Aaron really want to wear a scraggly beard and a fur hat on his head? my father asked. It was well known that the Hasidim turned converts against their own families. He didn't like to use the word *cult*, but if the shoe fit . . .

My mother interrupted him in an unnaturally cheerful voice. "Nobody likes to travel alone," she said.

"New York is so exciting. Felix has always wanted to go. The two of you can take in a show."

I reached Division Street and, as if the name itself conjured change, there were suddenly Hasids everywhere. Walking on the broken sidewalks, driving big old cars slowly up Bedford, talking on the steps of crumbling walkups. At first they all looked the same to me with their beards and hats and dark suits, but soon I began to make the ordinary discovery of their differences. A man of my own age was handsome and elegant, almost dandyish, in his white stockings and well-cut coat and the beautifully rich curls of his beard and sidelocks. Behind him on the sidewalk came a large-bellied man, slovenly, his brow damp from the heat, yarmulke askew, a cigarette in his mouth dripping ash. Some wore vests under their coats, some had their top shirt buttons undone. Most wore suits of black with pale pinstripes, but others wore dark blue. An old man in a flat hat hunched over his cane might have been traversing the cobblestones of Vilna. As for the women, they all wore brightly coloured dresses with high collars and opaque stockings. Those who were married wore kerchiefs or pretty hats or wigs. They pushed baby carriages or stood and talked in little groups, fanning themselves with their hands.

I drew from my pocket the address that the Hasid in the chess club had written for me and checked it for the dozenth time. I found the house just past Penn Street, squeezed between its neighbours, with a rose-coloured facade of decorative lintels that was turning to dust. Beside the stoop was a shop in the basement called Yidel's Hats. I obeyed the instruction not to approach the house but stood on the opposite side of the street. After a few moments the shape of a face appeared in an upper window and then another. The two faces disappeared, and the curtain fell back.

The door at the top of the stoop opened and Aaron stepped out. He squinted towards me as if he had not known daylight for some time. He wore the same university sweatshirt that I'd seen him in before he disappeared. The only difference was a couple of days' growth of beard on his chin, so fair that I could only see it after he had crossed to my side of the street. And he had replaced his brightly woven yarmulke with a plain black one.

"Hi, Felix," he said and grinned, sounding as though he'd just opened the door of his bedroom back home. I had an urge to put my arms around him but didn't even shake his hand. He said, "I hope you haven't been worrying about me."

"You hope?" My voice sounded more angry than I had intended. "It would have been nice if you had let me know where you'd gone."

"You're right, I should have. It was thoughtless of me."

"I've had to lie to Mom."

"I'm sorry. It wasn't my intention to put you in a difficult position. I'll do better, I promise. It would be nice if we could try to relax."

I took a deep breath. Aaron was right, this wasn't the way I had wanted the conversation to go. And it wasn't going to help me persuade him to come back to the Kemels'. "At least I know where you're staying," I said more calmly. "So whose house is this?"

"Someone I met in Toronto. He and his family have the second floor. Mordecai and his wife are younger than me and they've already got two kids. Actually there are three families in the house, a total of nine children. It's pretty wild. You want to get something to eat? There's a little grocery just up the street. You must have passed it."

"All right."

As we walked Aaron pointed out a few sights — a cheder, a religious goods store. We saw two boys dressed in long sleeves and wool pants going in with their mother.

I said, "It's got to be eighty-five degrees. Why can't the kids wear shorts?"

"I know," Aaron said. "It does seem like torture. Mordecai's wife dresses hers the same way. I asked him why the kids can't dress for summer weather. All he said was, 'A Jew should sweat.' It's not as if everything around here makes sense to me, Felix."

We reached the little bakery at the corner of Rutledge, three steps below the sidewalk, the window crowded with baked goods. I waited outside while Aaron went in and I could see him talking to a shrunken old Hasid behind the counter with a beard like a withered plant. Aaron emerged again, carrying cans of Coke and poppyseed Danishes. We leaned against the iron railing in front of the store and I bit into the Danish; dry on the outside but moist and sweet in the middle.

With his mouth half full, Aaron said, "The family I'm staying with has a business near here, right under the elevated train. You should see it, Felix, it's just like the photographs from seventy or eighty years ago, with the iron girders overhead and the trains shaking everything as they go by. The store sells calculators, adding machines, electric typewriters — all the latest office stuff. And they have another store in the Bronx. I've spent a morning with them to see how the business runs. It's actually quite interesting. What do you think of the Danish? It comes from the best bakery in Williamsburg."

Something about the way Aaron pretended to be at home here annoyed me.

He said, "There's a young guy who helps in the bakery. He's a cousin of the owner, just shy of mentally retarded. They take care of their own."

"People do that in the rest of the world too."

"Of course they do. I didn't mean otherwise."

"So tell me," I said, unable to get the tone of annoyance out of my voice, "what's with the slovenly look? Some of the men look neat but most of them are pretty sloppy. With their shirts hanging out and their ties loose."

"I know. And Kovner Hasidim won't even wear ties. It shows that appearance doesn't matter to them. That it's a worldly concern. Also, it separates them from the Gentiles among whom they do business."

Two young women walked by, slim and pretty, wearing identical long blue skirts and stockings, but Aaron avoided looking at them.

"You never told me how you even found out about this court. And how do you know Mordecai?"

"I never told you because I didn't think you particularly wanted to hear. It was back in January. I'd spent the day at the law courts on a school assignment and it got late so I called Mom and then went to Switzer's for a bite to eat. I was eating a pastrami sandwich and working out a chess problem when I noticed someone standing beside my table."

"Not a chess player, I gather."

"Hardly. A guy with a gaunt face and bad teeth and a workman's cap on his head. He said to me in a low voice, 'Are you a Jew?' I was taken aback. No one had ever asked me that before and even though I had no idea what he wanted this weird feeling came over me. I guess it was a kind of crisis. I thought to myself: who was I? What does the name Aaron Roth mean? A law student? A chess dropout? Somebody who still lived in his parents' house in Willowdale? I felt that nothing in my life allowed me to answer the guy. But finally I managed to mumble out that, yes, I was a Jew. And the man said, 'Come with me. We need one more for a *minyan*.'"

"And you went?"

"I didn't think I had any choice. So I followed the guy into Kensington Market. I hadn't been there for years. Even though it isn't really Jewish anymore I felt I was going back in time. He took me to a small brick building with a Star of David carved in the stone over the wooden door. I hadn't known that there were any open synagogues left in the market. We went inside and I could see light filtering in from the windows onto the benches and the embroidered tapestry in front of the Ark. But we didn't stay in the main sanctuary. We went down into the basement."

"They probably go into that restaurant to look for one or two people every day."

"I'm sure you're right, but for me it felt almost fated. The men were waiting for us in the basement, eight to be exact, so that the two of us made ten. Without saying a word to us they opened their prayer books and began. Nobody seemed to lead the service the way we're used to — they just went at their own pace. All of them were sixty or more except for one. There was this young Orthodox Jew, pale face, red beard, wearing a black coat that went past his knees. He prayed with such devotion that I couldn't stop watching him. The prayers ended abruptly, the old men slammed their books shut and shook hands before leaving. But this young Orthodox guy was different, I could see that. He belonged to something rich and alive."

"So you spoke to him?"

"It took some nerve, but I did. I asked if he was from around here and he said no, he lived in Brooklyn and was just here on a business trip. He was staying with cousins but had got caught late downtown at a meeting. We went on the subway together and he told me he was a member of the Kovner Hasidim. A small court, just seventy-five families. But the Kovner Rebbe was a great man, holy and wise, directly descended from the Rebbe who founded the court over a hundred years ago. They believed in many hours of prayer and days of fasting. He said that some of the other Hasidim considered them too solemn, but Reb Samuelson liked to say that even joy was a kind of solemnity when it grew out of reverence for the Almighty. I asked how I could find out more but he said there weren't any Kovner Hasidim in Toronto, not even his cousins. But he gave me his card and told me I could write to him and that if I ever came to Brooklyn the Rebbe would see me. He's a generous man and never turns anyone away. His advice is worth more than gold."

"And this young Orthodox Jew was Mordecai?"

"Right. I did write to him and he's been advising me on what to read and other matters. He even had his cousins help me find that teacher I've been studying with back home."

Aaron took his last bite of Danish and licked his finger. The street seemed to have become busier. A group of men were standing at the opposite corner talking earnestly with someone in a blue sedan. I said, "When are you going to see this Rebbe? Our flight home is tomorrow at noon. Your articling job is starting soon."

"Of course I know that, Felix. I'll probably see him tonight. The Rebbe has a lot of demands on his time. People come from all over to ask his advice. He studies for hours every day and his health isn't that good either. But he knows about me. In fact, the Rebbe said I should see you this afternoon."

"You had to get permission?"

"No, it's not like that. He told Mordecai to encourage me, that's all. Because it's wrong to worry my family, he said. Oh, I wanted to tell you, I went to a wedding this weekend. The groom was a second cousin of Mordecai's wife. Of course I knew the men and women wouldn't dance together, but I didn't know they actually had separate banquet halls. You should have seen the men dance, Aaron. Round and round, shouting and singing. We just never reach that level of ecstasy in our lives. Near the end the women were brought in from the other hall. The musicians began a slow melody, sombre almost, and the bride danced with her father, each of them holding the end of a handkerchief. Then she danced with her new husband, only she held his hand. I found it almost unspeakably moving."

"I can understand that," I said. "But maybe they

invited you to the wedding for that very purpose. To seduce you into joining them."

"I don't think so. Except for Mordecai, they're all pretty suspicious of me. They don't take to outsiders. You pretty well have to be born a Kovner Hasid or come from another court and join them through marriage. I haven't been allowed to attend any of the men's study groups, not that I would be able to follow anyway — they speak in Yiddish. I have to convince them of my dedication and faith, which I'm not even sure I have. To be honest, Felix, I find this the most exhilarating thing I've done but also the most scary. I'm a fish out of water, I know it. A part of me wants to run back home where it's safe."

"Well, come, then. No one says you have to stop studying. I've found a nice bed and breakfast here. We can stay together tonight and go to the airport tomorrow."

A couple of men ran past us on the sidewalk — running Hasids seemed strangely unlikely — and we watched them going down the street. Aaron said, as if he were in a daydream, "So tell me what you've been doing."

What could I possibly tell him? About Alice? Hadassah? Harry Winter? "Just hanging around," I said. "I went to a chess club on the Upper West Side. That's how I found you."

"Really?" He seemed to wake up. "So what was the club like? I used to dream of playing the hustlers in Washington Square Park."

"I remember. The club was packed with fanatics. They play fast. I could hardly keep up just watching."

"Did you play a game?"

"One."

"So?"

"I blew the opening, the middle, and the endgame."

Aaron smiled his beautiful smile.

"We can go right now," I said. I wasn't sure what to do about meeting Hadassah at Carnegie Hall, but I could worry about that later. "Just get your bag and we'll take the subway back to Manhattan."

"I wouldn't want to insult Mordecai. He's been so good to me. And I think I should get the most out of this experience that I can."

A sound made us both turn our heads. Across Bedford Avenue a man had broken out weeping. Others were talking loudly in Yiddish, and one grasped his own collar and ripped it away from his shirt. Women hurried past us on the sidewalk crying. Several teenage boys hurried into the grocery store.

"What's going on?" I said.

"I better find out."

Aaron walked over to a group of young men and began speaking to them. At first they ignored him but finally one turned and spoke to him. Meanwhile, the old man in the grocery store hung a Closed sign in the window. Cars had stopped on the street, blocking traffic.

Aaron returned. "Reb Shimon Markus has died."

"Who's that?"

"A very respected man. A famous teacher, a Satmar, almost ninety years old. I've heard his name but that's all I know. Apparently he had a heart attack and at first it wasn't certain whether he had died. But now it's been confirmed. All the businesses are closing."

The street was filling with people. I could hardly

tell where they all came from, hundreds of them and more every minute. All the women had disappeared. Someone jostled me from behind and I almost fell on Aaron, who steadied me with his hand. Bedford Avenue was suddenly a crush of people, so many that we were swept off the sidewalk and into the street. I could see nothing now but a sea of black hats, the brick apartments on either side barely containing them like flood walls.

Since childhood I had been afraid of crowds, and a panic rose in my throat. When I looked for Aaron again I saw that the crowd was pushing between us. An arm knocked Aaron's yarmulke from his head.

"Aaron!" I called above the clamour. I reached out to grab him but he was pushed farther away.

"I can't come back yet," he shouted; I could barely make out the words. "Tell Mom and Dad —"

A roar from the crowd drowned him out. "Don't do this!" I screamed. "I need you!"

"Don't worry," he shouted back. "You haven't lost me."

The pressure of bodies on every side lifted me momentarily from the ground. The brim of a fedora banged me hard on the bridge of my nose. I tried to see Aaron but he was gone. I called out his name but my words were swallowed by the din.

# 22

# How Do You Get to Carnegie Hall?

It took me almost two hours to get back to Manhattan, so difficult was it to make my way through the hordes of people. I could not find my way to a subway entrance and so had to cross the Williamsburg Bridge again on foot. The lowering sun, pulsing just above the city's skyscrapers, made my eyes ache and perspiration run down my face like blood.

I would have gladly sacrificed a piece of my last twenty dollars for a cab ride to Carnegie Hall, but on the Lower East Side I could not find a single cab. What I felt about my brother at that moment I could not have articulated even to myself, for a kind of seizure or paralysis gripped my heart. Or at least a part of it, for — in inverse proportion — my need to see Hadassah had grown even more urgent. It was as if my right ventricle had turned to ice while the left was pumping so hotly it might explode. Hadassah would save me; Hadassah would bring purpose to these last days. It was too much to ask of her, and perhaps I knew that even then, but I had no other hope.

The subway ride that I finally took up to Carnegie Hall was a blur even as I lived it. I could never afterwards remember what train I took or whether I had to transfer lines, but only that I arrived at the Fifty-seventh Street entrance sweating and with a painful stitch in my side. My watch showed six minutes to eight and people were making their way through the open doors. I couldn't see Hadassah anywhere and tried to calm myself by looking up at the chocolate brick and terra-cotta front and silently reciting the names of the famous who had walked through those same doors: Tchaikovsky, Gershwin, Ellington, Stravinsky, Fats Waller, Edith Piaf . . . Maybe the doorman of the Belnord had taken vengeance on me by tearing up my note. Or had Hadassah decided to have nothing more to do with me? I hurried inside and joined the line in front of the ticket window. The woman behind the grille wore a net over her hair and I thought how my mother would have disapproved and taken it as another sign of the decline of the civility she had known in her youth.

I reached the front of the line. "You're holding two tickets for my brother and me. The name's Roth."

"The brothers Roth," she said without smiling. People were rushing past me now — in New York they flocked even to see an orchestra from New Jersey — and a bell was sounding inside the hall. I took the tickets and went outside again to pace back and forth, only I kept bumping into other concertgoers and had to stop and just stand on the sidewalk. Where was

Hadassah? The cold from the right ventricle began seeping into the left. Without her I had no desire to see the concert but did not want to break the promise to my mother. Only a few stragglers were arriving now as the concert was about to begin, and after another couple of minutes there was only me and a tall and very thin man, Indian or Pakistani, with a beaky nose that reminded me of several relatives on my father's side. The disconnected thought floated through my mind that Jews and Indians looked like cousins.

An usher began closing the doors. The Indian gentleman — that was how I thought of him because of his air of sad gentility — was examining the posted program with the half-smile of someone who has nowhere particular to go.

I said, "Excuse me. I have an extra ticket to the concert."

"Oh, no, I am just looking." The man nodded quickly and took a step backwards.

"I'm not trying to sell it. It's just going to go to waste so you can have it if you want."

"Do you mean it?" He had a pleasant, musical accent.

"Please, take it."

"You are very kind. Mendelssohn is a big favourite of mine. Also Brahms, who they are playing first. But I am sorry that you have been disappointed by your companion."

"I guess I ought to have known better. We should get inside."

"Please, allow me." The Indian gentleman jumped to hold the door open. We passed through the dowdy lobby and I gave the young woman our tickets. The lights were already dimming as an usher showed us to a pair of seats halfway up the first balcony. The stage brightened again and the orchestra members came on as we applauded, followed by the first violinist and the conductor. My own image of the conductor came from the crazy-haired Leopold Stokowski as depicted in a Bugs Bunny cartoon that Aaron had particularly liked when we were kids, but this conductor was young and a little paunchy. The violinist, Stephanie Chan, came last, looking no more than fourteen years old. The conductor held up his hand — he didn't even use a baton — and brought it briskly down.

I hardly listened to the Brahms or the Mozart that followed, and during the intermission I made the uncharacteristic act of walking briskly to the bar and ordering a scotch. It burned in my throat and felt like a punch to my stomach, but it was calming like a shot of Novocaine and I went back to listen to the Mendelssohn Violin Concerto. The music was so familiar that I had a sudden image of myself as a kid back in our living room, my mother standing by the hi-fi gazing into space. She might even be doing the same thing now, imagining that she was here with me, and in a way I wished that she was because she would have appreciated it so much more. Still, even I could tell that Stephanie Chan played with energy and feeling, and the melody, which I had disliked for so long, became almost unbearably beautiful.

An odd sound made me turn my head. The Indian gentleman was humming under his breath while tears slipped down his cheeks.

*

By the time we came out onto Fifty-seventh Street darkness had fallen. I watched the headlights of the cars moving down Seventh Avenue. The night was still very warm, but not as humid, and so felt like something of a relief.

The Indian gentleman said, "It was kind of you to give me a ticket."

"Well, I'm just glad you enjoyed it."

"It is true, I react strongly to music. That has always been my nature. Would you allow me to return the kindness by inviting you for something to eat or drink? Perhaps you would like to go to the Carnegie Deli just down the street. It is quite well known, you know."

As I had nothing else to do with my time and did not feel ready to go back to the Kemels' for my last night in the city during which I would likely just lie there like a condemned man, I agreed and we crossed the avenue.

The restaurant air was redolent of spices and brine. A short line waited by the takeout counter displaying kasha varnishkas and blintzes, and as we joined them I examined the signed photos on the wall of Milton Berle and Barry Manilow and Woody Allen. A table for two came up almost immediately and we squeezed into two chairs against a wall. The clatter and shouts made it almost impossible to think.

The waiter flipped open his pad. "I'm not really very hungry," I said, trying to balance the giant menu without knocking over my water glass.

"Then you want the Stage Deli down the street," the waiter grumbled.

"Please, have something," the Indian gentleman pleaded. "Why not try the strudel? It is very good."

"All right. And coffee, please."

"The same for me."

"You must go to concerts often," I said, only too glad to hear about someone else's life.

"In my time I have seen many great performers. And at the opera too. I never missed a performance by Maria Callas. When I had my own business my wife and I went to a concert every Saturday. But I go rarely now. Unfortunately, my financial situation does not permit it. So as you can see, you have provided me with a great treat tonight."

"What was your business?"

"I am a photographer. I did all the best Indian weddings in the New York area. Hindu, Muslim, Parsi — I was in demand from them all."

"But how did you lose it?"

"It is not a very nice story. You see, I was married and with three beautiful children. A house in the Bronx. But fate was cruel to me. I fell in love, not with another woman but a man. He was only twenty years old. And suddenly nothing else was important to me. I was willing to sacrifice everything. In retrospect it seems to me that a kind of madness came over me. My wife threw me out and refused to let me see the children. The Indian community ostracized me. No one would hire me to photograph their weddings. Finally I had to sell all my equipment. Now I work in a one-hour photo lab in Times Square. The pay is not very good and I live in a single men's residence where all the others are alcoholics."

"And what about the young man?"

"He left me, of course. The foolish thing is that I knew he wouldn't stay with me and still I couldn't stop myself. He was extraordinarily beautiful. I threw my life away for a few short weeks of bliss."

"So you regret it?"

"Certainly I regret it. But even now I don't know if I could have behaved differently. Here are our desserts. Tonight I heard the Mendelssohn concerto, an unexpected pleasure! So what do you think of the strudel?"

"It's excellent."

"Yes," he sighed and took a bite of his own.

We ate our strudel and talked of trivial matters while plates and forks clanged around us and people raised their voices. A man nearby began choking and had to be slapped vigorously on the back. Neither of us seemed in any hurry to leave and when I finally looked at the clock on the wall it was almost midnight. We rose and shook hands and I let the Indian gentleman leave first, giving as a pretext a need to visit the washroom, so that I could be alone as I stepped again onto Seventh Avenue.

I stood outside and tried to rehearse telling Hannah Kemel that I didn't have the money to pay for my room. I would somehow pay for it, of course, not from any earnings from *Lowenstein's Sheet*, which I was determined to quit if Arthur didn't fire me, but from whatever job I could find back in Toronto. I felt sure that Hannah would trust me enough to let me send her the money, perhaps in instalments. Still, I was reluctant to go back and lie there staring at the French postcards on the wall. At this moment it felt like I would never sleep again.

"Felix."

I knew before I saw her that it was Hadassah. She stood under a street lamp. Her hair was pulled back in a ponytail and she wore a plain white T-shirt and a pair of cutoff shorts and she looked wonderful. But it was the way she looked at me, as if seeing me the way no one ever had before, that made me unable to speak. And as I looked into her eyes as we stood under that street lamp, a word came silently to me. Devotion. It was devotion that would save us all. I wanted to take her in my arms and kiss her but could not move.

"I've been waiting for you to come out," she said.

"But — but why didn't you come to the concert?"

"I wasn't going to come at all. But then I couldn't stop myself and I saw you leave the hall with that man. Somehow I didn't feel that I could approach you until he was gone. Felix, I haven't been fair to you."

"But you've been better to me than I deserve. Look, Hadassah —" and I drew the tattered manuscript from inside my blazer. "See, I'm not a liar, I did bring my story after all."

Suddenly I felt giddy, as if I would begin laughing for no reason. But Hadassah was frowning. "Here," I said, "you can read my story."

"Right now? I can't read it on the street, Felix."

"Of course. I'm an idiot. I don't care if you read it or not, or if your uncle Isaac reads it. I just want you to know it really exists. So you can have faith in me. Hadassah, I'm going home tomorrow. Everything has to happen tonight, like in Cinderella —"

"Please, Felix, slow down." She took my arm and led me to the curb. "We better go back to the Belnord. I'll get a cab."

And she did, taking one step onto the street and flagging a cab with a single pointed finger. She opened the door and ushered me inside. The driver went down a block to Fifty-fifth and over to Broadway to head uptown. But after that I saw nothing, for I pulled Hadassah to me and we kissed as heatedly as two teenagers in the back of the family sedan. I could not get enough of her. But why did she say that she had been unfair? Was she engaged to this Zazi, or whatever she called her boyfriend? Had she pretended interest in me just so she could marry and get out of Israel? Whatever the hurdle was I felt confident — that is, if a person could feel confident and absolutely desperate at the same time — that we could get over it. I had already lost Aaron; I was not going to lose Hadassah.

The cab stopped and I saw the archway of the Belnord through the cab window. With the last of my money I paid the fare and followed Hadassah out. The night doorman was a different fellow, unusually thin and with a beard like Abe Lincoln's, and he tipped his hat at us and said, "Evening, Miss Sussman." We crossed the dark courtyard and rode the elevator up to the fourteenth floor. Had it really been just two and a half days ago that I had first seen Hadassah in this hallway? She took keys from her bag and unlocked the door.

When she turned on the lights I stood there in surprise, for the apartment — Isaac Bashevis Singer's apartment — was nothing like I had imagined. Instead of heavy European furniture, rugs, books, I saw a modern, pristine apartment. Everything was white on white: the plush carpet, the blinds, even a white leather sofa in the raised living room. The dining table was bevelled glass, with high-backed steel chairs. On the walls were abstract canvases that reminded me of enlarged views of spermatozoa. There were no books at all.

"Your uncle likes it this way? I had no idea."

"Please, you must take off your shoes because of the carpet." I did as she told, leaving my running shoes beside a pair of matching Louis Vuitton suitcases standing in the entrance. Hadassah took my hand and led me past the modern kitchen, the mirrored bathroom, to a bedroom. It was the room of a privileged young girl, with a pink comforter on the bed and plush animals from F.A.O. Schwartz on the pillows and shelves of dolls and glass figures. This made no sense; Singer and his wife had no children together.

"Hadassah —" I began, but she pulled me to the bed and kissed my mouth. Then she unceremoniously pulled her T-shirt over her head. In moments my own clothes were on the floor.

How long we made love for I had no idea, for time had become suspended. I cannot — I will not — describe our lovemaking except to say that it did move beyond pleasure as I had long imagined; my own soul disappeared in hers. Finally we lay with our arms around one another and I closed my eyes and felt Hadassah breathing beside me. Under my breath I whispered, "*Oz mich looz.*"

"Felix, I have to tell you something."

I opened my eyes to the darkness of the room. "Hadassah," I said, "you sound different. Your accent — where is it?"

"This apartment belongs to my parents, Felix. This is my childhood room." She had no accent at all now, or rather she sounded like a New Yorker.

I said, "You're — you're not from Israel?"

"I was born in Manhattan. I grew up here on the Upper West Side. Although I did live on a kibbutz for two weeks when I was sixteen. Felix, I'm so sorry, I don't know what came over me when I saw you. I've been working on voice and character all summer — I'm a theatre major at UCLA — and when I saw you I just decided to stay in character. I didn't think it would go beyond meeting you in the hallway. Did you never really suspect?"

I sat up on the bed. "Suspect? I fell head over heels for someone who doesn't exist. Is Hadassah even your name?"

"It's Heidi. Heidi Sussman. But I'm thinking of changing it. Felix, you don't know how shitty I feel about this."

"I don't know what to say. I'm — I'm speechless. I should get up. What are we doing making love? Who did I just have sex with, anyway? I should go —"

"No, not yet."

"Maybe you're not really Heidi Sussman. If you want to know the truth it sounds even less convincing than Hadassah. Maybe you're a Russian spy."

"I was hoping you wouldn't be mad."

"I'm not mad. I'm too upset and confused and deranged to be mad. Where are your parents? What if they walk in?"

"They just left for New Orleans. My dad's got business there. He's very big in dental supplies."

"I'm so glad to hear it. And I suppose you don't actually know Singer."

"Sure, I know him. He has the apartment next door. We say hello all the time. He used to pat my head when I was little. In high school I even did a project on him. These days he's not here most of the time. He spends the winters in Miami Beach and the summers in Switzerland. For all I know he's not even in New York right now."

"So he never even heard of me or my story."

"I'm sure it's a very good story."

"And tell me, what does *Oz mich looz* really mean?"

"It means anything you want it to."

"I think I'm going insane."

But when I tried to get up she pulled me back to the bed and kissed me again and put my hands to her breasts. I had come to New York hungry for actuality and I was making love to a woman who was more chimera than real. But she was real when I kissed the corners of her mouth, her neck, her nipples. "Hadassah," I said, and then, "Heidi, Heidi . . . "

# 23

# Welcome to Life

I watched the arrival of dawn from the windows of the Sussmans' apartment. Somewhere on the New Jersey shore the giant Maxwell House cup dropped its glowing red drops, but all I could see from this corner view was a narrow strip down Eighty-sixth Street and the occasional cab cruising up Broadway along with a few delivery trucks. Somewhere out there Aaron was lying in a bed in Brooklyn and I hoped that at least he was sleeping contentedly. It was difficult to believe that he would not be coming back with me to begin his articling job. I was sure that my mother too was awake, lying next to my snoring father, unable to close her eyes from the expectation of our return. And here I stood, unable to find the wisdom that would give this *Bildungsroman* I was living a conclusion, that would transform the hero from boy to man.

I returned to the bedroom and watched Heidi sleep for a while, the sheet pulled up to her delicate shoulders.

Strangely, my feelings for her had not diminished and I wondered whether I could love Heidi Sussman as well as I could Hadassah, that in reality it was Hadassah who was a mirage and Heidi who was real.

I lay down beside her and dozed lightly for another couple of hours before getting up again and dressing. It was 7:30 by the hands of the sunflower clock on Heidi's wall. I would go to the Kemels' to pack my bag and explain the money situation. After fixing my tie in the mirror on the back of the door, I kissed her lightly on the cheek and put the manuscript of my story on her dresser. I wanted her to see it when she woke up so that she would not think that *I* had been the mirage.

Tuesday turned out to be garbage day on the Upper West Side and a truck rumbled along Eighty-second Street while two men hauled the dented metal cans, spilling a trail of refuse. Even the volume of New York's garbage was impressive. I took the stairs of the Kemels' brownstone two at a time and let myself in. Hannah was clearing dishes from the dining-room table.

"There you are, Felix," she said. "I was very concerned about you not coming in last night."

"I didn't mean to worry you. Do you mind if I have one of those rolls?"

"Help yourself. Sam and Hershel are already gone. Sam had an early appointment with a Dutch collector. I'm very glad not to have to meet these people. Sit down and have some coffee. Are you all right, Felix? You look a little run down."

"I didn't get a lot of sleep, that's all. I've come to get my things."

"I hate saying goodbye to our guests. I suppose it's foolish but I find it very upsetting. You mustn't forget that beautiful porcelain figurine in the sitting room."

"Hannah, I feel terrible about this, but the sad truth is that I've run out of money. Of course I'll pay for my room as soon as I can. In the meantime, perhaps you would accept the figurine as a gift."

"Felix, you don't have to look so concerned. Sometimes New York turns out to be more expensive than people expect. And you don't need to leave the figurine."

"No, I would really like you to have it. I think it looks right in your sitting room."

"Well, that's a lovely gesture. And it will remind us of your stay. How about we accept it as payment? But of course it must be worth more than that so I should give you something for it."

"I wouldn't take a cent. You're kind to accept it, Hannah. I better go and pack."

"Do take good care of yourself, Felix. Maybe you'll stay with us again some time."

She leaned over to kiss me on each cheek.

I packed my bag, including the copy of Singer's *Nobel Lecture* that Harry Winter had stolen for me, and checked to make sure I had my plane ticket. It was nine o'clock when I came out onto the street again and the day was already warm and the sky clear. It was going to be another scorcher. I carried my bag back to the Belnord and was relieved to find the doorman absent from his post under the archway, so that I could slink through the courtyard and take the elevator.

During the ride up I tried to rehearse what I might say to Heidi. It was possible that her deceiving me was as much my fault as hers, although I wasn't sure exactly how except to speculate that I had wanted to be deceived. In truth, I hoped that she was still in bed and that I could slip back in with her. My mother was right; sometimes words were of no use at all.

The door of the apartment was locked, so I put down my bag and knocked hard to make sure she could hear. There was no answer so I knocked again. A moment later I heard the sound of a vacuum cleaner. This was puzzling, as it seemed unlikely that Heidi was required to do housework, so I banged even louder. The vacuum did not stop. In a panic I pounded on the door with both fists until it opened so suddenly that I almost fell into the apartment.

A woman stood just inside, holding the hose of the vacuum, which was still on and making its awful noise. She was very big, with dimples in her cheeks and also her arms left bare by the polyester uniform.

"What is it, you want to break down the door?"

"I'm sorry. Would you please get Heidi for me."

"Heidi? She's gone."

"What do you mean, gone?

"Back to university in California. She left by taxi almost an hour ago."

I thought to look for the two suitcases I had noticed. They were missing.

The woman turned off the machine and yanked the cord from the wall. "I've got a lot of work to do," she said.

"Did Heidi leave anything for me? A message at least?"

"She did leave something. What's your name?"

"Felix Roth."

"Wait a minute."

She retreated inside and I resisted the urge to follow and search the apartment. What was taking her so long? Finally she lumbered into view, carrying the manuscript of my story. "This is for you," she said, thrusting it towards me. I took it from her and she closed the door hard.

I looked at the manuscript. It was curling, smudged, tattered. Heidi had written a few lines in the left-hand margin of the ripped first page.

*Dear Felix,*
*I didn't have the heart to tell you that my plane back to Los Angeles leaves this morning. Please forgive me for being "Hadassah." It was a great experience for me.*

*By the way, I read your story. I think it's very sweet.*

*Loads of love,*
*Heidi*

The first thing I felt was annoyance. Sweet? What did she mean by calling my story sweet? And then I realized that she was gone, and I knew that the only good thing I had managed to do in New York was meet her. Nothing had turned out the way I had planned or wanted. An overwhelming exhaustion came over me and without the slightest warning I started to cry. The sobs felt like a file being drawn up my insides and soon my face was soaked with tears.

And so I stood, on the fourteenth floor of the Belnord Apartments, weeping.

And heard a noise. The sound of a door lock turning. Perhaps the cleaning woman was coming out to threaten me with the police. But when I looked up I saw that it was not Heidi's apartment door but the next one that was opening. I saw someone peer out at me.

"Vat is dat crying? Is sometink going on?"

He opened the door a few more inches and I saw Isaac Bashevis Singer staring at me with surprise and distrust, the creases in his forehead rising to the few stray hairs left on his scalp. With his slightly bulging eyes, papery skin, and pointed ears he really did look like a wizened elf.

"Mr. Singer," I sniffled.

"I don't like crying. Did somebody die, God forbid?"

"No. I've lost someone. A woman."

"That's not a reason for crying. There are other women."

"Everything is such a disaster."

"Welcome to life. The history of mankind is the history of disaster. And still we cling to this world."

I found a tissue in my pocket and wiped my eyes and realized that I was holding the manuscript in my hand. "Mr. Singer, I know I shouldn't ask, but would you read something?"

He looked hard at me with his pale eyes. "What is this something?"

"A story." I hesitantly raised the manuscript.

"This is a story you've got? It looks like something for the bottom of the budgie's cage."

"I know. It's a disaster like everything else."

He sighed. "Come in and sit a minute. Maybe you need a cup of tea."

*

Two hours later I was walking with my bag slung on my shoulder down the chaos of Broadway. Ahead of me I could see Times Square and its enormous pixel sign flashing an advertisement for women's jeans. A workman was drilling the broken sidewalk but people ignored the yellow tape running between concrete posts, ducking under it instead. The soundtrack of *Rocky* blared from speakers hung from an open shopfront crammed with baseball jerseys and cheap handbags and miniature Statues of Liberty. The sun was relentless; it baked the sidewalks and made everything metal too hot to touch. In the doorway of a strip club a big-shouldered woman in a halter and skirt wiped her brow, an angry expression on her face. It took me a moment to realize that she was a transvestite.

I felt ravenously hungry and stopped to buy a hot knish from a vendor at the corner of Forty-sixth Street. The vendor handed me the paper bag and as I walked on I took a bite. The filling tasted like wallpaper paste but I chewed anyway. Blood pounded in my head.

A garbage truck ground its way down Broadway, and although it already looked full the men dumped in yet more cans of trash, food remains, broken furniture. I caught up with it, and as the hydraulic shovel came down, garbage clinging to it like food to a mouth, I took the manuscript of "The Goat Bride" from inside my blazer and tossed it in.

The pounding in my head eased, even if sweat continued to drip down my face. I took another bite of knish but might as well have been eating glue. Suddenly the pain in my head vanished completely.

In its place was a new story. I could hardly believe it was mine — my legs began to tremble — yet I knew that no one else could write it. I searched my jacket for a pen and then, swallowing the last glutinous wad of knish, I flattened the paper bag against the sign of a Chinese takeout. And while a stream of people jostled by, while Heidi Sussman flew towards California, while my brother Aaron said his prayers before the noon meal to a God who refused to reveal His face, while the Indian gentleman was developing somebody's snapshots and Harry Winter was hunched over a desk at the New York Public Library, while Alice was surprising Arthur Lowenstein in his office and my mother and father drove to the Toronto airport in anticipation of meeting their sons, while some poor bastard was being stabbed with a knife and another was eagerly shedding his clothes in a rented hotel room — while more than I could ever imagine was going on, I leaned against the sign of the Chinese takeout and wrote the first line of the new story on the greasy bag.

# Acknowledgements

I wish to thank the following people for their comments and support: Don Bastian, Bethany Gibson, Bernard Kelly, Anne McDermid, Shaun Oakey, Sherie Posesorski, and as always Joanne. And a most special thanks to David Diamond and Frank Carucci, who have been my family in New York for the last seventeen years.